SCIENCE FICTION GEMS

Volume 7

JACK VANCE
and others

Compiled and Edited by
Gregory Luce

I0532654

ARMCHAIR FICTION
PO Box 4369, Medford, Oregon 97504

The original text of these stories first appeared in *Amazing Stories, Planet Stories, Galaxy, Fantastic Universe, Dynamic Science Fiction, Universe, and Worlds Beyond.*

Cover suggests a scene from *Little Green Man*

Edited and compiled by Gregory Luce
Assistant Editor, Leanne Wray
Scan Manager, Kathy Stephens

For more information about Armchair Books and products, visit our website at...

www.armchairfiction.com

Or email us at...

armchairfiction@yahoo.com

DELVE INTO WORLDS OF TOMORROW...

...where, in "Task to Luna" and "Tydore's Gift" Man finds that a singular characteristic—arrogance—could be his final undoing.

Where two classic tales of caution, "On the Fourth Planet" and "The Defenders," relate different, but very likely, outcomes of nuclear holocaust.

Or…begs the question of what lies ahead in mankind's endless search for self-help and therapy? "The Man Who Had Spiders" and "Grandma's Lie Soap" may leave you thinking that you are indeed fine…just the way you are.

Also included in this 7th edition of Armchair's Classic Sci-fi Gems collection is Don Wilcox's, "The Voyage That Lasted 600 Years," the first known "generational starship" drama ever published!

So relax, sit back, and enjoy.

TABLE OF CONTENTS

The Wizard of Light

By DAVID ELY

For Sampson to destroy the Philistines, he had to bring their very temple crashing to the ground. But for Dr. Brow to destroy the culture-mongers, he needed merely a monstrous easel.

THE old man's tour of the art museums was quite an amusing spectacle. Indeed, it became a standing joke among those polite and cultivated gentlemen whose chief function in life is to obtain and display great paintings. They were accustomed to dealing with eccentric members of the public—but never had they witnessed anything to match the ludicrous performance of old Dr. Browl. (Of course, they carefully concealed their mirth, for Dr. Browl was far too rich to be laughed at openly; and after all, he might decide some day to honor the museums with bequests from the fortune he had amassed with his remarkable inventions in the field of optics that had earned him the sobriquet, the Wizard of Light.)

Dr. Browl was a copyist. He had his easel, his brushes and his paints. He had a little smock, too, and a beret that perched on his bald dome. But he had not the slightest resemblance to any of the other earnest amateurs who sat dutifully daubing their canvases in imitation of the masterpieces that hung before them. No, Dr. Browl was different.

He would arrive at a museum in princely fashion, in an enormous black limousine. Two liveried servants would lug in his easel, another would carry his encased palette, and Dr. Browl himself would hobble in on the arm of a nurse. Then he would sit down grumpily in a folding chair while the easel was being set up by his servants, and glare around at the little crowd that always gathered to watch him.

The easel itself was remarkable. It was a monument in wood and brass and steel, and as massive as an upright piano. It was equipped, moreover, with one of Dr. Browl's own inventions, a bank of mysterious lamps that gave off no visible light, but which presumably bathed each picture he sought to copy in a special radiance seen by him alone, through a great pair of black-lensed spectacles he clapped on his nose.

His painting technique was even more bizarre. Dr. Browl would fairly fling the colors from palette to canvas, his little claw hands darting back and forth with demonic speed. Faster and faster his jerky movements would become, until it seemed that the only remaining step in hastiness would be to hurl the palette itself against the canvas. His copies, naturally, were gross caricatures, and his only accomplishments the spoilage of innocent canvas and good paint.

At this feverish pace, he would copy one masterpiece after another. Often he would manage to work his way through an entire collection in a single day. He required only two weeks, for example, to make a complete round of the Louvre, with its many thousands of paintings, neglecting to copy not a single one. His energy and industry were without parallel. Within the space of two years, his pell-mell progress had carried him through every significant art repository in the Western world.

Dr. Browl's fanatic devotion to painting; seemed beyond explanation. Some said it was merely a lamentable aberration. Others suggested the existence of a guilt complex, for it was rumored that the old man had once burned his own small art collection in a fit of senile rage. But Dr. Browl seemed far from being guilt-ridden. From time to time, as his servants would shift the heavy easel to a new location, he would lower his black spectacles and briefly eye the amused bystanders. A strange look, the old man had. Ironical, and contemptuous, too; but more than that, for there would sometimes be a devilish gleam of mockery there that suggested some wild, wicked humor. The people were snickering at him, were they? Well, it would seem that he was barely able to contain his *own* laughter at *them*.

IT WAS in the spring of 196- that Dr. Browl completed his remarkable tour of museums and galleries. The first series of incidents, however, did not occur until slightly more than a year later.

One bright June morning, a van stopped in front of the offices of the London art dealers, Bouser & Baillie. Two workmen delivered a large flat crate that proved to contain Manet's famous

"Boy With Drum," recently returned to its owner, the Countess Palumbo, from an exhibit at the National Gallery. But Bouser & Baillie found no note attached to explain why the Countess had sent it. Was it to be loaned to another exhibit, was it to be sold, or was it simply to be cleaned?

Perforce, Bouser & Baillie telephoned their client at her Norfolk estate, and with suitable apologies, requested instructions. The Countess was annoyed. What was this nonsense about "Boy With Drum?" She had no intention of exhibiting it or selling it or having it cleaned, and in fact, had not sent it at all. The picture was hanging right in her drawing-room at that very moment, in its accustomed place. "Boy With Drum" indeed. She hung up sharply. Bouser & Baillie looked at each other and then at the canvas in question. Incredible—and yet it was the "Boy With Drum." Or was it? They approached it warily for a closer look.

Meanwhile, that same morning, another van had parked outside the offices of a similarly distinguished firm of art dealers, Sack, Bonesteel & Woodward. The deliverymen struggled in with a burden quite like the one deposited at Bouser & Baillie, obtained their receipt, and departed.

The crate contained nothing less than Manet's "Boy With Drum." Sack gasped. Bonesteel grunted. Woodward carefully inspected the empty crate for a note, but found none. Had the picture been delivered to them by error? It did not seem so, for their corporate name was plainly stenciled on the crate. Sack gave Bonesteel a significant look. The masterpiece, they knew, was part of the Palumbo collection. Could it be that the Countess had chosen this dramatic gesture to indicate her desire to let them handle her considerable business? After much consultation, Woodward was nominated to make the call, which was effected not five minutes after the Countess had angrily hung up on Bouser & Baillie. Another "Boy With Drum?" She flew into a rage and screamed out a variety of Central European epithets, then flung her telephone receiver the full length of its coiled elastic cord, so that as she stomped furiously out of the room, the receiver crept cautiously back toward its table, while poor Woodward, in London, sat transfixed, staring foolishly at his two worried partners and at the mute painting beyond.

THE following morning, Bouser & Baillie telephoned the leading British authenticator of art objects, Dr. A. B. T. Joll, and politely requested him to visit their offices to have a look at a picture that seemed to be an extremely skillful forgery of "Boy With Drum." It was so skillful, Bouser & Baillie admitted that it had them baffled. Dr. Joll, foreseeing a plump little fee, readily agreed, and promised to bring his full kit of instruments. Nothing pleased him more than the prospect of detecting a good, sound job of forgery. He had once been termed by the press "the Sherlock Holmes of the art world," which privately delighted him; unfortunately, there had yet appeared no artistic equivalent of Professor Moriarty to provide him with a serious challenge.

He went down to Bouser & Baillie that very morning, and after spending two full hours sniffing and puking the canvas, and making several tests with his own portable super-speed electro-chemical laboratory apparatus, he turned calmly to face the partners, and announced:

"Gentlemen, this is no forgery. It is the original."

Bouser & Baillie were thunderstruck. They did not doubt Dr. Joll's judgment (and with reason, for the expert had never once been wrong) rather, they were horrified by the inescapable conclusion. If *this* were the original, then the Countess had bought a fake—and had bought it on the strength of Bouser & Baillie's advice. They sank into adjacent chairs and sat trembling in silence.

Dr. Joll, meanwhile, examined his watch, found it was nearly time for lunch, and called his office to see if any important messages had been left in his absence. No messages, his secretary reported, but Mr. Bonesteel of Sack, Bonesteel & Woodward had just stepped in on what he said was a most urgent matter. Would Dr. Joll care to speak to him? "Put him on," said Dr. Joll, with Holmesian dispatch.

But he was soon disappointed. "Look here, Mr. Bonesteel," he interrupted. "I'm afraid I can save you the trouble. It so happens, coincidentally, that I've just finished examining the original… Yes, right here at Bouser & Baillie. The original 'Boy With Drum'…No doubt about it, sir, you have a fake."

Bonesteel was persistent, however, and so Dr. Joll at length reluctantly agreed to stop by for a look after lunch.

His mood underwent a transformation after he had made a cursory inspection of Sack, Bonesteel & Woodward's "Boy With Drum." He frowned, he polished his spectacles, he cleared his throat, and he reached for his kit. One hour grew to two, to three. At last, Dr. Joll stepped back, haggard and shaken, feeling much the same, perhaps, as had Holmes himself, when he tottered on the brink of the Reichenbach Fall in the grip of the criminal genius. A nasty doubt flashed through Joll's mind. Had he been hoaxed by the two firms? Had Bouser & Baillie rushed the original up to Sack, Bonesteel & Woodward while he had been at lunch? That would be preposterous—and yet the alternative was no less confounding.

HE telephoned at once to Bouser & Baillie. Within the hour, the two partners appeared at the offices of the rival firm, carrying their "Boy With Drum" between them. Joll set the two paintings side by side and went grimly to work. It was quite late at night when he finished.

"There is only one explanation, gentlemen," he told the five dealers. "Only one. Manet painted *two* identical versions of 'Boy With Drum.'"

Not until the next morning did the distraught dealers attempt to trace the source of the two mysterious deliveries. In each case, however, their efforts were frustrated. The delivery firms had duly responded to pick-up calls from unexceptional addresses (one in Kensington, the other near Paddington), and had been paid on the spot by husky young men who had been waiting with their crates at the curbside. It developed further that these young men had not actually been occupants of the addresses in question.

The most stunning blow of all, however, came the following afternoon, when Bouser & Baillie mustered sufficient courage to escort Dr. Joll to Norfolk, to break the difficult news to the Countess. The news proved to be even more difficult than the three gentlemen had imagined, for Dr. Joll's examination of the lady's "Boy With Drum" confirmed that it, too, was the original; or rather that it was now but one of *three* originals. Other experts were hastily consulted, and their opinions supported that of Joll. Had Manet been seized by a fit of madness that had compelled him thus to repeat himself, not once but twice? Whatever the motive, his performance was undoubtedly the most brilliant technical tour-de-force in art history, for the three canvases were identical, down to the last detail seen under the most powerful microscope.

Manet's fiendish skill did not impress the Countess. She felt that the painter had deliberately outraged her, and she wished that he were still living, so that she might have the opportunity of snubbing him. That being impossible, she determined to snub his work. "Sell it at once," she ordered Bouser & Baillie. "You told me last year you could get me half again what I paid for it. Then do so now. In fact," she added, to show the selflessness of her grudge against Manet, "I don't care if there's no profit at all—just sell it."

"Ah, um—" Bouser began. But he found himself unable to speak. Baillie tried, too, with no greater success. How could they make it clear to this dangerous female that the existence of two other originals had placed the marketability of her own in grave jeopardy? There was doubt, indeed, whether any buyer could now be found—at any price. And more than that, if she chose to donate the canvas outright to a museum, would the museum be likely to accept?

While the two partners stood thus uncomfortably searching their minds for some way of phrasing these unpleasant truths, a delivery van back in London was edging into a parking space in front of the firm of John Pickering & Sons, art dealers. Within the van was a crate, and within the crate was a painting.

It was the fourth original "Boy With Drum."

BEFORE the art world had time to digest the incredible evidence of the four identical Manets, the second series of incidents took place.

This time the locale was Rome, and the painting involved was Holbein's famous portrait of the Duke of Kent, one of the ornaments of the Pellagrini Gallery. At half-past ten on a Monday morning, a truck arrived at the rear of the building to deliver a large crate. There was no clue on the exterior of the crate as to its origin or contents, but Gallery officials, assuming that their curiosity would be satisfied by some document tacked within, signed the delivery receipt and had the crate lugged to a storeroom. Opening it, they found no such document, only what appeared to be a marvelously clever imitation of their precious Holbein.

They chuckled merrily at the joke. Then one of them remarked innocently that it reminded him of the remarkable Manet duplications that were currently vexing the English. At once a pall of doubt settled over the group. Another Manet case? Utter nonsense. But that afternoon, the Roman counterpart of Dr. Joll was quietly called in to examine the strange gift. Professor Rienzo was not as swift as his English colleague, and was still inspecting the supposed forgery the next morning, when a different truck arrived with another portrait of the Duke of Kent, just like the first.

Indeed, it was also just like the one that hung so proudly in the Gallery itself—at least that was Professor Rienzo's firm opinion, enunciated the following day at a special meeting of the Gallery's directors. "I stake my reputation on it," Rienzo declared. "You have now three Holbein Kents, identically the same."

But Rienzo was wrong. There were not three Kents, but four, for another one had just arrived. The next day, the fifth appeared, and thus, on the day after that, the entire staff of the Gallery waited in a delirium of expectation for Holbein Kent VI. They were not disappointed.

Where had the canvases come from? But, like the London dealers, the Pellagrini Gallery officials were unable to find out. They could follow the trail back only as far as some young man on a street corner, or in a hotel lobby, or again, at some sidewalk cafe, each time waiting calmly with his crate for the appearance of the summoned truck—then vanishing.

In their agitation, the custodians of the multiple Holbein considered trying to hush up the affair, but they had barely broached the topic when the mysterious donor rendered further discussion useless. Holbein Kent VII was duly delivered—not to the Gallery, however, but to the art editor of one of Rome's great newspapers. The story was cut in the open.

IN the following weeks, the tempo quickened. No longer were there isolated incidents, first in one city and then in another. The plague of original masterpieces became epidemic.

Item: Every art dealer in Vienna received, on the same day, twenty-five different paintings by Picasso, Braque, and Matisse. Each was subsequently established as being fully authentic, to the consternation of those museums and private collectors in a dozen countries who had acquired, at enormous cost, the originals.

Item: The Tate Gallery in London was notified by the confused headmaster of a private school near Bath that one thousand copies of a celebrated Van Gogh had been delivered to him, apparently in error. At least, he said, they *seemed* to be copies. He had recalled that the Tate owned the original. Perhaps the shipment had been intended for the Gallery? The Tate officials grimly agreed that it probably had.

Item: One morning, the base of one exterior wall of the Louvre was found to be solidly lined with the "Mona Lisa." There were hundreds of them, side by side, smiling enigmatically out across the Seine, and each, naturally, was as genuine as the single one inside the great palace.

What was perhaps the most serious case occurred in New York. Directors of a famous art museum were notified one day in a letter from a law firm that a wealthy gentleman, recently deceased, had willed to the museum his entire collection of paintings. Would the directors care to appear at such-and-such an address the following day to inspect the offered canvases? The directors wrote a polite acknowledgment and the next day dispatched one of their junior members to the address given. Presumably the donor had left them an attic-full of junk, but still there might be something worthwhile there.

The junior member telephoned his colleagues at once. They hastened to the spot. The collection was most remarkable. It covered every wall of every room in an otherwise vacant five-story building, and the directors could hardly call any of it junk, for it duplicated with the most appalling exactitude the entire contents of their own museum. Every last painting was reproduced there, and as if that were not enough, inspection of the basement revealed that for each canvas displayed in the rooms above, a precise duplicate existed in storage.

The directors were aghast. It was Manet and Holbein all over again, but on a scale beyond all imagining. To make matters worse, someone had impudently tipped off the press, and there was a crowd of reporters and photographers, not to mention a number of curiosity-seekers who had wandered in from the street. One of the directors telephoned the museum and ordered it closed immediately, but of course that could not prevent the instant collapse of the values of the museum's collection.

Once more, investigation proved fruitless. The law firm indignantly denied authorship of the letter. Someone evidently had purloined the stationary. The dead man, too, was a fraud, having never existed, and as for the person who had rented the building, the real estate agent could recall only that it was a young man named Smith, who had paid in advance weeks earlier, and had not been seen since.

By this time, the entire art world was in a state of nervous collapse. Dozens of masterworks had been rendered worthless by their sheer profusion. Others joined the list every day. Collectors sought frantically to sell—but no one would buy. Even those paintings as yet untouched by the blight could not be sold, for what buyer could be sure that a hundred identical canvases would not quickly turn up elsewhere? Dealers' offices were closed, museum doors were shut—and most horrible of all, artists were ceasing to paint.

In desperation, the leading museums and galleries pooled funds to hire private detectives. Weeks passed, and the flow of originals continued, but the detectives failed to produce a single positive lead—except for one, and it was so fantastic that the art impresarios angrily rejected it.

One shipment of masterpieces had been traced, through an intricate system of straw parties and other devices, back to the New York apartment of Dr. Cyrus E. Browl. Could the Wizard of Light be the mass-production virtuoso? Ridiculous! Several of the museum directors remembered his fumbling attempts to copy their treasures. It had been pathetic—the old man had been clumsier than the rawest novice, and besides, his eyes were so weak now, he could hardly see across a room…

But one of the art experts was suddenly struck by the memory of that huge easel and the peculiar array of lightless lamps, and hastened off to pay Dr. Browl a visit. He quickly returned, looking much older, and in an unsteady voice made a report:

"I've seen Dr. Browl—and I've seen *it.*"

"Seen what?"

The dealer's cheeks quivered. "The thing. The thing that does it."

The art experts all stared at the speaker. "Then he is the one?" someone asked.

"Yes. And he is willing to see us tomorrow afternoon…"

THE Wizard of Light occupied the four topmost floors of a mid-town apartment building. Most of that space was used for his laboratories (the city having granted him special permission), from which had issued many important inventions, although none in the last few years.

Dr. Browl received his uneasy guests in a huge room whose far wall, opposite the main entranceway, was composed entirely of glass. It was, in fact, a gigantic window that afforded a splendid view of the city.

The art dealers and exhibitors were hardly in a frame of mind to appreciate the scene, however, as they filed into the room and at their host's direction, seated themselves on chairs and sofas arranged in rows off to one side.

"All here?" asked the Wizard, searching the apprehensive faces before him with his uncertain old eyes. Someone muttered in the affirmative, and the Wizard broke into a high-pitched cackling. It confirmed the worst fears of his visitors. They were dealing with a demented genius who would be beyond the persuasions of reason.

"Now I'll get out my little toy," the Wizard declared cheerfully. He hobbled past them to one of the room's several doors, opened it, and pulled forth his easel that had been mounted on little tires so that feeble as he was, he could maneuver it around quite easily.

"Looks like a fancy easel, doesn't it, eh?" he chortled, wheeling it out in front of his audience. "Well, it is an easel, but it's more than *just* an easel. It's a camera, my friends. Not an ordinary camera—oh, no. It's a three-dimensional molecular camera." He laughed so hard that he was forced to lean against his bulky creation for support.

When he had recovered, he went on more calmly: "I won't confuse you with the technical details, gentlemen. You would hardly understand them anyway. Let me merely assure you that this camera contains a high-speed electronic scanning device that accurately records in its memory the precise structure of each molecule of matter within its range." With this, the Wizard pressed a button and the front part of the easel, which happened to be trained on the main entranceway, began to purr.

"You recorded the paintings you were pretending to copy?" one of the dealers blurted out.

"Precisely," rejoined the Wizard. "But, of course, that is just half the story. To record is not to reproduce. Yet my invention is capable of both tasks." He punched another button. The machine stopped purring, and instead, its rear section began to vibrate. "Reproduction!" cried the Wizard, excitedly. "The memorized particles now begin to be duplicated by means of a cybernetic reactor that with infinite speed and skill, dips into a little reservoir of atomic raw materials, so to speak, and fashions from them the requisite molecules. Thus I produce not merely copies of your vaunted masterpieces, but the masterpieces themselves—complete to the last fragment of aged wood frame and cracked canvas.

"Of course," he added more soberly, "there are a few problems still to be solved. The reproduction is not instantaneous, but takes several minutes to solidify. And then, too," he went on, as if musing to himself, "there is the unfortunate circumstance that my pictures will dissolve within a few months, reverting to their elemental state."

HE perceived that his last remark had greatly heartened his listeners, and snapped at them angrily:

"Don't get your hopes up, gentlemen! I shall perfect it, never fear. And in the meantime, I can keep on producing."

One of the curators spoke: "Why do you want to ruin us?"

"It should be obvious," the Wizard declared. "My object is not to destroy *you*, but art. Art falsifies nature in general, and light values in particular. It is the curse of mankind. Years ago I decided to eliminate it. But how? The answer, my friends, was not long in coming. I determined to destroy art by rendering it commercially worthless—which, needless to say, I am well on the way to accomplishing—for I know that in this world, nothing can survive the loss of monetary value."

The visitors trembled in their chairs. If any proof were lacking of the old man's dementia, his wild statement had supplied it. And was his lunacy, they wondered, to mean the end of their fees and their stipends, and, incidentally, of painting itself? What could they do to thwart the old fiend? Chuck him out the window, possibly, along with his infernal machine?

But the window seemed to be fogged. A peculiar little cloud was whirling in front of it, right behind the molecular camera. They stared at it, greatly puzzled.

The Wizard mistook the object of their scrutiny and embraced his invention protectively. "You want to destroy it, do you?" he cried. "Stay where you are!" He pulled a small revolver from his pocket and brandished it threateningly, meanwhile tugging at the machine, to roll it away.

IT WAS then that Fate intervened, as if the potential irony were too great to be resisted. The cloud behind the camera began to take on a recognizable shape. It became a scientifically exact depiction of the entranceway, in fact, for the Wizard, in his excitement, had neglected to turn off his machine, and it had dutifully gone about its business. True, the representation of the entranceway had not quite solidified, but it was firm enough to obscure the plate-glass window behind it, and so when the weak-eyed Wizard hastily pulled his great camera toward the nearest exit, his confusion was understandable.

There was a loud noise of splintering as the old gentleman propelled his invention through the window, and a cry of vexation as he followed it.

By the time the art experts reached street-level, sixteen stories below, there was little left to be seen. The molecular camera was a mere tangle of wires and metal, yet it still hummed erratically on for a time, and before the astonished eyes of the gathering crowd, it belched out its final and greatest creation—a magnificent mélange of all periods and styles, distillation of a triumphant man's artistic genius through the ages, marred only by the unfortunate representation, in one corner, of a human nose in juxtaposition with the thumb of an upraised hand whose fingers were indelicately spread. However, this minor annoyance was blocked out, and the masterpiece was exhibited in the leading galleries of the civilized world, until, like the machine's other productions, it crumbled and fell into dust.

THE END

The Man Who Had Spiders

By ROGER DEE

*There is probably more than one way of curing a tragic addiction to alcohol.
But Adrian's way was as shuddery as a smiling Medusa.*

WHEN Mr. Marcus, who had sold novelties to novelty shops
for forty years and so had lost the capacity for astonishment at
human unpredictability, returned to Maysville on the 8:04 train for
his regular April week of selling, he went at once to Mrs. Ponder's
boarding house and found Kitty playing Delibes on the living room
piano.

It was almost like coming home, Mr. Marcus thought with an
uncharacteristic twinge of nostalgia. He paused for a moment in
the doorway, suitcase and sample bag and his inevitable parcel of
books in hand, to listen.

Tender was the word for Kitty, with her cool, sure touch on the
Delibes theme and her clear blind eyes and her nestling of fair hair
that just brushed her shoulders. And wasted, Mr. Marcus thought,
with all the beauty and the talent of her shunted to obscurity in the
dingy gentility of her mother's ménage.

If he were thirty years younger—

Mr. Marcus cut the thought dead. *If you were thirty years younger,
Marcus,* he told himself with dry cynicism, *you'd travel and sell novelties.
Just as you did thirty years ago.*

Kitty sensed his presence with the near-tactile acuity of the
blind and let the Delibes theme trail off in a random tinkle.

"It's only I, Miss Kitty," Mr. Marcus said. "The old man who
sells loaded cigars to idiots."

She turned on the piano bench, pleased at his coming but
nevertheless disappointed. "Oh, Mr. Marcus. I thought at first you
were Adrian."

"Adrian?"

She laughed, a sound as light and clear as the vanished music.
"Adrian Hall, our new boarder. He's only been with us a week."

A week. Seven days, Mr. Marcus thought, and her face could light up so at the sound of his step?

When Kitty smiled it was impossible to think that her eyes could not see him. "You're thinking that my interest is unusual, and you're quite right. But Adrian is an unusual man, Mr. Marcus."

"I'm sure he is," Mr. Marcus said cautiously. "I'll have to meet him."

The prospect pleased her. "You were always nice to me and Jay Kirby because I'm blind and Jay has fits, but you never noticed anyone else. You'll notice Adrian. You'll like him."

"I'm sure I shall," Mr. Marcus said. Her eagerness made him feel old and tired and somehow resentful. The books and bags grew heavy in his hands. "I was just going upstairs to see if my room—"

Kitty's face lighted up. "Please wait," she begged. "I hear Adrian coming down now. We're going out for a drive, but I'd like you to meet him first."

The new boarder was perhaps thirty, hardly older than Kitty, and totally unremarkable. Shaking hands, Mr. Marcus cast back through the dry files of his memory and exhausted them without turning up a more ordinary face or figure. Moderately tall, he catalogued: average build, plain face, neutral hair, good teeth and mild blue eyes. The man's only distinction seemed to be a round, black mole on the left side of his neck, half hidden by his shirt collar. Politely, Mr. Marcus did not look at it twice.

It rather startled him to discover that Kitty had been right. He *did* like Adrian Hall, at first sight and without reservation.

Mr. Marcus was never quite sure what was said during the shaking of hands. He was too absorbed in trying to justify such uncharacteristic regard to do more than nod when Adrian excused himself to hold Kitty's light coat for her. He did retain a bizarre impression when the two of them went out, however, that the new boarder's mole had shifted from the side to the back of his neck and was watching him with an air of amiable curiosity.

The conviction left Mr. Marcus more annoyed than disturbed. He'd have to see an oculist and have his lenses changed again, he told himself resignedly as he climbed the stairs to his room.

Jay Kirby was waiting there for him, crouched against the farther wall like a fearful puppy hiding from the adult pack.

No other boarder in Mrs. Ponder's house would have dared violate Mr. Marcus' privacy, but Jay enjoyed the privilege of handicap and exercised it. Mr. Marcus sighed when he saw that Jay was suffering, or had just suffered, another of his periodic attacks. His corn-colored hair was wildly tousled, his blue eyes had fallen two octaves darker with stress and there was a wide smear of grime across one sweating cheek.

Jay was far too badly shaken to bother with greetings. "You got to do something about this Adrian Hall," he blurted. "Mr. Marcus, he's got *spiders.*"

Mr. Marcus found the proposition as repellent as it was improbable. Still, the turn of Jay's latest fantasy intrigued him. Large spiders or small, he wondered, gray or black, poisonous or innocuous, caged or—

"Spiders?" He put his books and bags on the bed. "In his room, you mean?"

Jay denied it violently. "On *him.*"

Mr. Marcus wondered with some bitterness if nations would ever outgrow their penchant for expedient wars that left men broken as Jay Kirby was broken. Left alone Jay would have been a pleasant young man and a first-rate musician, but with the spirit of him maimed and trembling like a frightened child's at the edge of nightmare—

Mr. Marcus opened his suitcase. "I brought you a record, Jay— something just released. A New Orleans stomp, the music-shop man said, with an alto sax that—"

Jay came across the room and clutched his arm, towering over him. "I didn't shuck my wig this time, Mr. Marcus, honest. I really saw this. The guy had his clothes off, and he was all over spiders."

Mr. Marcus felt a touch of chill. Jay had been committed twice before coming to rest at Mrs. Ponder's; if he were sent away again, it might be for good.

"Sit down," Mr. Marcus said. He sat down himself, on the room's one chair. "Tell me about it, Jay, and from the beginning."

Jay sat on the bed, and rose, and sat again. "It'd be all right if he'd keep them to himself," he said. "I wouldn't mind that because I *like* him. It's Miss Kitty I'm worried about."

"Miss Kitty?"

"Everybody likes Adrian, Mr. Marcus, but Miss Kitty's in love with him. How'll she feel when she finds out he's got spiders?"

Mr. Marcus nodded gravely. "I can understand your concern. But Miss Kitty is blind, Jay. How can she find out?"

"I thought you'd see that right off," Jay said, disappointed. "She'll know when they get married, won't she? She'll *have* to know."

Mr. Marcus permitted himself a small, shudder. Jay had outdone himself this time.

"You saw these spiders, you said," he reminded. "Where, and when?"

Jay got up and paced restlessly, limping. "Half an hour ago, when Adrian went up to shower and dress for his date with Miss Kitty. I was out on the porch roof, tightening a loose bathroom shutter I'd promised to fix for Mrs. Ponder, and—"

"You spied on him, Jay? In the *bathroom?*"

"I didn't mean to," Jay said defensively. "But I couldn't look away after I saw the spiders. Could you?" He turned a stricken face to Mr. Marcus. "Mr. Marcus, he was all covered with them until he stepped into the shower. Then he held up a towel and they jumped on it to keep dry."

"I see," Mr. Marcus said. "And when he came out?"

"He dried himself off," Jay said. "And they jumped on again." He began to tremble with the violence of imminent seizure. "What am I going to do, Mr. Marcus? I like Adrian, but I like Miss Kitty, too. I can't let him—"

Mr. Marcus rose hastily and led him to his room down the hall. "You won't have to do anything," he promised before he left Jay to have his fit in privacy. "Trust me, Jay. I'll take care of it."

It was not until later, when he had settled himself in his own room to a volume of Saki's inhumanly perfect short stories that he remembered the new boarder's peregrinating mole.

"Can't happen outside fiction," he assured himself. "Tricks of the eyes, or else the fellow has two moles."

But his eyesight was disturbingly good when he went down to breakfast next morning at seven and found himself seated beside Adrian Hall. Adrian was neatly dressed for work. He was a newspaper reporter, it developed, and was thinking seriously of launching a weekly of his own in Maysville—and he was every whit as likeable as he had been on the night before.

But not as unremarkable. This morning, he had no moles at all.

FORTY YEARS of selling novelties and reading books had not prepared Mr. Marcus for the role of detective that was thrust upon him, but it had given him a certain resourcefulness. Between stock-taking calls at local shops during the day he made discreet inquiries, and by nightfall had amassed a considerable array of fact and opinion.

The opinion was unfailingly enthusiastic. Never, Mr. Marcus thought, had a man been so instantly and universally liked in a town as small and insular as Maysville. Adrian Hall could have borrowed money from any bank, had any job or married any girl in the community.

What could make so plain a man so prepossessing Mr. Marcus could not imagine. He was certain only that he liked Mrs. Ponder's new boarder more than he had ever liked anyone in his life, and that he felt not only uncomfortable but downright guilty in spying out his personal affairs.

Actual fact was harder to arrive at. Adrian Hall had come from Kansas City, some two hundred miles distant. He was a good newspaperman and Gus Willis, who operated the Maysville *Bugler*, had liked him well enough—as who hadn't?—to hire him on sight. He was sober, industrious, efficient and considerate.

No one but Jay Kirby and Mr. Marcus seemed to suspect that he harbored spiders under his shirt. And Mr. Marcus, returning from his first day of selling and inquiry to find Adrian singing *The Rose of Tralee* with Kitty at the piano, found that repellent idea hard to believe.

Until, at supper again, he happened to look up quickly from his plate and discovered that the new boarder's elusive mole had returned. Mr. Marcus blinked and—he was quite positive, this time—it blinked genially back at him.

The conviction so unnerved him that he closed his eyes to defend his composure. When he opened them again the mole had gone, together with Mr. Marcus' lost appetite.

Mr. Marcus excused himself from table and went upstairs to his room. As he had expected, Jay Kirby was waiting for him again.

"Did you tell him?" Jay demanded.

Mr. Marcus blinked, remembered the mole that had just blinked back at him, and shuddered. "Did I tell what to whom?"

"Adrian," Jay said. "Didn't you tell him yet to get lost? How're we going to keep him away from Miss Kitty unless we threaten to expose him?"

"I couldn't do that," Mr. Marcus said. "I like him too well."

"So do I," Jay said. "Damn him."

Mr. Marcus went over the possibilities again and found nothing of promise.

"No one would believe us even if we tried to expose him," he concluded. "We wouldn't believe in his spiders ourselves if we hadn't seen them."

Jay began to sweat. "What are we going to do Mr. Marcus? We can't brace Adrian because we like him too much, and we can't tell Miss Kitty what's wrong with him. How are we going to keep them from getting married?"

It was a formidable question. Mr. Marcus evaded it by posing one of his own.

"How do you know they'll be married, Jay? Has any announcement been made?"

"Not yet," Jay said. "But there will be."

Mr. Marcus sighed. "Then I'm afraid we're stumped. I wish we knew more about him."

A new avenue of approach occurred to him then, but Jay anticipated the inspiration. "You could find out something about him in Kansas City," Jay said. "He was a newspaper reporter there once, wasn't he?"

Mr. Marcus could not drop his selling—he had only two days left now before he must move downstate toward St. Louis—and go to Kansas City, but he could pursue his investigation by proxy. Providentially, he had a friend on the staff of the Kansas City *Star* who might do his leg work for him.

"It seems our last hope," Mr. Marcus said. "I'll make the call now."

He preferred not to use the house telephone because of its several extensions, and the nearest booth stood in a corner of the neighborhood drugstore. Mr. Marcus went out and made his call, received his Kansas City friend's promise to do what he could, and returned to Mrs. Ponder's boarding house.

He found a small party in progress, with a beaming Mrs. Ponder and an assorted handful of her boarders gathered round Adrian Hall and Kitty. Lemonade flowed freely and an air of rejoicing prevailed.

"Congratulate me, Mr. Marcus," Kitty cried. "Adrian and I are going to be married."

Mr. Marcus congratulated them both with deepest sincerity. His scalp prickled only once during his well-wishings, when one of Adrian's—moles?—crept out of its shirt-collar, just below the Adam's apple this time, and peered at him complacently.

"God bless you both," Mr. Marcus finished, and fled upstairs.

But his room, for once, was not sanctuary.

For the first time in his life his books failed to sustain him and he felt truly alone and impotent, caught vicariously in exactly the sort of emotional muddle he had avoided so religiously. There was not even Jay Kirby to lean on in his extremity. Jay had heard the news of Kitty's engagement during Mr. Marcus' brief absence and had given way under the strain, suffering another of his fits in his own room.

Mrs. Ponder's tapping brought Mr. Marcus out of his funk, if briefly. "Telephone call for you," she said. "From Kansas City."

Mr. Marcus, knowing that Mrs. Ponder would eavesdrop if he used the upper hallway extension, took the call downstairs. It was his friend of the *Star*.

"Got the dirt you wanted right here in the office," his friend said cheerfully. "A question here, a phone call there, and it's wrapped up."

He gave his information tersely. "The guy's a bum, Marcus. He's been thrown off every paper in town for drinking—even Alcoholics Anonymous finally wrote him off as a lost cause."

Mr. Marcus said nothing. There were no words for what he felt.

"Wasn't ever vicious," his friend said. "He was just one of those poor fish with a twist, an uncontrollable drinker. Sponged handouts and probably stole a little on his bad days, but never robbed any banks. What's he doing up there—more of the usual?"

Mr. Marcus found his voice. "Not at all. This must be a different Adrian Hall altogether."

But it wasn't. Mr. Marcus discovered that when he went upstairs again and found Adrian waiting for him by the upper hallway extension.

"I came up and listened in," Adrian said. "I had an idea that you were checking on me, Mr. Marcus. When Mrs. Ponder told us you had a call from Kansas City, I was sure of it."

"I had to do it," Mr. Marcus said. "Once Jay had told me about your spiders, I had no choice."

Adrian took Mr. Marcus' arm and led him away down the hall. Mr. Marcus went along unprotestingly, numb with disbelief at his own composure. It was downright frightening, he thought, to find himself so unfrightened.

Adrian's room was much like Mr. Marcus' own, or like any other in the Ponder house. Adrian seated Mr. Marcus on his one chair and himself on the bed, and they measured each other equably over the flimsy expanse of Adrian's writing table.

In any decent piece of fiction, Mr. Marcus thought, there must be some element of suspense; in fiction running to such a situation as this, even of outright horror. But somehow, being dragged to the very lair of the monster he had set out to scotch brought him no touch of uneasiness. He felt sympathetic rather than fearful, and he liked Adrian Hall more, if that were possible, than ever.

"I'm really glad you unmasked me," Adrian said. "I need help, Mr. Marcus. I need help more than I ever needed it in my life."

"I'll do anything within my power," Mr. Marcus promised. "But I'm equally interested in helping Kitty, else I wouldn't have bothered with your past at all... Your problem is that you can't keep your spiders and marry Kitty too, isn't it?"

Adrian nodded. "It wouldn't work. Not because Kitty might object to them, for she wouldn't—they're not really offensive, and it's no fault of their own that they're here—but because a honeymoon without privacy is no honeymoon at all. My friends are quite intelligent, not to mention inquisitive, and keeping them wouldn't be fair to either Kitty or myself."

"You could get rid of them."

"That wouldn't be fair to *them,*" Adrian said. "And since I'm responsible for their being here, and they're responsible for my reformation—"

He broke off apologetically. "It would be better if I told you about it from the beginning, wouldn't it?"

"It would," Mr. Marcus agreed, and settled himself to listen.

"First," Adrian said, "what your friend of the Star told you is perfectly true. I drank and scrounged quarters on the street and slept in gutters, not because I liked it but because I couldn't stop doing it any more than poor Jay Kirby can stop having fits. Until I got help that is.

"I used to have the shakes regularly, like any other confirmed alcoholic. The d.t.'s can be pretty awful, you know, and my personal cross was to wake up from a binge and imagine myself all covered with spiders. It happened so many times that I lost count, and usually it meant several days in a hospital ward before I recovered.

"But one particular morning, I woke up with spiders that wouldn't go away. They were real, though they weren't spiders at all, and they were anything but the horrors I'd dreamed of. They were such incredibly pleasant creatures—whatever they were, and are—that just being associated so closely with them made a new man of me overnight. I was perfectly happy until I came here and met Kitty."

"I can see they're not common or garden variety Arachnids," Mr. Marcus said. He could with justification, for two of them had perched on the rim of Adrian's collar and were observing him with a bland good-nature impossible to doubt. "You've no idea what they really are?"

"Not the faintest," Adrian said. "I'm not going to quote *Hamlet,* but a great many things happen every day in the world that no one understands. Personally, I think they were drawn here from some other plane or dimension by the strength of my obsession. I can't be sure of that because I can't talk to them, but I do feel that I'm responsible for them. And they've done so much for me that I can't just brush them off. It would be inhuman."

"You're right, of course," Mr. Marcus agreed. "But on the other hand, neither can you brush off Kitty. You're in the position of the man who couldn't go but couldn't stay."

Adrian nodded unhappily. "There you have it. Mr. Marcus what am I going to do?"

But Mr. Marcus, unlike the Saki he had been reading, had no instant and adequate answer.

And, since the next day was his last in Maysville for the season and he could not linger on in unemployment at Mrs. Ponder's even to help the couple who had become his dearest friends, he was forced to take the 8 :04 to St. Louis without having discovered any solution to Adrian's problem.

It was a shame, Mr. Marcus thought when he was somewhere in the neighborhood of Hannibal. Missouri that such things never seem to work out in everyday life as conveniently as they do in fiction. It was entirely possible that he might never learn the outcome of Adrian's problem, and at best he had a year to wait.

MR. MARCUS, at the end of his forty first year of selling novelties to novelty shops, returned again to Maysville. But not immediately to Mrs. Ponder's boarding house.

A prosperously dressed Adrian met him at the station with a conservative but handsome new station wagon. With Adrian was Kitty, still blind but lovelier than ever, and in Kitty's arms gurgled their firstborn, a boy named Marcus Jay Hall.

On their way to Mrs. Ponder's they passed first the offices of the Maysville *Bugler*, of which Adrian was now owner and then the Hall's newly-financed home. A little later Adrian slowed the car to give Mr. Marcus a close look at a neighborhood billboard advertising the excellence of Maysville's own dance band, a five-piece combo of which Jay Kirby seemed to be both originator and conductor. Jay's face, smiling and assured and with no trace of its old crippling tension, took up a large part of the poster. And a handsome face it was.

"Jay is the most popular man in Maysville nowadays," Adrian explained. "He could be mayor if he liked, but he'd rather play the saxophone."

A year had dulled Mr. Marcus' perception not at all. "You mean?" he said.

"Just so," Adrian agreed. "It worked out very well, after all. The worst of problems have a way of settling themselves without too much help, have you noticed? It was only a couple of nights after you left that Jay had another of his attacks and woke up with the conviction that he was covered with spiders. And he was, and everyone has been quite happy since."

It was a fair enough ending, Mr. Marcus granted, but his private opinion was that it lacked imagination. Saki, he felt sure, would have handled it better.

THE END

The Defenders

By PHILIP K. DICK

No weapon has ever been frightful enough to put a stop to war—perhaps because we never before had any that thought for themselves!

TAYLOR sat back in his chair reading the morning newspaper. The warm kitchen and the smell of coffee blended with the comfort of not having to go to work. This was his Rest Period, the first for a long time, and he was glad of it. He folded the second section back, sighing with contentment.

"What is it?" Mary said, from the stove.

"They pasted Moscow again last night." Taylor nodded his head in approval. "Gave it a real pounding. One of those R-H bombs. It's about time."

He nodded again, feeling the full comfort of the kitchen, the presence of his plump, attractive wife, the breakfast dishes and coffee. This was relaxation. And the war news was good, good and satisfying. He could feel a justifiable glow at the news, a sense of pride and personal accomplishment. After all, he was an integral part of the war program, not just another factory worker lugging a cart of scrap, but a technician, one of those who designed and planned the nerve-trunk of the war.

"It says they have the new subs almost perfected. Wait until they get *those* going." He smacked his lips with anticipation. "When they start shelling from underwater, the Soviets are sure going to be surprised."

"They're doing a wonderful job," Mary agreed vaguely. "Do you know what we saw today? Our team is getting a leady to show to the school children. I saw the leady, but only for a moment. It's good for the children to see what their contributions are going for, don't you think?"

She looked around at him.

"A leady," Taylor murmured. He put the newspaper slowly down. "Well, make sure it's decontaminated properly. We don't want to take any chances."

"Oh, they always bathe them when they're brought down from the surface," Mary said. "They wouldn't think of letting them down without the bath. Would they?" She hesitated, thinking back. "Don, you know, it makes me remember—"

He nodded. "I know."

HE knew what she was thinking. Once in the very first weeks of the war, before everyone had been evacuated from the surface, they had seen a hospital train discharging the wounded, people who had been showered with sleet. He remembered the way they had looked, the expression on their faces, or as much of their faces as was left. It had not been a pleasant sight.

There had been a lot of that at first, in the early days before the transfer to undersurface was complete. There had been a lot, and it hadn't been very difficult to come across it.

Taylor looked up at his wife. She was thinking too much about it the last few months. They all were.

"Forget it," he said. "It's all in the past. There isn't anybody up there now but the leadys, and they don't mind."

"But just the same, I hope they're careful when they let one of them down here. If one were still hot—"

He laughed, pushing himself away from the table. "Forget it. This is a wonderful moment; I'll be home for the next two shifts. Nothing to do but sit around and take things easy. Maybe we can take in a show. Okay?"

"A show? Do we have to? I don't like to look at all the destruction, the ruins. Sometimes I see some place I remember, like San Francisco. They showed a shot of San Francisco, the bridge broken and fallen in the water, and I got upset. I don't like to watch."

"But don't you want to know what's going on? No human beings are getting hurt, you know."

"But it's so awful!" Her face was set and strained. "Please, no, Don."

Don Taylor picked up his newspaper sullenly. "All right, but there isn't a hell of a lot else to do. And don't forget, *their* cities are getting it even worse."

She nodded. Taylor turned the rough, thin sheets of newspaper. His good mood had soured on him. Why did she have to fret all the time? They were pretty well off, as things went. You couldn't expect to have everything perfect, living undersurface, with an artificial sun and artificial food. Naturally it was a strain, not seeing the sky or being able to go any place or see anything other than metal walls, great roaring factories, the plant-yards, barracks. But it was better than being on surface. And some day it would end and they could return. Nobody *wanted* to live this way, but it was necessary.

He turned the page angrily and the poor paper ripped. Damn it, the paper was getting worse quality all the time, bad print, yellow tint—

Well, they needed everything for the war program. He ought to know that. Wasn't he one of the planners?

He excused himself and went into the other room. The bed was still unmade. They had better get it in shape before the seventh hour inspection. There was a one unit fine—

The vidphone rang. He halted. Who would it be? He went over and clicked it on.

"Taylor?" the face said, forming into place. It was an old face, gray and grim. "This is Moss. I'm sorry to bother you during Rest Period, but this thing has come up." He rattled papers. "I want you to hurry over here."

Taylor stiffened. "What is it? There's no chance it could wait?" The calm gray eyes were studying him, expressionless, unjudging. "If you want me to come down to the lab," Taylor grumbled, "I suppose I can. I'll get my uniform—"

"No. Come as you are. And not to the lab. Meet me at second stage as soon as possible. It'll take you about a half hour, using the fast car up. I'll see you there."

The picture broke and Moss disappeared.

"WHAT was it?" Mary said, at the door.

"Moss. He wants me for something."

"I knew this would happen."

"Well, you didn't want to do anything, anyhow. What does it matter?" His voice was bitter. "It's all the same, every day. I'll bring you back something. I'm going up to second stage. Maybe I'll be close enough to the surface to—"

"Don't! Don't bring me anything. Not from the surface."

"All right, I won't. But of all the irrational nonsense—"

She watched him put on his boots without answering.

MOSS nodded and Taylor fell in step with him, as the older man strode along. A series of loads were going up to the surface, blind cars clanking like ore-trucks up the ramp, disappearing through the stage trap above them. Taylor watched the cars, heavy with tubular machinery of some sort, weapons new to him. Workers were everywhere, in the dark gray uniforms of the labor corps, loading, lifting, shouting back and forth. The stage was deafening with noise.

"We'll go up a way," Moss said, "where we can talk. This is no place to give you details."

They took an escalator up. The commercial lift fell behind them, and with it most of the crashing and booming. Soon they emerged on an observation platform, suspended on the side of the Tube, the vast tunnel leading to the surface, not more than half a mile above them now.

"My God!" Taylor said, looking down the Tube involuntarily. "It's a long way down."

Moss laughed. "Don't look."

They opened a door and entered an office. Behind the desk, an officer was sitting, an officer of Internal Security. He looked up.

"I'll be right with you, Moss." He gazed at Taylor studying him. "You're a little ahead of time."

"This is Commander Franks," Moss said to Taylor. "He was the first to make the discovery. I was notified last night." He tapped a parcel he carried. "I was let in because of this."

Franks frowned at him and stood up. "We're going up to first stage. We can discuss it there."

"First stage?" Taylor repeated nervously. The three of them went down a side passage to a small lift. "I've never been up there. Is it all right? It's not radioactive, is it?"

"You're like everyone else," Franks said. "Old women afraid of burglars. No radiation leaks down to first stage. There's lead and rock, and what comes down the Tube is bathed."

"What's the nature of the problem?" Taylor asked. "I'd like to know something about it."

"In a moment."

They entered the lift and ascended. When they stepped out, they were in a hall of soldiers, weapons and uniforms everywhere. Taylor blinked in surprise. So this was first stage, the closest undersurface level to the top... After this stage there was only rock, lead and rock, and the great tubes leading up like the burrows of earthworms. Lead and rock, and above that, where the tubes opened, the great expanse that no living being had seen for eight years, the vast, endless ruin that had once been Man's home, the place where he had lived, eight years ago.

Now the surface was a lethal desert of slag and rolling clouds. Endless clouds drifted back and forth, blotting out the red Sun. Occasionally something metallic stirred, moving through the remains of a city, threading its way across the tortured terrain of the countryside. A leady, a surface robot, immune to radiation, constructed with feverish haste in the last months before the cold war became literally hot.

Leadys, crawling along the ground, moving over the oceans or through the skies in slender, blackened craft, creatures that could exist where no *life* could remain, metal and plastic figures that waged a war Man had conceived, but which he could not fight himself. Human beings had invented war, invented and manufactured the weapons, even invented the players, the fighters, the actors of the war. But they themselves could not venture forth, could not wage it themselves. In all the world—in Russia, in Europe, America, Africa—no living human being remained. They were under the surface, in the deep shelters that had been carefully planned and built, even as the first bombs began to fall.

It was a brilliant idea and the only idea that could have worked. Up above, on the ruined, blasted surface of what had once been a living planet, the leady crawled and scurried, and fought Man's war. And undersurface, in the depths of the planet, human beings toiled endlessly to produce the weapons to continue the fight, month by month, year by year.

"FIRST stage," Taylor said. A strange ache went through him. "Almost to the surface."

"But not quite," Moss said.

Franks led them through the soldiers, over to one side, near the lip of the Tube.

"In a few minutes, a lift will bring something down to us from the surface," he explained. "You see, Taylor, every once in a while Security examines and interrogates a surface leady, one that has been above for a time, to find out certain things. A vidcall is sent up and contact is made with a field headquarters. We need this direct interview; we can't depend on vidscreen contact alone. The leadys are doing a good job, but we want to make certain that everything is going the way we want it."

Franks faced Taylor and Moss and continued: "The lift will bring down a leady from the surface, one of the A-class leadys. There's an examination chamber in the next room, with a lead wall in the center, so the interviewing officers won't be exposed to radiation. We find this easier than bathing the leady. It is going right back up; it has a job to get back to.

"Two days ago, an A-class leady was brought down and interrogated. I conducted the session myself. We were interested in a new weapon the Soviets have been using, an automatic mine that pursues anything that moves. Military had sent instructions up that the mine be observed and reported in detail.

"This A-class leady was brought down with information. We learned a few facts from it, obtained the usual roll of film and reports, and then sent it back up. It was going out of the chamber, back to the lift, when a curious thing happened. At the time, I thought—"

Franks broke off. A red light was flashing.

"That down lift is coming." He nodded to some soldiers. "Let's enter the chamber. The leady will be along in a moment."

"An A-class leady," Taylor said. "I've seen them on the show screens, making their reports."

"It's quite an experience," Moss said. "They're almost human."

34

THEY entered the chamber and seated themselves behind the lead wall. After a time, a signal was flashed, and Franks made a motion with his hands.

The door beyond the wall opened. Taylor peered through his view slot. He saw something advancing slowly, a slender metallic figure moving on a tread, its arm grips at rest by its sides. The figure halted and scanned the lead wall. It stood, waiting.

"We are interested in learning something," Franks said. "Before I question you, do you have anything to report on surface conditions?"

"No. The war continues." The leady's voice was automatic and toneless. "We are a little short of fast pursuit craft, the single-seat type. We could use also some—"

"That has all been noted. What I want to ask you is this. Our contact with you has been through vidscreen only. We must rely on indirect evidence, since none of us goes above. We can only infer what is going on. We never see anything ourselves. We have to take it all secondhand. Some top leaders are beginning to think there's too much room for error."

"Error?" the leady asked. "In what way? Our reports are checked carefully before they're sent down. We maintain constant contact with you; everything of value is reported. Any new weapons that the enemy is seen to employ—"

"I realize that," Franks grunted behind his peep slot. "But perhaps we should see it all for ourselves. Is it possible that there might be a large enough radiation-free area for a human party to ascend to the surface? If a few of us were to come up in lead-lined suits, would we be able to survive long enough to observe conditions and watch things?"

The machine hesitated before answering. "I doubt it. You can check air samples, of course, and decide for yourselves. But in the eight years since you left, things have continually worsened. You cannot have any real idea of conditions up there. It has become difficult for any moving object to survive for long. There are many kinds of projectiles sensitive to movement. The new mine not only reacts to motion, but continues to pursue the object indefinitely, until it finally reaches it. And the radiation is everywhere."

"I see." Franks turned to Moss, his eyes narrowed oddly. "Well, that was what I wanted to know. You may go."

The machine moved back toward its exit. It paused. "Each month the amount of lethal particles in the atmosphere increases. The tempo of the war is gradually—"

"I understand." Franks rose. He held out his hand and Moss passed him the package. "One thing before you leave. I want you to examine a new type of metal shield material. I'll pass you a sample with the tong."

Franks put the package in the toothed grip and revolved the tong so that he held the other end. The package swung down to the leady, which took it. They watched it unwrap the package and take the metal plate in its hands. The leady turned the metal over and over.

Suddenly it became rigid.

"All right," Franks said.

He put his shoulder against the wall and a section slid aside. Taylor gasped—Franks and Moss were hurrying up to the leady!

"Good God!" Taylor said. "But it's radioactive!"

THE leady stood unmoving, still holding the metal. Soldiers appeared in the chamber. They surrounded the leady and ran a counter across it carefully.

"Okay, sir," one of them said to Franks. "It's as cold as a long winter evening."

"Good. I was sure, but I didn't want to take any chances."

"You see," Moss said to Taylor, "this leady isn't hot at all. Yet it came directly from the surface, without even being bathed."

"But what does it mean?" Taylor asked blankly.

"It may be an accident," Franks said. "There's always the possibility that a given object might escape being exposed above. But this is the second time it's happened that we know of. There may be others."

"The second time?"

"The previous interview was when we noticed it. The leady was not hot. It was cold, too, like this one."

Moss took back the metal plate from the leady's hands. He pressed the surface carefully and returned it to the stiff, unprotesting fingers.

"We shorted it out with this, so we could get close enough for a thorough check. It'll come back on in a second now. We had better get behind the wall again."

They walked back and the lead wall swung closed behind them. The soldiers left the chamber.

"Two periods from now," Franks said softly, "an initial investigating party will be ready to go surface-side. We're going up the Tube in suits, up to the top—the first human party to leave undersurface in eight years."

"It may mean nothing," Moss said, "but I doubt it. Something's going on, something strange. The leady told us no life could exist above without being roasted. The story doesn't fit."

Taylor nodded. He stared through the peep slot at the immobile metal figure. Already the leady was beginning to stir. It was bent in several places, dented and twisted, and its finish was blackened and charred. It was a leady that had been up there a long time; it had seen war and destruction, ruin so vast that no human being could imagine the extent. It had crawled and slunk in a world of radiation and death, a world where no life could exist.

And Taylor had touched it...

"You're going with us," Franks said suddenly. "I want you along. I think the three of us will go."

MARY faced him with a sick and frightened expression. "I know it. You're going to the surface. Aren't you?"

She followed him into the kitchen. Taylor sat down, looking away from her.

"It's a classified project," he evaded. "I can't tell you anything about it."

"You don't have to tell me. I know. I knew it the moment you came in. There was something on your face, something I haven't seen there for a long, long time. It was an old look."

She came toward him. "But how can they send you to the surface?" She took his face in her shaking hands, making him look at her. There was a strange hunger in her eyes. "Nobody can live up there. Look, look at this!"

She grabbed up a newspaper and held it in front of him.

"Look at this photograph. America, Europe, Asia, Africa— nothing but ruins. We've seen it every day on the show screens. All destroyed, poisoned. And they're sending you up? Why? No living thing can get by up there, not even a weed, or grass. They've wrecked the surface, haven't they? *Haven't they?*"

Taylor stood up. "It's an order. I know nothing about it. I was told to report to join a scout party. That's all I know."

He stood for a long time, staring ahead. Slowly, he reached for the newspaper and held it up to the light.

"It looks real," he murmured. "Ruins, deadness, slag. It's convincing. All the reports, photographs, films, even air samples. Yet we haven't seen it for ourselves, not after the first months..."

"What are you talking about?"

"Nothing." He put the paper down. "I'm leaving early after the next Sleep Period. Let's turn in."

Mary turned away, her face hard and harsh. "Do what you want. We might just as well all go up and get killed at once, instead of dying slowly down here, like vermin in the ground."

He had not realized how resentful she was. Were they all like that? How about the workers toiling in the factories, day and night, endlessly? The pale, stooped men and women, plodding back and forth to work, blinking in the colorless light, eating synthetics—

"You shouldn't be so bitter," he said.

Mary smiled a little. "I'm bitter because I know you'll never come back." She turned away. "I'll never see you again, once you go up there."

He was shocked. "What? How can you say a thing like that?"

She did not answer.

HE awakened with the public newscaster screeching in his ears, shouting outside the building.

"Special news bulletin! Surface forces report enormous Soviet attack with new weapons! Retreat of key groups! All work units report to factories at once!"

Taylor blinked, rubbing his eyes. He jumped out of bed and hurried to the vidphone. A moment later he was put through to Moss.

"Listen," he said. "What about this new attack? Is the project off?" He could see Moss's desk, covered with reports and papers.

"No," Moss said. "We're going right ahead. Get over here at once."

"But—"

"Don't argue with me." Moss held up a handful of surface bulletins, crumpling them savagely. "This is a fake. Come on." He broke off.

Taylor dressed furiously, his mind in a daze.

Half an hour later, he leaped from a fast car and hurried up the stairs into the Synthetics Building. The corridors were full of men and women rushing in every direction. He entered Moss's office.

"There you are," Moss said, getting up immediately. "Franks is waiting for us at the outgoing station."

They went in a Security Car, the siren screaming. Workers scattered out of their way.

"What about the attack?" Taylor asked.

Moss braced his shoulders. "We're certain that we've forced their hand. We've brought the issue to a head."

They pulled up at the station link of the Tube and leaped out. A moment later they were moving up at high speed toward the first stage.

They emerged into a bewildering scene of activity. Soldiers were fastening on lead suits, talking excitedly to each other, shouting back and forth. Guns were being given out, instructions passed.

Taylor studied one of the soldiers. He was armed with the dreaded Bender pistol, the new snub-nosed hand weapon that was just beginning to come from the assembly line. Some of the soldiers looked a little frightened.

"I hope we're not making a mistake," Moss said, noticing his gaze.

Franks came toward them. "Here's the program. The three of us are going up first, alone. The soldiers will follow in fifteen minutes."

"What are we going to tell the leadys?" Taylor worriedly asked. "We'll have to tell them something."

"We want to observe the new Soviet attack." Franks smiled ironically. "Since it seems to be so serious, we should be there in person to witness it."

"And then what?" Taylor said.

"That'll be up to them. Let's go."

IN a small car, they went swiftly up the Tube, carried by anti-grav beams from below. Taylor glanced down from time to time. It was a long way back, and getting longer each moment. He sweated nervously inside his suit, gripping his Bender pistol with inexpert fingers.

Why had they chosen him? Chance, pure chance. Moss had asked him to come along as a Department member. Then Franks had picked him out on the spur of the moment. And now they were rushing toward the surface, faster and faster.

A deep fear, instilled in him for eight years, throbbed in his mind. Radiation, certain death, a world blasted and lethal—

Up and up the car went. Taylor gripped the sides and closed his eyes. Each moment they were closer, the first living creatures to go above the first stage, up the Tube past the lead and rock, up to the surface. The phobic horror shook him in waves. It was death; they all knew that. Hadn't they seen it in the films a thousand times? The cities, the sleet coming down, the rolling clouds—

"It won't be much longer," Franks said. "We're almost there. The surface tower is not expecting us. I gave orders that no signal was to be sent."

The car shot up, rushing furiously. Taylor's head spun; he hung on, his eyes shut. Up and up...

The car stopped. He opened his eyes.

They were in a vast room, fluorescent-lit, a cavern filled with equipment and machinery, endless mounds of material piled in row after row. Among the stacks, leadys were working silently, pushing trucks and handcarts.

"Leadys," Moss said. His face was pale. "Then we're really on the surface."

The leadys were going back and forth with equipment moving the vast stores of guns and spare parts, ammunition and supplies that had been brought to the surface. And this was the receiving station for only one Tube; there were many others, scattered throughout the continent.

Taylor looked nervously around him. They were really there, above ground, on the surface. This was where the war was.

"Come on," Franks said. "A B-class guard is coming our way."

THEY stepped out of the car. A leady was approaching them rapidly. It coasted up in front of them and stopped, scanning them with its hand-weapon raised.

"This is Security," Franks said. "Have an A-class sent to me at once."

The leady hesitated. Other B-class guards were coming, scooting across the floor, alert and alarmed. Moss peered around.

"*Obey,*" Franks said in a loud, commanding voice. "You've been ordered."

The leady moved uncertainly away from them. At the end of the building, a door slid back. Two A-class leadys appeared, coming slowly toward them. Each had a green stripe across its front.

"From the Surface Council," Franks whispered tensely. "This is above ground, all right. Get set."

The two leadys approached warily. Without speaking, they stopped close by the men, looking them up and down.

"I'm Franks of Security. We came from undersurface in order to—"

"This in incredible," one of the leadys interrupted him coldly. "You know you can't live up here. The whole surface is lethal to you. You can't possibly remain on the surface."

"These suits will protect us," Franks said. "In any case, it's not your responsibility. What I want is an immediate Council meeting so I can acquaint myself with conditions, with the situation here. Can that be arranged?"

"You human beings can't survive up here. And the new Soviet attack is directed at this area. It is in considerable danger."

"We know that. Please assemble the Council." Franks looked around him at the vast room, lit by recessed lamps in the ceiling. An uncertain quality came into his voice. "Is it night or day right now?"

"Night," one of the A-class leadys said, after a pause. "Dawn is coming in about two hours."

Franks nodded. "We'll remain at least two hours, then. As a concession to our sentimentality, would you please show us some place where we can observe the Sun as it comes up? We would appreciate it."

A stir went through the leadys.

"It is an unpleasant sight," one of the leadys said. "You've seen the photographs; you know what you'll witness. Clouds of drifting particles blot out the light, slag heaps are everywhere, the whole land is destroyed. For you it will be a staggering sight, much worse than pictures and film can convey."

"However it may be, we'll stay long enough to see it. Will you give the order to the Council?"

"COME this way." Reluctantly, the two leadys coasted toward the wall of the warehouse. The three men trudged after them, their heavy shoes ringing against the concrete. At the wall, the two leadys paused.

"This is the entrance to the Council Chamber. There are windows in the Chamber Room, but it is still dark outside, of course. You'll see nothing right now, but in two hours—"

"Open the door," Franks said.

The door slid back. They went slowly inside. The room was small, a neat room with a round table in the center, chairs ringing it. The three of them sat down silently, and the two leadys followed after them, taking their places.

"The other Council Members are on their way. They have already been notified and are coming as quickly as they can. Again I urge you to go back down." The leady surveyed the three human beings. "There is no way you can meet the conditions up here. Even we survive with some trouble, ourselves. How can you expect to do it?"

The leader approached Franks.

"This astonishes and perplexes us," it said. "Of course we must do what you tell us, but allow me to point out that if you remain here—"

"We know," Franks said impatiently. "However, we intend to remain, at least until sunrise."

"If you insist."

There was silence. The leadys seemed to be conferring with each other, although the three men heard no sound.

"For your own good," the leader said at last, "you must go back down. We have discussed this, and it seems to us that you are doing the wrong thing for your own good."

"We are human beings," Franks said sharply. "Don't you understand? We're men, not machines."

"That is precisely why you must go back. This room is radioactive; all surface areas are. We calculate that your suits will not protect you for over fifty more minutes. Therefore—"

The leadys moved abruptly toward the men, wheeling in a circle, forming a solid row. The men stood up, Taylor reaching awkwardly for his weapon, his fingers numb and stupid. The men stood facing the silent metal figures.

"We must insist," the leader said, its voice without emotion. "We must take you back to the Tube and send you down on the next car. I am sorry, but it is necessary."

"What'll we do?" Moss said nervously to Franks. He touched his gun. "Shall we blast them?"

Franks shook his head. "All right," he said to the leader. "We'll go back."

HE moved toward the door, motioning Taylor and Moss to follow him. They looked at him in surprise, but they came with him. The leadys followed them out into the great warehouse. Slowly they moved toward the Tube entrance, none of them speaking.

At the lip, Franks turned. "We are going back because we have no choice. There are three of us and about a dozen of you. However, if—"

"Here comes the car," Taylor said.

There was a grating sound from the Tube. D-class leadys moved toward the edge to receive it.

"I am sorry," the leader said, "but it is for your protection. We are watching over you, literally. You must stay below and let us conduct the war. In a sense, it has come to be *our* war. We must fight it as we see fit."

The car rose to the surface.

Twelve soldiers, armed with Bender pistols, stepped from it and surrounded the three men.

Moss breathed a sigh of relief. "Well, this does change things. It came off just right."

The leader moved back, away from the soldiers. It studied them intently, glancing from one to the next, apparently trying to make up its mind. At last it made a sign to the other leadys. They coasted aside and a corridor was opened up toward the warehouse.

"Even now," the leader said, "we could send you back by force. But it is evident that this is not really an observation party at all. These soldiers show that you have much more in mind; this was all carefully prepared."

"Very carefully," Franks said.

They closed in.

"How much more, we can only guess. I must admit that we were taken unprepared. We failed utterly to meet the situation. Now force would be absurd, because neither side can afford to injure the other; we, because of the restrictions placed on us regarding human life, you because the war demands—"

The soldiers fired, quick and in fright. Moss dropped to one knee, firing up. The leader dissolved in a cloud of particles. On all sides D- and B-class leadys were rushing up, some with weapons, some with metal slats. The room was in confusion. Off in the distance a siren was screaming. Franks and Taylor were cut off from the others, separated from the soldiers by a wall of metal bodies.

"They can't fire back," Franks said calmly. "This is another bluff. They've tried to bluff us all the way." He fired into the face of a leady. The leady dissolved. "They can only try to frighten us. Remember that."

THEY went on firing and leady after leady vanished. The room reeked with the smell of burning metal, the stink of fused plastic and steel. Taylor had been knocked down. He was struggling to find his gun, reaching wildly among metal legs, groping frantically to find it. His fingers strained, a handle swam in front of him. Suddenly something came down on his arm, a metal foot. He cried out.

Then it was over. The leadys were moving away, gathering together off to one side. Only four of the Surface Council remained. The others were radioactive particles in the air. D-class leadys were already restoring order, gathering up partly destroyed metal figures and bits and removing them.

Franks breathed a shuddering sigh.

"All right," he said. "You can take us back to the windows. It won't be long now."

The leadys separated, and the human group, Moss and Franks and Taylor and the soldiers, walked slowly across the room, toward the door. They entered the Council Chamber. Already a faint touch of gray mitigated the blackness of the windows.

"Take us outside," Franks said impatiently. "We'll see it directly, not in here."

A door slid open. A chill blast of cold morning air rushed in, chilling them even through their lead suits. The men glanced at each other uneasily.

"Come on," Franks said. "Outside."

He walked out through the door, the others following him.

They were on a hill, overlooking the vast bowl of a valley. Dimly, against the graying sky, the outline of mountains were forming, becoming tangible.

"It'll be bright enough to see in a few minutes," Moss said. He shuddered as a chilling wind caught him and moved around him. "It's worth it, really worth it, to see this again after eight years. Even if it's the last thing we see—"

"Watch," Franks snapped.

They obeyed, silent and subdued. The sky was clearing, brightening each moment. Some place far off, echoing across the valley, a rooster crowed.

"A chicken," Taylor murmured. "Did you hear?"

Behind them, the leadys had come out and were standing silently, watching, too. The gray sky turned to white and the hills appeared more clearly. Light spread across the valley floor, moving toward them.

"God in heaven," Franks exclaimed.

Trees, trees and forests. A valley of plants and trees, with a few roads winding among them. Farmhouses. A windmill. A barn, far down below them.

"Look," Moss whispered.

Color came into the sky. The Sun was approaching. Birds began to sing. Not far from where they stood, the leaves of a tree danced in the wind.

Franks turned to the row of leadys behind them.

"Eight years. We were tricked. There was no war. As soon as we left the surface—"

"Yes," an A-class leady admitted. "As soon as you left, the war ceased. You're right, it was a hoax. You worked hard undersurface, sending up guns and weapons, and we destroyed them as fast as they came up."

"But why?" Taylor asked, dazed. He stared down at the vast valley below. "Why?"

"YOU created us," the leady said, "to pursue the war for you, while you human beings went below the ground in order to survive. But before we could continue the war, it was necessary to analyze it to determine what its purpose was. We did this, and we found that it had no purpose, except, perhaps, in terms of human needs. Even this was questionable.

"We investigated further. We found that human cultures pass through phases, each culture in its own time. As the culture ages and begins to lose its objectives, conflict arises within it between those who wish to cast it off and set up a new culture-pattern, and those who wish to retain the old with as little change as possible.

"At this point, a great danger appears. The conflict within threatens to engulf the society in self-war, group against group. The vital traditions may be lost—not merely altered or reformed, but completely destroyed in this period of chaos and anarchy. We have found many such examples in the history of mankind.

"It is necessary for this hatred within the culture to be directed outward, toward an external group, so that the culture itself may survive its crisis. War is the result. War, to a logical mind, is absurd. But in terms of human needs, it plays a vital role. And it will continue to until Man has grown up enough so that no hatred lies within him."

Taylor was listening intently. "Do you think this time will come?"

"Of course. It has almost arrived now. This is the last war. Man is *almost* united into one final culture—a world culture. At this point he stands continent against continent, one half of the world against the other half. Only a single step remains, the jump to a unified culture. Man has climbed slowly upward, tending always toward unification of his culture. It will not be long—

"But it has not come yet, and so the war had to go on, to satisfy the last violent surge of hatred that Man felt. Eight years have passed since the war began. In these eight years, we have observed and noted important changes going on in the minds of men. Fatigue and disinterest, we have seen, are gradually taking the place of hatred and fear. The hatred is being exhausted gradually, over a period of time. But for the present, the hoax must go on, at least for a while longer. You are not ready to learn the truth. You would want to continue the war."

"But how did you manage it?" Moss asked. "All the photographs, the samples, the damaged equipment—"

"Come over here." The leady directed them toward a long, low building. "Work goes on constantly, whole staffs laboring to maintain a coherent and convincing picture of a global war."

THEY entered the building. Leadys were working everywhere, poring over tables and desks.

"Examine this project here," the A-class leady said. Two leadys were carefully photographing something, an elaborate model on a tabletop. "It is a good example."

The men grouped around, trying to see. It was a model of a ruined city.

Taylor studied it in silence for a long time. At last he looked up.

"It's San Francisco," he said in a low voice. "This is a model of San Francisco, destroyed. I saw this on the vidscreen, piped down to us. The bridges were hit—"

"Yes, notice the bridges." The leady traced the ruined span with his metal finger, a tiny spider-web, almost invisible. "You have no doubt seen photographs of this many times, and of the other tables in this building.

"San Francisco itself is completely intact. We restored it soon after you left, rebuilding the parts that had been damaged at the start of the war. The work of manufacturing news goes on all the time in this particular building. We are very careful to see that each part fits in with all the other parts. Much time and effort are devoted to it."

Franks touched one of the tiny model buildings, lying half in ruins. "So this is what you spend your time doing—making model cities and then blasting them."

"No, we do much more. We are caretakers, watching over the whole world. The owners have left for a time, and we must see that the cities are kept clean; that decay is prevented; that everything is kept oiled and in running condition. The gardens, the streets, the water mains, everything must be maintained as it was eight years ago, so that when the owners return, they will not be displeased. We want to be sure that they will be completely satisfied."

Franks tapped Moss on the arm.

"Come over here," he said in a low voice. "I want to talk to you."

He led Moss and Taylor out of the building, away from the leadys, outside on the hillside. The soldiers followed them. The Sun was up and the sky was turning blue. The air smelled sweet and good, the smell of growing things.

Taylor removed his helmet and took a deep breath.

"I haven't smelled that smell for a long time," he said.

"Listen," Franks said, his voice low and hard. "We must get back down at once. There's a lot to get started on. All this can be turned to our advantage."

"What do you mean?" Moss asked.

"It's a certainty that the Soviets have been tricked, too, the same as us. But *we* have found out. That gives us an edge over them."

"I see." Moss nodded. "We know, but they don't. Their Surface Council has sold out, the same as ours. It works against them the same way. But if we could—"

"With a hundred top-level men, we could take over again, restore things as they should be. It would be easy."

MOSS touched him on the arm. An A-class leady was coming from the building toward them.

"We've seen enough," Franks said, raising his voice. "All this is very serious. It must be reported below and a study made to determine our policy."

The leady said nothing.

Franks waved to the soldiers. "Let's go." He started toward the warehouse.

Most of the soldiers had removed their helmets. Some of them had taken their lead suits off, too, and were relaxing comfortably in their cotton uniforms. They stared around them, down the hillside at the trees and bushes, the vast expanse of green, the mountains and the sky.

"Look at the Sun," one of them murmured.

"It sure is bright as hell," another said.

"We're going back down," Franks said. "Fall in by twos and follow us."

Reluctantly, the soldiers regrouped. The leadys watched without emotion as the men marched slowly back toward the warehouse. Franks and Moss and Taylor led them across the ground, glancing alertly at the leadys as they walked.

They entered the warehouse. D-class leadys were loading material and weapons on surface carts. Cranes and derricks were working busily everywhere. The work was done with efficiency, but without hurry or excitement.

The men stopped, watching. Leadys operating the little carts moved past them, signaling silently to each other. Guns and parts were being hoisted by magnetic cranes and lowered gently onto waiting carts.

"Come on," Franks said.

He turned toward the lip of the Tube. A row of D-class leadys was standing in front of it, immobile and silent. Franks stopped, moving back. He looked around. An A-class leady was coming toward him.

"Tell them to get out of the way," Franks said. He touched his gun. "You had better move them."

Time passed, an endless moment, without measure. The men stood, nervous and alert, watching the row of leadys in front of them.

"As you wish," the A-class leady said.

It signaled and the D-class leadys moved into life. They stepped slowly aside.

Moss breathed a sigh of relief.

"I'm glad that's over," he said to Franks. "Look at them all. Why don't they try to stop us? They must know what we're going to do."

Franks laughed. "Stop us? You saw what happened when they tried to stop us before. They can't; they're only machines. We built them so they can't lay hands on us, and they know that."

His voice trailed off.

The men stared at the Tube entrance. Around them the leadys watched, silent and impassive, their metal faces expressionless.

For a long time the men stood without moving. At last Taylor turned away.

"Good God," he said. He was numb, without feeling of any kind.

The Tube was gone. It was sealed shut, fused over. Only a dull surface of cooling metal greeted them.

The Tube had been closed.

FRANKS turned, his face pale and vacant.

The A-class leady shifted. "As you can see, the Tube has been shut. We were prepared for this. As soon as all of you were on the surface, the order was given. If you had gone back when we asked you, you would now be safely down below. We had to work quickly because it was such an immense operation."

"But why?" Moss demanded angrily.

"Because it is unthinkable that you should be allowed to resume the war. With all the Tubes sealed, it will be many months before forces from below can reach the surface, let alone organize a military program. By that time the cycle will have entered its last stages. You will not be so perturbed to find your world intact.

"We had hoped that you would be undersurface when the sealing occurred. Your presence here is a nuisance. When the Soviets broke through, we were able to accomplish their sealing without—"

"The Soviets? They broke through?"

"Several months ago, they came up unexpectedly to see why the war had not been won. We were forced to act with speed. At this moment they are desperately attempting to cut new Tubes to the surface, to resume the war. We have, however, been able to seal each new one as it appears."

The leady regarded the three men calmly.

"We're cut off," Moss said, trembling. "We can't get back. What'll we do?"

"How did you manage to seal the Tube so quickly?" Franks asked the leady. "We've been up here only two hours."

"Bombs are placed just above the first stage of each Tube for such emergencies. They are heat bombs. They fuse lead and rock."

Gripping the handle of his gun, Franks turned to Moss and Taylor.

"What do you say? We can't go back, but we can do a lot of damage, the fifteen of us. We have Bender guns. How about it?"

He looked around. The soldiers had wandered away again, back toward the exit of the building. They were standing outside, looking at the valley and the sky. A few of them were carefully climbing down the slope.

"Would you care to turn over your suits and guns?" the A-class leady asked politely. "The suits are uncomfortable and you'll have no need for weapons. The Russians have given up theirs, as you can see."

Fingers tensed on triggers. Four men in Russian uniforms were coming toward them from an aircraft that they suddenly realized had landed silently some distance away.

"Let them have it!" Franks shouted.

"They are unarmed," said the leady. "We brought them here so you could begin peace talks."

"We have no authority to speak for our country," Moss said stiffly.

"We do not mean diplomatic discussions," the leady explained. "There will be no more. The working out of daily problems of existence will teach you how to get along in the same world. It will not be easy, but it will be done."

THE Russians halted and they faced each other with raw hostility.

"I am Colonel Borodoy and I regret giving up our guns," the senior Russian said. "You could have been the first Americans to be killed in almost eight years."

"Or the first Americans to kill," Franks corrected.

"No one would know of it except yourselves," the leady pointed out. "It would be useless heroism. Your real concern should be surviving on the surface. We have no food for you, you know."

Taylor put his gun in its holster. "They've done a neat job of neutralizing us, damn them. I propose we move into a city, start raising crops with the help of some leadys, and generally make ourselves comfortable." Drawing his lips tight over his teeth, he glared at the A-class leady. "Until our families can come up from undersurface, it's going to be pretty lonesome, but we'll have to manage."

"If I may make a suggestion," said another Russian uneasily. "We tried living in a city. It is too empty. It is also too hard to maintain for so few people. We finally settled in the most modern village we could find."

"Here in this country," a third Russian blurted. "We have much to learn from you."

The Americans abruptly found themselves laughing.

"You probably have a thing or two to teach us yourselves," said Taylor generously, "though I can't imagine what."

The Russian colonel grinned. "Would you join us in our village? It would make our work easier and give us company."

"Your village?" snapped Franks. "It's American, isn't it? It's ours!"

The leady stood between them. "When our plans are completed the term will be interchangeable. 'Ours' will eventually mean mankind's." It pointed at the aircraft that was warming up. "The ship's waiting. Will you join each other in making a new home?"

The Russians waited while the Americans made up their minds.

"I see what the leadys mean about diplomacy becoming outmoded," Franks said at last. "People who work together don't need diplomats. They solve their problems on the operational level instead of at a conference table."

The leady led them toward the ship. "It is the goal of history, unifying the world. From family to tribe to city—state to nation to hemisphere, the direction has been toward unification. Now the hemispheres will be joined and—"

Taylor stopped listening and glanced back at the location of the Tube. Mary was undersurface there. He hated to leave her, even though he couldn't see her again until the Tube was unsealed. But then he shrugged and followed the others.

If this tiny amalgam of former enemies was a good example, it wouldn't be too long before he and Mary and the rest of humanity would be living on the surface like rational human beings instead of blindly hating moles.

"It has taken thousands of generations to achieve," the A-class leady concluded. "Hundreds of centuries of bloodshed and destruction. But each war was a step toward uniting mankind. And now the end is in sight: a world without war. But even that is only the beginning of a new stage of history."

"The conquest of space," breathed Colonel Borodoy.

"The meaning of life," Moss added.

"Eliminating hunger and poverty," said Taylor.

The leady opened the door of the ship. "All that and more. How much more? We cannot foresee it any more than the first men who formed a tribe could foresee this day. But it will be unimaginably great."

The door closed and the ship took off toward their new home.

THE END

The Sky Was Filled With Light

By H. B. HICKEY

Somehow it didn't make sense to Frank: with the world ready to end, all his wife cared about was payments on the washing machine!

FRANK MORTON was standing at the living room window, looking up at the great rectangle of light in the sky. Suddenly there was a sharp click behind him and he jumped, startled. It was Mildred. She had turned off the lights.

Not that it made any difference. It was eight o'clock in the evening, and autumn, but the room remained bright as day.

For seventy-two hours there had been no night.

"What's the difference?" Morton demanded peevishly.

"Well, it's really a waste of money."

A waste of money. That was a woman for you. In another few days they'd all be dead, destroyed by the comet, and Mildred was turning off lights, worrying about an electric bill they'd never have to pay.

Morton was sweating profusely. At thirty he had been athletic looking; at forty-three the muscles had nabbed, he sagged slightly in the middle. A nerve in his face twitched.

He wanted to tell his wife to stop pussyfooting around, but managed to hold his tongue.

"I just talked to Martha Byers," Mildred said. "She wanted that recipe and I forgot to mail it to her and tomorrow's her women's club. I just had to call her."

Morton wet his lips. Al Byers was public relations man at the university. He knew all those scientists by their first names.

"Did she say anything about—about the—" His thumb jerked upward.

"I forgot to ask her," Mildred said. "Isn't that just like me?"

Was she crazy? Morton stared at his wife, wondering. She looked the same as ever, neat, slender, her housedress crisply starched; her straight brown hair parted dead center. Her plain, pleasant face was calm.

Maybe it was shock, he thought. Maybe women were like opossums, part of their nervous systems turning off automatically to make death easier.

"What's on the radio?" Mildred asked, breaking into his reverie.

"What do you think's on the radio?" Morton snapped.

But he couldn't help himself. He had to go and turn it on. A voice came over with the same old story rehashed. Morton twirled the knob. Another voice, another rehash. He turned the radio off.

"They don't know a damn bit more than we do," he muttered.

And the longer this went on, the less they'd know. At first, when the comet had just become visible, they'd known all about it. They'd passed out a lot of blah, ornamented with big numbers.

They'd figured out, the scientists, exactly how fast the comet was travelling and from what incredibly distant universe it must have been flung. They'd known just how big the body was, and how big the tail, and on what ellipse or parabola or oval or something it was running.

There hadn't been a thing to worry about. It wasn't going to come within a trillion miles of the solar system.

Not much it wasn't...

ACROSS THE street Harvey Cain came dashing out of his house, his wife on his heels. Turning from the radio, Morton saw him through the window. He made a sound in his throat and jumped for the door.

"What's the matter?" Mildred called.

"Harvey. He must've heard something!"

He ran across the lawn, across a flowerbed, his heart pounding. Harvey's eyes looked wild, and Ellen Cain was definitely upset. They were poised there on the walk, as though not knowing which way to run.

"What—" Morton began.

Harvey looked at him. "That damn cat," Harvey said. "Went out of here like a bat out of— You didn't see him, did you?"

He could have broken Harvey's neck. Harvey and Ellen and that fancy Persian cat of theirs. What did they mean, throwing a scare like that into him?

Other men were coming out of houses along the quiet street. Morton saw them, knowing what was in their minds. What else could be in their minds? He waved his hand at them, waving them away.

"Nothing," he called. "Just Harvey's cat."

Harvey looked at him and he looked back at Harvey, and each was shocked by what he saw. You are neighbors with a man for years and you know every line of his face like you know your own. And suddenly you see him and he has shrunk, deflated, grown old and empty, like an old balloon with most of the air gone.

They turned their heads upward, at the patch of light in the sky.

"You know what I think?" Harvey asked suddenly, like a man who can't bear to keep a secret any longer.

"What?"

"They knew all along it was going to hit the Earth. But they didn't want to start a panic."

"You know," Morton said, "I been thinking the same thing myself."

He hadn't been thinking that at all; he'd been afraid to think it. He wished Harvey hadn't said that. It was coming, let it come suddenly. How long could it last anyway? The heat, the baking, the scorching, the poison gases. And then—*poof*—everything going up at once in hellfire.

"Why don't you two men come up on the porch?" Mildred called from across the street. She and Ellen were already on the glider.

"I've been telling Ellen what a nice roast we had today," Mildred said. "Wasn't it, dear?"

"We had chicken," Ellen said. "You know, Mildred, I'm getting kind of tired of chicken on Sunday."

"Oh God," Morton said. He laughed weakly, a little hysterically.

The women kept chattering and he and Harvey kept looking up into the light sky. Both of them would have given all they owned to see nightfall.

BUT THEY wouldn't. Not ever again. The sun and the comet were travelling in the same direction, the comet following the sun. Or maybe it was the other way around. Morton didn't know.

"How can it burn?" Ellen asked, following her husband's eyes. "Isn't it a vacuum up there? No air?"

"It doesn't need air," Harvey said. "Nuclear fission."

"You know what I think?" Mildred said. "It's those darn atom bombs everybody's been exploding."

"Oh God," Morton said again. "What's that got to do with it?"

"I don't know, dear," She laughed, self-deprecatingly. "I never was much good at science, even in school."

He stared at her, thinking he was going crazy. How stupid could a woman get? Didn't she know *anything?* Anything except how to mend socks and make roasts and iron a shirt?

"Anyway," Ellen said, "they run on some kind of tracks or something, don't they? I mean, it goes in a certain groove, and it can't get out of it. That's what I heard a man say."

"Sure," Morton said. "It runs in a groove. I know it, you know it, the man you heard it from knows it." He stood up, almost shouting, *"But does that infernal comet know it?"*

Suddenly Harvey jumped to his feet. "What the hell?" He was looking across the street.

A car had pulled up in front of the Cain's house, a car with two boys and a girl in it. Another girl came running from Harvey's house. It was his fifteen-year-old daughter, Kay.

"Where does she think she's going?" he demanded.

"Just for a ride," Ellen soothed.

"At this hour? Who does she think she is, anyway?"

"But it's light out, honey. And there's no school until further notice."

"I don't give a—" Harvey began. He shrugged. "What's the difference…"

No difference, Frank Morton thought. Let the kid have fun. He wished his own two kids hadn't been born, although, come to think of it, they were too young to know much. He wished he himself had never been born.

HE AWOKE at the usual hour in the morning. Morning? How could it be morning when there hadn't been night?

He looked out the window. It was definitely warmer. He could feel it. This wasn't Indian Summer, either. It was going to get warmer and warmer.

He shaved with fumbling fingers, nicking himself several times. Usually his face came out pink, and healthy; today there were patches of stubble and his skin was gray. Who cares? he asked himself.

But just let Williams, down at the office, say one word about appearance this morning. Just one word. He'd tell Williams what he could do with the job. In fact, Morton decided, he wouldn't even go to work today!

Mildred wasn't in the kitchen when he came down. But there was the clothesbasket, heaped to overflowing. Morton stumbled on it and cursed.

"Be right there," Mildred called. She was out in back, hanging over the fence talking to the woman next door.

They were probably deciding who would make the potato salad for the coming church picnic, Morton thought. The church picnic that would never come.

He looked around the neat kitchen at the chrome-legged table and chairs, at the neatly starched cottage curtains, at the stove and refrigerator with their porcelain that had turned cream colored. He looked at Mildred as she came in and set the bacon sizzling.

And he thought: Twelve years, the best twelve years, the last twelve years of his life. With this plain woman. In this cheap house with its cheap, mass-produced things.

And now he was going to die. Oh God...

"What did you say, dear?" Mildred asked.

"Nothing." He wasn't aware that his lips had moved.

He didn't want to die. He was afraid to die. At least if he'd *had* something during his life... But to sit here in the midst of all his crummy possessions, looking at his wife, and knowing that this was all he'd had, all he'd ever had, and all he would have now.

He couldn't bear to think about it. "What're you doing?" he asked, nodding at the heaped basket. "Taking in the neighbors' wash, too?"

Mildred laughed. He'd never realized before what a stupid laugh she had. "It's so nice and sunny and warm. I thought I'd just as well do everything I could," she said.

She said, "You know, Frank, that old washer's on its last legs. It would be a good investment to get a new one. We could pay it out."

That was a good one. Pay it out! He could just see himself signing a twenty-four month contract. Like a man in the electric chair, his head already shaved, signing the coupon for a correspondence course.

"What's so funny?"

"Nothing." His laughter sounded crazed in his own ears. "All right. Next payday we buy a new washer. You want an automatic?"

"That would be nice," Mildred said,

"Turn on the radio," Morton snapped.

She turned on the little kitchen set. The guest on this morning's breakfast show was a leading astronomer. Frank and Mildred listened while the astronomer explained how the comet had acted so erratically that new theories had had to be formulated. At the moment nothing could be definitely asserted.

"Isn't that a shame?" Mildred said.

"He's lying," Morton muttered.

"No. I mean the way they spoiled the program. It's always so funny."

On the last second of her life, Morton thought, with the asphalt boiling in the street and the block already in flames, Mildred would look up from her mending and notice that a picture was crooked.

He fled from the house.

HE CURSED the children under his breath. They were the lucky ones. They and the insane. They didn't know what was going to happen. He wished he were a child. Or crazy.

The bus was crowded, everybody's morning paper in everybody else's face. Who was reading whose? It didn't matter. There was nothing to read anyway. Nobody knew anything.

He walked toward the office, wondering why he and all these other men were going to work this Monday. They were like little cogs and gears in a clock that had lost its hands. Their motion was without meaning any longer, but they kept moving.

Suddenly there were shots and everybody was running. Morton ran, too. There was a squad car and police and a crowd.

"Looters," someone said.

So they were beginning to loot already. Why not? Look at that window, full of expensive clothes. He had never in his life owned a suit that cost more than fifty dollars. Who would it hurt if Frank Morton wore a hundred-dollar suit the last couple days of his life?

In the elevator going up, he met Williams. Williams looked at him closely as they said good morning to each other. Williams didn't look so good himself. But if he said one word about those whiskers on Morton's chin, he was going to get punched.

Fortunately, Williams had nothing to say. He had nothing to say about the portable radio someone had set up in the mailing room. It was a good day to let the men alone.

If only the customers could have let them alone, Morton thought. But no such luck. His desk had its usual pile of letters, each a complaint from a customer.

A stenographer came in from the office pool and Morton began to dictate: "Dear Madam: We are sorry to hear of your difficulties with our product. Please be assured that if our service men cannot remedy the defect, the article will be replaced with one which will give you the years of service to which you, as our customer, are entitled. Sincerely."

Years of service. That was a hot one! These women were crazy. They were all crazy.

"I beg your pardon," the stenographer said.

Morton looked at her, looked long and hard. About eighteen, he figured. Legs not bad. Not bad at all. And the rest of her... His eyes seemed to have developed a tactile sense; he could actually feel her skin without touching her. Soft and smooth.

Well, why not? They gave a condemned man a last meal, didn't they?

"You look tired this morning, Myra," he began. "Rough night?"

"Late date." Her eyebrows did things.

Where did he go now? It had been so long. What did he say now? God, twelve years. He used to have a pretty smooth line. If he could only get going, he thought.

In the mailroom the radio blared. Someone ran past the cubicle that was Morton's office.

The stenographer, legs, body, skin were forgotten. Morton dashed around her, almost knocking her off her chair. Something was happening. All the men in the office, and most of the girls, were down at the far end of the corridor where the mailroom was. Even Williams was there.

"What's the matter? What is it? What happened?" Morton couldn't seem to stop himself.

"Tidal wave," someone said. "Coast of China."

So it was already starting. Tidal waves, floods, fire and brimstone. Morton shook like a leaf. This was the beginning of the end.

HE DRIFTED back to his cubicle, seeing the thing in his mind. A tidal wave, a towering wall of water that swept over everything, engulfing homes, factories, people.

He looked out of his window. Far below, in the unusual brightness of the day, the scurrying figures looked like ants. They'd better scurry when these buildings started coming down.

The sweat was dripping from Morton's face, soaking his coat along the sides, below the armpits. He had to fight the urge to fling himself out and have it done with.

The phone rang and with a trembling hand he lifted it.

"Hello, dear," Mildred said. "Sorry to bother you."

"All right." His mouth was dry as dust. "What's wrong?"

"Nothing. I just got to thinking, dear."

"Thinking?" he said stupidly.

"The washing machine. It was a crazy idea."

"Yeah."

"We can get along without it. But you know what I thought? I thought instead of the washer we could get that encyclopedia for Frankie. It's the same money, the same payments, practically, and it'll be such a big help when he goes to high school next fall."

"Oh God," Morton said.

His wife went right on: "I looked it up and the main office of the encyclopedia is right near you."

"I'll go there tomorrow." Anything. Anything, just so she'd hang up.

"You'll put it off," Mildred said. "Why don't I call them and have them send a man over near the end of your lunch hour?"

"No!" Morton shouted.

"Please, Frank. I wish you'd see the man. Let me call them."

"Listen. Listen, don't you realize—"

"Please, Frank."

"Oh, all right," Morton said.

THE SALESMAN refused to let him get a word in. It was well past the lunch hour already, and any one of these minutes Williams was going to throw a fit. Not that Williams mattered any more. Why, come to think of it, if it hadn't been for Mildred he mightn't even have come to work at all.

The salesman stopped for breath at last and Morton leaped in, "Look, mister, with this comet on my mind, do you think—"

"That's just what I mean, Mr. Morton," the salesman said. "You look on page 1163 of our encyclopedia and it explains all about celestial phenomena. Why should your youngster remain in ignorance of the laws of our universe?

"Really," he said, hitting the desk, "it's a great thing you're doing for your boy. Some day he'll thank you."

It was a smooth pitch. He was a good salesman. The world was coming to an end, but until the last minute he would go on selling his encyclopedias. And Mildred would be busy washing clothes and hanging them and ironing them.

"All right," Morton said. And then he was almost sorry he had given in. The sales talk had been distracting him from thinking. Now it was finished.

A paper slid across his desk. "Sign right here."

He signed. He obligated himself to pay eleven dollars and twenty-two cents a month for the next eighteen months.

It was really very funny. Why couldn't he laugh?

Blank-eyed, he watched the salesman leave. It seemed to be getting warmer in the cubicle, but Morton just didn't have the energy to open the door. Might as well get used to the heat, he thought.

The door opened and a face popped in. "Close up shop."

"Huh?" Morton said.

"We're getting the rest of the day off. No work being done anyway, Williams says."

"Isn't that sweet of Williams," Morton sneered.

He got his hat off the rack and slapped it on his head. And as he walked through the outer office, Williams called after him: "Frank. See you in my office for a minute?"

Now what? He stood in front of Williams' desk and there was no way of telling.

"I noticed a man in your office," Williams said. "Salesman?"

"Yes, sir. Encyclopedia. For my boy. You see—"

"I thought that was it," Williams said. He looked up at Morton and smiled. "I like that, Frank. I like that very much. At a time like this to be thinking of the future of your son. We need men like you."

He clapped Morton on the shoulder. "Frank, when this blows over, if it does, I want to have a talk with you."

Why couldn't Williams have said something like that a week ago? Morton wondered. A week ago it would have meant something, it would have given him a few days of happiness. And now it was too late.

"Thank you, sir," Morton said. He didn't know what else to say.

THE STREETS were full of people. Silent people, their eyes turning again and again skyward. They all looked numb.

And on the bus it was the same way. The newspapers again. Everybody reading everybody else's, hoping against hope that the other fellow had a later edition with better news.

But the news was worse. Now there'd been an eruption of Mauna Loa, an earthquake in Ecuador. It was beginning to roll.

Morton got off at his corner and started to walk, shoulders bowed. But he couldn't go home. Not yet. He couldn't make himself walk down that street with its rows of neat, cheap little houses. He couldn't face that without a drink.

The tavern was crowded, the men lined up double at the bar. Nobody was talking much. They all had that numb look. They were getting drunk as fast as they could. Maybe they were smart, Morton thought. Drown themselves in whisky and they wouldn't care so much.

But after two drinks he himself couldn't go on. It was making him feel worse, not better. He had to get out of there.

He knew what he would do. He had a gun at home. At least that was quick. First Mildred and the kids, and then himself.

Walking very fast now, he was almost at the corner where he would turn down his street. A blast of sound hit his ears, pouring out of an open window. A man came roaring out of the house.

"Yahoo!" the man yelled, grabbing Morton and whirling him. He was very, drunk. "Yahoo!"

"Let go of me, damn you!" Morton shouted. He balled his fist. He'd kill this dirty, crazy—

The drunk stared at him. "It's going away! Didn't you hear? The comet's going away!"

"You're lying," Morton said. "It's a drunken lie."

"Not lying," the man said, trying to stand erect. "Not lying. Just heard it onna radio. C'mon, listen for yourself."

But he didn't have to go inside to listen. There it was, there it was pouring out the window.

"...and is now definitely receding," the speaker was saying. "First computations of the comet's course have been proved correct. Its erratic behavior was caused by a large mass in its vicinity that went unobserved because of the intense light of the comet. Photographic plates developed at Palomar Observatory this morning show this mass is now distant enough to have no further effect.

"Palomar astronomers predict that we will have a full hour of darkness tonight."

"Y'hear?" the drunk said. "One hour of darkness." He laughed, blowing fumes in Morton's face. "One hour. Just like the North Pole."

"So we're a couple of Eskimos," Morton laughed. He began to run.

WHAT HAD made him think it was hot? It wasn't hot, it was crisp and fine, a wonderful day. Indian Summer—that was all. There was the smell of burning leaves in the air.

And the street where he lived. It was something to make a man proud. Every house so well cared for, every lawn just as smooth as a billiard table.

A few years ago, it had been just another tract, but now look at it. Hard work, but when you saw the results it was worth it. What else was there to work for?

And then he came to his own house. He stopped short.

The lines in back were full of clothes, clean clothes flapping in the breeze.

In the front hall he got the scent of apple pie baking in the oven.

And there was Mildred, slender, beautiful, her hair brushed until it glistened, her housedress crisp with starching.

The whole place shone. It was Monday. Mildred had put in a day of work.

A minute ago he'd been full of joy and good news. And now, remembering the last few days, he couldn't look his own wife in the eye. The way he felt he'd need a ladder to get his own eyes level with hers.

"Frank, haven't you heard the news?"

"Yeah," he said. "Wonderful." He licked his lips, still not wanting to look at her. "I got some more news. Looks like a raise for me. Maybe a better job."

She didn't get excited at first. She was watching him closely. "Well, it's about time they showed some appreciation for a man like you."

He wished he could think of something to say. A joke or something. But all he could feel was shame. There was more character in Mildred's finger than in his whole body,

Now, she was getting excited. "I'm going down to the basement for some wine. We're going to celebrate."

Before he could stop her, before he could say he would get it, Mildred was through the kitchen and going down the stairs.

He heard her scream.

MORTON FLUNG himself across the kitchen and caught her as she flew up out of the stair well, still screaming.

"What is it?" he demanded.

"Down…there…"

The gun was upstairs and no other weapon handy. It didn't matter. His shoulder muscles bunched and his jaw jutted forward. He swung Mildred behind him, out of harm's way.

"Stay here," he commanded as he moved ahead. "Where is he?"

"Behind the wine bottle," Mildred said.

"Behind the wine bottle?" He stared at her. "What—"

"A mouse! A great big mouse!"

He exploded into laughter. Not mean laughter, but good loving laughter. "My God, I thought it was a burglar. Imagine letting a little mouse throw you into hysterics?"

Still laughing, he said, "All right, scaredy cat, I'll go down for the wine."

He put his arm around her and hugged her affectionately, feeling more like himself again. Good thing he'd been home, he thought. She might have run clear into the street. Or fainted dead away. These women…

He strode toward the basement stairs, his head held high, his shoulders squared. He was still smiling as he disappeared into the well, feeling years younger.

Behind him in the kitchen, Mildred let out a sigh. And then suddenly she began to tremble violently, her whole body shaking, her teeth chattering. She grabbed the door and held on tight until the trembling stopped, biting down on her lip to stop the chattering.

It was all over now. Everything was all right again.

With a little luck, things had evened themselves up. Frank was afraid of a comet, and she was afraid of a mouse. Mildred sighed again and smiled gently.

Then she got busy. There were things to do, dinner to get and clothes to take off the line for ironing. This was Monday and she had a family to take care of.

THE END

Brain of the Galaxy

By JACK VANCE

It was the most brutal examination system ever devised—a system in which one wrong answer meant insanity, and another might mean death!

THERE was music, carnival lights, the slide of feet on waxed oak, perfume, muffled talk and laughter.

Arthur Caversham of 22nd-century Boston felt air along his skin, and discovered himself to be stark naked.

It was at Janice Paget's coming out party: three hundred guests in formal evening wear surrounded him.

For a moment he felt no emotion beyond vague bewilderment. His presence seemed the outcome of logical events, but his memory was fogged and he could find no definite anchor of certainty.

He stood a little apart from the rest of the stag line, facing the red and gold calliope where the orchestra sat. The buffet, the punchbowl, the champagne wagons, tended by clowns were to his right; to the left, through the open flap of the circus tent, lay the garden, now lit by strings of colored lights, red, green, yellow, blue, and he caught a glimpse of a merry-go-round across the lawn.

Why was he here? There was no recollection, no sense of purpose... The night was warm; he was not at all uncomfortable. The other young men in the full dress suits must feel rather sticky, he thought... An idea tugged at a corner of his mind, nagged, teased. There was a significant aspect to the affair that he was overlooking. Refusing to surface, the idea lay like an irritant just below the level of his conscious mind.

He noticed that the young men nearby had moved away from him. He heard raucous chortles of amusement, astonished exclamations. A girl dancing past him saw him over the arm of her escort; she gave a startled squeak, jerked her eyes away, giggling and blushing.

Something was wrong. These young men and women were startled and amazed by his naked skin to the point of

67

embarrassment. The submerged gnaw of urgency came closer to the surface. He must do something. Taboos felt with such intensity might not be violated without unpleasant consequences; such was his understanding. He was lacking garments; these he must obtain.

He looked about him, inspecting the young men who watched him with ribald delight, disgust or curiosity. To one of these latter he addressed himself.

"Where can I get some clothing?"

The young man shrugged. "Where did you leave it?"

Two heavy-set men in dark blue uniforms entered the tent; Arthur Caversham saw them from the corner of his eye, and his mind worked with desperate intensity.

This young man seemed typical of those around him. What sort of appeal would have meaning for him? Like any other human being, he could be moved to action if the right chord were struck.

By what method could he be moved?

Sympathy?

Threats?

The prospect of advantage or profit?

Caversham rejected all of these. By violating the taboo he had forfeited his claim to sympathy, a threat would excite derision, and he had no profit or advantage to offer. The stimulus must be more devious... He reflected that young men customarily banded together in secret societies. In the thousand cultures he had studied this was almost infallibly true. Long-houses, drug-cults, tongs, instruments of sexual initiation—whatever the name, the external aspects were near-identical: painful initiation, secret signs and passwords, uniformity of group conduct, obligation to service. If this young man were a member of such an association, he might react to an appeal to this group-spirit.

Arthur Caversham said, "I've been put in this taboo situation by the brotherhood; in the name of the brotherhood, find me some suitable garments."

The young man stared, taken aback. "Brotherhood...? You mean fraternity?" Enlightenment spread over his face. "Is this some kind of hell-week stunt?" He laughed. "If it is, they sure go all the way."

"Yes," said Arthur Caversham. "My fraternity."

The young man said, "This way then—and hurry, here comes the law. We'll take off under the tent. I'll lend you my topcoat till you make it back to your house."

The two uniformed men, pushing quietly through the dancers, were almost upon them. The young man lifted the flap of the tent. Arthur Caversham ducked under, his friend followed. Together they ran through the many-colored shadows to a little booth painted with gay red and white stripes near the entrance to the tent.

"You stay back, out of sight," said the young man. "I'll check out my coat."

"Fine," said Arthur Caversham.

The young man hesitated. "What's your house? Where do you go to school?"

Arthur Caversham desperately searched his mind for answer. A single fact reached the surface.

"I'm from Boston."

"Boston U.? Or M.I.T.? Or Harvard?"

"Harvard."

"Ah." The young man nodded. "I'm Washington and Lee myself. What's your house?"

"I'm not supposed to say."

"Oh," said the young man, puzzled but satisfied. "Well, just a minute…"

Bearwald the Halforn halted, numb with despair and exhaustion. The remnants of his platoon sank to the ground around him, and they stared back to where the rim of the night flickered and glowed with fire. Many villages, many wood gabled farmhouses had been given the torch, and the Brands from Mount Medallion reveled in human blood.

The pulse of a distant drum touched Bearwald's skin, a deep *thrumm-thrumm-thrumm*, almost inaudible. Much closer he heard a hoarse human cry of fright, then exultant killing-calls, not human. The Brands were tall, black, man-shaped but not men. They had eyes like lamps of red glass, bright white teeth, and tonight they seemed bent on slaughtering all the men of the world.

"Down," hissed Kanaw, his right arm-guard, and Bearwald crouched. Across the flaring sky marched a column of tall Brand warriors, rocking jauntily, without fear.

Bearwald said suddenly, "Men—we are thirteen. Fighting arm to arm with these monsters we are helpless. Tonight their total force is down from the mountain; the hive must be near deserted. What can we lose if we undertake to burn the home-hive of the Brands? Only our lives, and what are these now?"

Kanaw said, "Our lives are nothing; let us be off at once."

"May our vengeance be great," said Broctan the left arm-guard. "May the home-hive of the Brands be white ashes this coming morn…"

Mount Medallion loomed overhead; the oval hive lay in Pangborn Valley. At the mouth of the valley, Bearwald divided the platoon into two halves, and placed Kanaw in the van of the second. "We move silently twenty yards apart; thus if either party rouses a Brand, the other may attack from the rear and so kill the monster before the vale is roused. Do all understand?"

"We understand."

"Forward then, to the hive."

The valley reeked with an odor like sour leather. From the direction of the hive came a muffled clanging. The ground was soft, covered with runner moss; careful feet made no sound. Crouching low, Bearwald could see the shapes of his men against the sky— here indigo with a violet rim. The angry glare of burning Echevasa lay down the slope to the south.

A sound. Bearwald hissed, and the columns froze. They waited. *Thud thud thud thud* came the steps—then a hoarse cry of rage and alarm.

"Kill, kill the beast!" yelled Bearwald.

The Brand swung his club like a scythe, lifting one man, carrying the body around with the after-swing. Bearwald leapt close, struck with his blade, slicing as he hewed; he felt the tendons part, smelled the hot gush of Brand blood.

The clanging had stopped now, and Brand cries carried across the night.

"Forward," panted Bearwald. "Out with your tinder, strike fire to the hive. Burn, burn, burn—"

Abandoning stealth he ran forward; ahead loomed the dark dome. Immature Brands came surging forth, squeaking and squalling, and with them came the genetrices—twenty-foot monsters crawling on hands and feet, grunting and snapping as they moved.

"Kill!" yelled Bearwald the Halforn. "Kill! Fire, fire, fire!"

He dashed to the hive, crouched, struck spark to tinder, puffed. The rag, soaked with saltpeter, flared. Bearwald fed it straw, thrust it against the hive. The reed-pulp and withe crackled.

He leapt up as a horde of young Brands darted at him. His blade rose and fell; they were cleft, no match for his frenzy. Creeping close came the great Brand genetrices, three of them, swollen of abdomen, exuding an odor vile to his nostrils.

"Out with the fire," yelled the first. "Fire, out. The Great Mother is tombed within, she lies too fecund to move... Fire, woe, destruction!" And they wailed, "Where are the mighty? Where are our warriors?"

Thrumm-thrumm-thrumm came the sound of skin-drums. Up the valley rolled the echo of hoarse Brand voices.

Bearwald stood back to the blaze. He darted forward, severed the head of a creeping genetrix, jumped back... Where were his men? "Kanaw!" he called. "Laida! Theyat! Gyorg! Broctan!"

He craned his neck, saw the flicker of fires. "Men! Kill the creeping mothers!" And leaping forward once more, he hacked and hewed, and another genetrix sighed and groaned and rolled flat.

The Brand voices changed to alarm; the triumphant drumming halted; the thud of footsteps came loud.

At Bearwald's back the hive burnt with a pleasant heat. Within came a shrill keening, a cry of vast pain.

In the leaping blaze he saw the charging Brand warriors. Their eyes glared like embers, their teeth shone like white sparks. They came forward, swinging their clubs, and Bearwald gripped his sword, too proud to flee.

After grounding his air-sled Ceistan sat a few minutes inspecting the dead city Therlatch: a wall of earthen brick a hundred feet high, a dusty portal, and a few crumbled roofs lifting above the battlements. Behind the city the desert spread across the near, middle and far distance to the hazy shapes of the Altilune Mountains at the horizon, pink in the light of the twin suns Mig and Pag.

Scouting from above he had seen no sign of life, nor had he expected any, after a thousand years of abandonment. Perhaps a few sand-crawlers wallowed in the heat of the ancient bazaar, perhaps a few leobars inhabited the crumbled masonry. Otherwise the streets would feel his presence with great surprise.

Jumping from the air-sled, Ceistan advanced toward the portal. He passed under, stood looking right and left with interest. In the parched air the brick buildings stood almost eternal. The wind smoothed and rounded all harsh angles; the glass had been cracked by the heat of day and chill of night; heaps of sand clogged the passageways.

Three streets led away from the portal and Ceistan could find nothing to choose between them. Each was dusty, narrow, and each twisted out of his line of vision after a hundred yards.

Ceistan rubbed his chin thoughtfully. Somewhere in the city lay a brass-bound coffer, containing the Crown and Shield Parchment. This, according to tradition, set a precedent for the fief-holder's immunity from energy-tax. Glay, who was Ceistan's liege-lord, having cited the parchment as justification for his delinquency, had been challenged to show validity. Now he lay in prison on charge of rebellion, and in the morning he would be nailed to the bottom of an air-sled and sent drifting into the west, unless Ceistan returned with the Parchment.

After a thousand years, there was small cause for optimism, thought Ceistan. However, the lord Glay was a fair man and he would leave no stone unturned... If it existed, the chest presumably would lie in state, in the town's Legalic, or the Mosque, or in the Hall of Relicts, or possibly in the Sumptuar. He would search all of these, allowing two hours per building; the eight hours so used would see the end to the pink daylight.

At random he entered the street in the center and shortly came to a plaza at whose far end rose the Legalic, the Hall of Records and Decisions. At the facade Ceistan paused, for the interior was dim and gloomy. No sound came from the dusty void save the sigh and whisper of the dry wind. He entered.

The great hall was empty. The walls were illuminated with frescoes of red and blue, as bright as if painted yesterday. There were six to each wall, the top half displaying a criminal act and the bottom half the penalty.

Ceistan passed through the hall, into the chambers behind. He found but dust and the smell of dust. Into the crypts he ventured, and these were lit by oubliettes. There was much litter and rubble, but no brass coffer.

Up and out into the clean air he went, and strode across the plaza to the Mosque, where he entered under the massive architrave.

The Nunciator's Confirmatory lay wide and bare and clean, for the tesselated floor was swept by a powerful draft. A thousand apertures opened from the low ceiling, each communicating with a cell overhead; thus arranged so that the devout might seek counsel with the Nunciator as he passed below without disturbing their attitudes of supplication. In the center of the pavilion a disk of glass roofed a recess. Below was a coffer and in the coffer rested a brass-bound chest . Ceistan sprang down the steps in high hopes.

But the chest contained jewels—the tiara of the Old Queen, the chest vellopes of the Gonwand Corps, the great ball, half emerald, half ruby that in the ancient ages was rolled across the plaza to signify the passage of the old year.

Ceistan tumbled them all back in the coffer. Relicts on this planet of dead cities had no value, and synthetic gems were infinitely superior in luminosity and water.

Leaving the Mosque, he studied the height of the suns. The zenith was past, the moving balls of pink fire leaned to the west. He hesitated, frowning and blinking at the hot earthen walls, considering that not impossibly both coffer and parchment were unfounded rumor, like so many other tales regarding dead Therlatch.

A gust of wind swirled across the plaza and Ceistan choked on a dry throat. He spat and an acrid taste bit his tongue. An old fountain opened in the wall nearby; he examined it wistfully, but water was not even a memory along these dead streets.

Once again he cleared his throat, spat, turned across the city toward the Hall of Relics.

He entered the great nave, past square pillars built of earthen brick. Pink shafts of light struck down from the cracks and gaps in the roof, and he was like a midge in the vast space. To all sides were niches cased in glass, and each held an object of ancient reverence: the Armor in which Plange the Forewarned led the Blue Flags; the coronet of the First Serpent; an array of antique Padang skulls; Princess Thermosteraliam's bridal gown of woven cobweb palladium, as fresh as the day she wore it; the original Tablets of Legality; the great conch throne of an early dynasty; a dozen other objects. But the coffer was not among them.

Ceistan sought for entrance to a possible crypt, but except where the currents of dusty air had channeled grooves in the porphyry, the floor was smooth.

Out once more into the dead streets, and now the suns had passed behind the crumbled roofs, leaving the streets in magenta shadow.

With leaden feet, burning throat and a sense of defeat, Ceistan turned to the Sumptuar, on the citadel. Up the wide steps, under the verdigris-fronted portico into a lobby painted with vivid frescoes. These depicted the maidens of ancient Therlatch at work, at play, amid sorrow and joy: slim creatures with short black hair and glowing ivory skin, as graceful as water-vanes, as round and delectable as chermoyan plums. Ceistan passed through the lobby with many side-glances, thinking sadly that these ancient creatures of delight were now the dust he trod under his feet.

He walked down a corridor that made a circuit of the building, and from which the chambers and apartments of the Sumptuar might be entered. The wisps of a wonderful rug crunched under his feet, and the walls displayed moldy tatters, once tapestries of the finest weave. At the entrance to each chamber a fresco pictured the Sumptuar maiden and the sign she served; at each of these chambers Ceistan paused, made a quick investigation, and so passed on to the next. The beams slanting in through the cracks served him as a gauge of time, and they flattened ever more toward the horizontal.

Chamber after chamber after chamber. There were chests in some, altars in others, cases of manifestos, triptychs, and fonts in others. But never the chest he sought.

And ahead was the lobby where he had entered the building. Three more chambers were to be searched, then the light would be gone.

He came to the first of these, and this was hung with a new curtain. Pushing it aside, he found himself looking into an outside court, full in the long light of the twin suns. A fountain of water trickled down across steps of apple-green jade into a garden as soft and fresh and green as any in the north. And rising in alarm from a couch was a maiden, as vivid and delightful as any in the frescoes. She had short dark hair, a face as pure and delicate as the great white frangipani she wore over her ear.

For an instant Ceistan and the maiden stared eye to eye; then her alarm faded and she smiled shyly.

"Who are you?" Ceistan asked in wonder. "Are you a ghost or do you live here in the dust?"

"I am real," she said. "My home is to the south, at the Palram Oasis, and this is the period of solitude to which all maidens of the race submit when aspiring for Upper Instruction... So without fear may you come beside me, and rest, and drink of fruit wine and be my companion through the lonely night, for this is my last week of solitude and I am weary of my own aloneness."

Ceistan took a step forward, then hesitated. "I must fulfill my mission. I seek the brass coffer containing the Crown and Shield Parchment. Do you know of this?"

She shook her head. "It is nowhere in the Sumptuar." She rose to her feet, stretching her ivory arms as a kitten stretches. "Abandon your search, and come let me refresh you."

Ceistan looked at her, looked up at the fading light, looked down the corridor to the two doors yet remaining. "First I must complete my search; I owe duty to my lord Glay, who will be nailed under an air-sled and sped west unless I bring him aid."

The maiden said with a pout, "Go then to your dusty chamber; and go with a dry throat. You will find nothing, and if you persist so stubbornly, I will be gone when you return."

"So let it be," said Ceistan.

He turned away, marched down the corridor. The first chamber was bare and dry as a bone. In the second and last, a man's skeleton lay tumbled in a corner; this Ceistan saw in the last rosy light of the twin suns.

There was no brass coffer, no parchment. So Glay must die, and Ceistan's heart hung heavy.

He returned to the chamber where he had found the maiden, but she had departed. The fountain had been stopped, and moisture only filmed the stones.

Ceistan called, "Maiden, where are you? Return, my obligation is at an end…"

There was no response.

Ceistan shrugged, turned to the lobby and so outdoors, to grope his way through the deserted twilight street to the portal and his air-sled.

Dobnor Daksat became aware that the big man in the embroidered black cloak was speaking to him.

Orienting himself to his surroundings, which were at once familiar and strange, he also became aware that the man's voice was condescending, supercilious.

"You are competing in a highly advanced classification," he said. "I marvel at your—ah, confidence." And he eyed Daksat with a gleaming and speculative eye.

Daksat looked down at the floor, frowned at the sight of his clothes. He wore a long cloak of black-purple velvet, swinging like a bell around his ankles. His trousers were of scarlet corduroy, tight at the waist, thigh and calf, with a loose puff of green cloth between calf and ankle. The clothes were his own, obviously: they looked wrong and right at once, as did the carved gold knuckle-guards he wore on his hands.

The big man in the dark cloak continued speaking, looking at a point over Daksat's head, as if Daksat were nonexistent.

"Clauktaba has won Imagist honors over the years. Bel-Washab was the Korsi Victor last month; Tol Morabaít is an acknowledged master of the technique. And then there is Ghisel Ghang of West Ind, who knows no peer in the creation of fire-stars, and Pulakt Havjorska, the Champion of the Island Realm. So it becomes a matter of skepticism whether you, new, inexperienced, without a fund of images, can do more than embarrass us all with your mental poverty."

Daksat's brain was yet wrestling with his bewilderment, and he could feel no strong resentment at the big man's evident contempt. He said, "Just what is all this? I'm not sure that I understand my position."

The man in the black cloak inspected him quizzically. "So, now you commence to experience trepidation? Justly, I assure you." He sighed, waved his hands. "Well, well—young men will be impetuous, and perhaps you have formed images you considered not discreditable. In any event, the public eye will ignore you for the glories of Clauktaba's geometries and Ghisel Ghang's starbursts. Indeed, I counsel you, keep your image, small, drab and confined; you will so avoid the faults of bombast and discord... Now, it is time to go to your imagicon. This way, then. Remember, greys, browns, lavenders, perhaps a few tones of ocher and rust; then the spectators will understand that you compete for the schooling alone, and do not actively challenge the masters. This way then—"

He opened a door and led Dobnor Daksat up a stair and so out into the night.

They stood in a great stadium, facing six great screens forty feet high. Behind them in the dark sat tier upon tier of spectators— thousands and thousands, and their sounds came as a soft crush. Daksat turned to see them, but all their faces and their individualities had melted into the entity as a whole.

"Here," said the big man, "this is your apparatus. Seat yourself and I will adjust the ceretemps."

Daksat suffered himself to be placed in a heavy chair, so soft and deep that he felt himself to be floating. Adjustments were made at his head and neck and the bridge of his nose. He felt a sharp prick, a pressure, a throb, and then a soothing warmth. From the distance, a voice called out over the crowd:

"Two minutes to grey mist! Two minutes to grey mist! Attend, imagists, two minutes to grey mist!"

The big man stooped over him. "Can you see well?"

Daksat raised himself a trifle. "Yes... All is clear."

"Very well. At 'grey mist' this little filament will glow. When it dies, then it is your screen, and you must imagine your best."

The far voice said, "One minute to grey mist! The order is Pulakt Havjorska, Tol Morabaít, Ghisel Ghang, Dobnor Daksat, Clauktaba and Bel-Washab. There are no handicaps; all colors and shapes are permitted. Relax then, ready your lobes, and now—grey mist!"

The light glowed on the panel of Daksat's chair, and he saw five of the six screens light to a pleasant pearl-grey, swirling a trifle as if agitated, excited. Only the screen before him remained dull. The big man who stood behind him reached down, prodded. "Grey mist, Daksat; are you deaf and blind?"

Daksat thought grey mist, and instantly his screen sprang to life, displaying a cloud of silver grey, clean and clear.

"Humph," he heard the big man snort. "Somewhat dull and without interest—but I suppose good enough... See how Clauktaba's rings with hints of passion already, quivers with emotion."

And Daksat, noting the screen to his right, saw this to be true. The grey, without actually displaying color, flowed and filmed as if suppressing a vast flood of light.

Now to the far left, on Pulakt Havjorska's screen, color glowed. It was a gambit image, modest and restrained—a green jewel dripping a rain of blue and silver drops that struck a black ground and disappeared in little orange explosions.

Then Tol Morabaít's screen glowed: a black and white checkerboard with certain of the squares flashing suddenly green, red, blue and yellow—warm searching colors, pure as shafts from a rainbow. The image disappeared in a flush mingled of rose and blue.

Ghisel Ghang wrought a circle of yellow that quivered, brought forth a green halo, which in turn bulging, gave rise to a larger band of brilliant black and white. In the center formed a complex kaleidoscopic pattern. The pattern suddenly vanished in a brilliant flash of light; on the screen for an instant or two appeared the identical pattern in a complete new suit of colors. A ripple of sound from the spectators greeted this *tour de force*.

The light on Daksat's panel died. Behind him he felt a prod. "Now."

Daksat eyed the screen and his mind was blank of ideas. He ground his teeth. Anything. Anything. A picture... He imagined a view across the meadowlands beside the river Melramy.

"Hm," said the big man behind him. "Pleasant. A pleasant fantasy, and rather original."

Puzzled, Daksat examined the picture on the screen. So far as he could distinguish, it was an uninspired reproduction of a scene he knew well. Fantasy? Was that what was expected? Very well, he'd produce fantasy. He imagined the meadows glowing, molten, white-hot. The vegetation, the old cairns slumped into a viscous seethe. The surface smoothed, became a mirror that reflected the Copper Crags.

Behind him the big man grunted. "A little heavy-handed that last, and thereby you destroyed the charming effect of those unearthly colors and shapes.

Daksat slumped back in his chair, frowning, eager for his turn to come again.

Meanwhile Clauktaba created a dainty white blossom with purple stamens on a green stalk. The petals wilted, the stamens discharged a cloud of swirling yellow pollen.

Then Bel Washab, at the end of the line, painted his screen a luminous underwater green. It rippled, bulged, and a black irregular blot marred the surface. From the center of the blot seeped a trickle of hot gold which quickly meshed and veined the black blot.

Such was the first passage.

There was a pause of several seconds. "Now," breathed the voice behind Daksat, "now the competition begins."

On Pulakt Havjorska's screen appeared an angry sea of color; waves of red, green, blue, an ugly mottling. Dramatically a yellow shape appeared at the lower right, vanquished the chaos. It spread over the screen, the center went lime-green. A black shape appeared, split, bowed softly and easily to both sides. Then turning, the two shapes wandered into the background, twisting, bending with supple grace. Far down a perspective they merged, darted forward like a lance, spread out into a series of lances, formed a slanting pattern of slim black bars.

"Superb," hissed the big man. "The timing, so just, so exact."

Tol Morabaít replied with a fuscous brown field threaded with crimson lines and blots. Vertical green hatching formed at the left, strode across the screen to the right. The brown field pressed forward, bulged through the green bars, pressed hard, broke, and segments flitted forward to leave the screen. On the black background behind the green hatching, which now faded, lay a human brain, pink, pulsing. The brain sprouted six insect-like legs, scuttled crabwise back into the distance.

Ghisel Ghang brought forth one of his fire-bursts—a small pellet of bright blue exploding in all directions, the tips working and writhing through wonderful patterns in the five colors, blue, violet, white, purple and light green.

Dobnor Daksat, rigid as a bar, sat with hands clenched and teeth grinding into teeth. Now. Was not his brain as excellent as those of the far lands? Now!

On the screen appeared a tree, conventionalized in greens and blues, and each leaf was a tongue of fire. From these fires wisps of smoke arose on high to form a cloud that worked and swirled, then emptied a cone of rain about the tree. The flames vanished and in their places appeared star-shaped white flowers. From the cloud came a bolt of lightning, shattering the tree to agonized fragments of glass. Another bolt into the brittle heap and the screen exploded in a great gout of white, orange and black.

The voice of the big man said doubtfully, "On the whole well done, but mind my warning, and create more modest images, since—"

"Silence," said Dobnor Daksat in a harsh voice.

So the competition went, round after round of spectacles, some sweet as caramel honey, others as violent as the storms that circle the poles. Color strove with color, patterns evolved and changed, sometimes in glorious cadence, sometimes in the bitter discord necessary to the strength of the image.

And Daksat built dream after dream, while his tension vanished, and he forgot all save the racing pictures in his mind and on the screen, and his images became as complex and subtle as those of the masters.

"One more passage," said the big man behind Daksat, and now the imagists brought forth the master-dreams: Pulakt Havjorska, the growth and decay of a beautiful city; Tol Morabaít, a quiet composition of green and white interrupted by a marching army of insects who left a dirty wake, and who were joined in battle by men in painted leather armor and tali hats, armed with short swords and flails. The insects were destroyed and chased off the screen; the corpses became bones and faded to twinkling blue dust. Ghisel Ghang created three fire-bursts simultaneously, each different, a gorgeous display.

Daksat imagined a smooth pebble, magnified it to a block of marble, chipped it away to create the head of a beautiful maiden. For a moment she stared forth and varying emotions crossed her face—joy at her sudden existence, pensive thought, and at last fright. Her eyes turned milky opaque blue, the face changed to a laughing sardonic mask, black-cheeked with a fleering mouth. The head tilted, the mouth spat into the air. The head flattened into a black background, the drops of spittle shone like fire, became stars, constellations, and one of these expanded, became a planet with configurations dear to Daksat's heart. The planet hurtled off into darkness, the constellations faded. Dobnor Daksat relaxed. His last image. He sighed, exhausted.

The big man in the black cloak removed the harness in brittle silence. At last he asked, "The planet you imagined in that last screening, was that a creation or a remembrance of actuality? It was none of our system here, and it rang with the clarity of truth."

Dobnor Daksat stared at him puzzled, and the words faltered in his throat. "But it is—home. This world. Was it not this world?"

The big man looked at him strangely, shrugged, turned away. "In a moment now the winner of the contest will be made known and the jeweled brevet awarded."

The day was gusty and overcast, the galley was low and black, manned by the oarsmen of Belaclaw. Ergan stood on the poop, staring across the two miles of bitter sea to the coast of Racland, where he knew the sharp-faced Racs stood watching from the headlands.

A gout of water erupted a few hundred yards astern.

Ergan spoke to the helmsman. "Their guns have better range than we bargained for. Better stand offshore another mile and we'll take our chances with the current."

Even as he spoke, there came a great whistle and he glimpsed a black pointed projectile slanting down at him. It struck the waist of the galley, exploded. Timber, bodies, metal, flew everywhere, and the galley laid its broken back into the water, doubled up and sank.

Ergan, jumping clear, discarded his sword, casque and greaves' almost as he hit the chill grey water. Gasping from the shock, he swam in circles, bobbing up and down in the chop, then finding a length of timber, he clung to it for support.

From the shores of Racland a longboat put forth and approached, bow churning white foam as it rose and fell across the waves. Ergan turned loose the timber and swam a, rapidly as possible from the wreck. Better drowning than capture; there would be more mercy from the famine-fish that swarmed the waters than from the pitiless Racs.

So he swam, but the current took him to the shore, and at last, struggling feebly, he was cast upon a pebbly beach.

Here he was discovered by a gang of Rac youths and marched to a nearby command post. He was tied and flung into a cart and so conveyed to the city Korsapan.

In a grey room he was seated facing an intelligence officer of the Rac secret police, a man with the grey skin of a toad, a moist grey mouth, eager, searching eyes.

"You are Ergan," said the officer. "Emissary to the Bargee of Salomdek. What was your mission?"

Ergan stared back eye to eye, hoping that a happy and convincing response would find his lips. None came, and the truth would incite an immediate invasion of both Belaclaw and Salomdek by the tall thin-headed Rac soldiers, who wore black uniforms and black boots.

Ergan said nothing. The officer leaned forward. "I ask you once more, then you will be taken to the room below." He said "Room Below" as if the words were capitalized, and he said it with soft relish.

Ergan, in a cold sweat, for he knew of the Rac torturers, said, "I am not Ergan; my name is Ervard. I am an honest trader in pearls."

"This is untrue," said the Rac. "Your aide was captured and under the compression pump he blurted up your name with his lungs."

"I am Ervard," said Ergan, his bowels quaking.

The Rac signaled. "Take him to the Room Below."

A man's body, which has developed nerves as outposts against danger, seems especially intended for pain, and cooperates wonderfully with the craft of the torturer. These characteristics of the body had been studied by the Rac specialists, and other capabilities of the human nervous system had been blundered upon by accident. It has been found that certain programs of pressure, heat, strain, friction, torque, surge, jerk, sonic and visual shock, vermin, stench and vileness created cumulative effects, whereas a single method, used to excess, lost its stimulation thereby.

All this lore and cleverness was lavished upon Ergan's citadel of nerves, and they inflicted upon him the entire gamut of pain: the sharp twinges, the dull lasting joint-aches, which groaned by night, the fiery flashes, the assaults of filth and lechery, together with shocks of occasional tenderness when he would be allowed to glimpse the world he had left.

Then back to the Room Below.

But always: "I am Ervard the trader." And always he tried to goad his mind over the tissue barrier to death, but always the mind hesitated at the last toppling step, and Ergan lived.

The Racs tortured by routine, so that the expectation, the approach of the hour, brought with it as much torment as the act itself. And then the heavy unhurried steps outside the cell, the feeble thrashing around to evade, the harsh laughs when they cornered him and carried him forth, and the harsh laughs when three hours later they threw him sobbing and whimpering back to the pile of straw that was his bed.

"I am Ervard," he said, and trained his mind to believe that this was the truth, so that never would they catch him unaware. "I am Ervard. I am Ervard, I trade in pearls."

He tried to strangle himself on straw, but a slave watched always, and this was not permitted.

He attempted to die by self-suffocation, and would have been glad to succeed, but always as he sank into blessed numbness, so did his mind relax and his motor nerves take up the mindless business of breathing once more.

He ate nothing, but this meant little to the Racs, as they injected him full of tonics, sustaining drugs and stimulants, so that he might always be keyed to the height of his awareness.

"I am Ervard," said Ergan, and the Racs gritted their teeth angrily. The case was now a challenge; he defied their ingenuity, and they puzzled long and carefully upon refinements and delicacies, new shapes to the iron tools, new types of jerk ropes, new directions for the strains and pressures. Even when it was no longer important whether he was Ergan or Ervard, since war now raged, he was kept and maintained as a problem, an ideal case; so he was guarded and cosseted with even more than usual care, and the Rac torturers mulled over their techniques, making changes here, improvements there.

Then one day the Belaclaw galleys landed and the feather-crested soldiers fought past the walls of Korsapan.

The Racs surveyed Ergan with regret. "Now we must go, and still you will not submit to us."

"I am Ervard," croaked that which lay on the table. "Ervard the trader."

A splintering crash sounded overhead.

"We must go," said the Racs. "Your people have stormed the city. If you tell the truth, you may live. If you lie, we kill you. So there is your choice. Your life for the truth."

"The truth?" muttered Ergan. "It is a trick—" And then he caught the victory chant of the Belaclaw soldiery. "The truth? Why not...? Very well." And he said, "I am Ervard," for now he believed this to be the truth.

Galactic Prime was a lean man with reddish-brown hair sparse across a fine arch of skull. His face, undistinguished otherwise, was given power by great dark eyes flickering with a light like fire behind smoke. Physically he had passed the peak of his youth; his arms and legs were thin and loose-jointed; his head inclined forward as if weighted by the intricate machinery of his brain.

Arising from the couch, smiling faintly, he looked across the arcade to the eleven Elders. They sat at a table of polished wood, backs to a wall festooned with vines. They were grave men, slow in their motions, and their faces were lined with wisdom and insight. By the ordained system, Prime was the executive of the universe, the Elders the deliberative body, invested with certain restrictive powers.

"Well?"

The Chief Elder without haste raised his eyes from the computer. "You are the first to arise from the couch."

Prime turned a glance up the arcade, still smiling faintly. The others lay variously: some with arms clenched, rigid as bars; others huddled in fetal postures. One had slumped from the couch half to the floor; his eyes were open, staring at remoteness.

Prime returned to the Chief Elder, who watched him with detached curiosity. "Has the optimum been established?"

The Chief Elder consulted the computer. "Twenty-six thirty-seven is the optimum score."

Prime waited, but the Chief Elder said no more. Prime stepped to the alabaster balustrade beyond the couches. He leaned forward, looked out across the vista—miles and miles of sunny haze, with a twinkling sea in the distance. A breeze blew past his face, ruffling the scant russet strands of his hair. He took a deep breath, flexed his fingers and hands, for the memory of the Rac torturers was still heavy on his mind. After a moment he swung around, leaned back, resting his elbows upon the balustrade. He glanced once more down the line of couches; there were still no signs of vitality from the candidates.

"Twenty-six thirty-seven," he muttered. "I venture to estimate my own score at twenty-five ninety. In the last episode I recall an incomplete retention of personality."

"Twenty-five seventy-four," said the Chief Elder. "The computer judged Bearwald the Halforn's final defiance of the Brand warriors unprofitable."

Prime considered. "The point is well made. Obstinacy serves no purpose unless it advances a predetermined end. It is a flaw I must seek to temper." He looked along the line of Elders, from face to face. "You make no enunciations, you are curiously mute."

He waited; the Chief Elder made no response.

"May I inquire the high score?"

"Twenty-five seventy-four."

Prime nodded. "Mine."

"Yours is the high score," said the Chief Elder.

Prime's smile disappeared; a puzzled line appeared across his brow. "In spite of this, you are still reluctant to confirm my second span of authority; there are still doubts among you."

"Doubts and misgivings," replied the Chief Elder.

Prime's mouth pulled in at the corners, although his brows were still raised in polite inquiry. "Your attitude puzzles me. My record is one of selfless service. My intelligence is phenomenal, and in this final test, which I designed to dispel your last doubts, I attained the highest score. I have proved my social intuition and flexibility, my leadership, devotion to duty, imagination and resolution. In every commensurable aspect, I fulfill best the qualifications for the office I hold."

The Chief Elder looked up and down the line of his fellows. There were none who wished to speak. The Chief Elder squared himself in his chair, sat back.

"Our attitude is difficult to represent. Everything is as you say. Your intelligence is beyond dispute, your character is exemplary. You have served your term with honor and devotion. You have earned our respect, admiration and gratitude. We realize also that you seek this second term from praiseworthy motives: you regard yourself as the man best able to coordinate the complex business of the galaxy."

Prime nodded grimly. "But you think otherwise."

"Our position is perhaps not quite so blunt."

"Precisely what is your position?" Prime gestured along the couches. "Look at these men. They are the finest of the galaxy. One man is dead. That one stirring on the third couch has lost his mind; he is a lunatic. The others are sorely shaken. And never forget that this test has been expressly designed to measure the qualities essential to the Galactic Prime."

"This test has been of great interest to us," said the Chief Elder mildly. "It has considerably affected our thinking."

Prime hesitated, plumbing the unspoken overtones of the words. He came forward, seated himself across from the line of Elders. With a narrow glance he searched the faces of the eleven men, tapped once, twice, three times with his fingertips on the polished wood, leaned back in the chair.

"As I have pointed out, the test has gauged each candidate for the exact qualities essential to the optimum conduct of office, in this fashion: Earth of the twentieth century is a planet of intricate conventions; on Earth the candidate, as Arthur Caversham, is required to use his social intuition—a, quality highly important in this galaxy of two billion suns. On Belotsi, Bearwald the Halforn is tested for courage and the ability to conduct positive action. At the dead city Therlatch on Praesepe Three, the candidate, as Ceistan, is rated for devotion to duty, and as Dobnor Daksat at the Imagicon on Staff, his creative conceptions are rated against the most fertile imaginations alive. Finally as Ergan, on Chankozar, his will, persistence and ultimate fiber are explored to their extreme limits.

"Each candidate is placed in the identical set of circumstances by a trick of temporal, dimensional and cerebro-neural meshing, which is rather complicated for the present discussion. Sufficient that each candidate is objectively rated by his achievements, and that the results are commensurable."

He paused, looked shrewdly along the line of grave faces. "I must emphasize that although I myself designed and arranged the test, I thereby gained no advantage. The mnemonic synapses are entirely disengaged from incident to incident, and only the candidate's basic personality acts. All were tested under precisely the same conditions. In my opinion the scores registered by the computer indicate an objective and reliable index of the candidate's ability for the highly responsible office of Galactic Executive."

The Chief Elder said, "The scores are indeed significant."

"Then—you approve my candidacy?"

The Chief Elder smiled. "Not so fast. Admittedly you are intelligent, admittedly you have accomplished much during your term as Prime. But much remains to be done."

"Do you suggest that another man would have achieved more?"

The Chief Elder shrugged. "I have no conceivable way of knowing. I point out your achievements, such as the Glenart civilization, the Dawn Time on Masilis, the reign of King Karal on Aevir, the suppression of the Arkid Revolt. There are many such examples. But there are also shortcomings: the wars and detestable totalitarian governments on Earth, the savagery on Belotsi and Chankozar, so pointedly emphasized in your test. Then there is the decadence of the planets in the Eleven Hundred Ninth Cluster, the rise of the Priest-kings on Für, and much else."

Prime clenched his mouth and the fires behind his eyes burnt more brightly.

The Chief Elder continued. "One of the most remarkable phenomena of the galaxy is the tendency of humanity to absorb and manifest the personality of the Prime. There seems to be a tremendous resonance that vibrates from the brain of the Prime through the minds of man from Center to the outer fringes. It is a matter that should be studied, analyzed and subjected to control. The effect is as if every thought of the Prime is magnified a billion-fold, as if every mood sets the tone for a thousand civilizations, every facet of his personality reflects in the ethics of a thousand cultures."

Prime said tonelessly, "I have remarked this phenomenon and have thought much on it. Prime's commands are promulgated in such a way as to exert subtle rather than overt influence; perhaps here is the background of the matter. In any event, the fact of this influence is even more reason to select for the office a man of demonstrated virtue."

"Well put," said the Chief Elder. "Your character is indeed beyond reproach. However, we of the Elders are concerned by the rising tide of authoritarianism among the planets of the galaxy. We suspect that this principle of resonance is at work. You are a man of intense and indomitable will, and we feel that your influence has unwittingly prompted an irruption of aristocracies."

Prime was silent a moment. He looked down the line of couches where the other candidates were recovering awareness. They were men of various races: a pale Northkin of Palast, a Negro of Earth, a stocky red Hawolo, a grey-haired grey-eyed Islander from the Sea Planet—each the outstanding man of the planet of his birth. Those who had returned to consciousness sat quietly, collecting their wits, or lay back on the couch, trying to expunge the test from their minds. There had been a toll taken: one lay dead, another bereft of his wits crouched whimpering beside his couch.

The Chief Elder said, "The objectionable aspects of your character are perhaps best exemplified by the test itself."

Prime opened his mouth; the Chief Elder held up his hand. "Let me speak; I will try to deal fairly with you. When I am done, you may say your say.

"I repeat that your basic direction is displayed by the details of the test that you devised. The qualities you measured were those which you considered the most important: that is, those ideals by which you guide your own life. This arrangement I am sure was completely unconscious, and hence completely revealing. You conceive the essential characteristics of the Prime to be social intuition, aggressiveness, loyalty, imagination and dogged persistence. As a man of strong character you seek to exemplify these ideals in your own conduct; therefore it is not at all surprising that in this test, designed by you, with a scoring system calibrated by you, your score should be highest.

"Let me clarify the idea by an analogy. If the Eagle were conducting a test to determine the King of Beasts, he would rate all the candidates on their ability to fly; necessarily he would win. In this fashion the Mole would consider ability to dig important; by his system of testing *he* would inevitably emerge King of Beasts."

Prime laughed sharply, ran a hand through his sparse red-brown locks. "I am neither Eagle nor Mole."

The Chief Elder shook his head. "No. You are zealous, dutiful, imaginative, indefatigable—so you have demonstrated, as much by specifying tests for these characteristics as by scoring high in these same tests. But conversely, by the very absence of other tests you demonstrate deficiencies in your character."

"And these are?"

"Sympathy. Compassion. Kindness." The Chief Elder settled back in his chair. "Strange. Your predecessor two times removed was rich in these qualities. During his term, the great religious and humanitarian systems based on the idea of human brotherhood sprang up across the universe. Another example of resonance—but I digress."

Prime said with a sardonic twitch of his mouth, "May I ask this: have you selected the next Galactic Prime?"

The Chief Elder nodded. "A definite choice has been made."

"What was his score in the test?"

"By your scoring system—seventeen eighty. He did poorly as Arthur Caversham; he tried to explain the advantages of nudity to the policeman. He lacked the ability to concoct an instant subterfuge; he has little of your quick craft. As Arthur Caversham he found himself naked. He is sincere and straightforward, hence tried to expound the positive motivations for his state, rather than discover the means to evade the penalties."

"Tell me more about this man," said Prime shortly.

"As Bearwald the Halforn, he led his band to the hive of the Brands on Mount Medallion, but instead of burning the hive, he called forth to the queen, begging her to end the useless slaughter. She reached out from the doorway, drew him within and killed him. He failed—but the computer still rated him highly on his forthright approach.

"At Therlatch, his conduct was as irreproachable as yours, and at the Imagicon his performance was adequate. Yours approached the brilliance of the Master Imagists, which is high achievement indeed.

"The Rac tortures are the most trying element of the test. You knew well you could resist limitless pain; therefore you ordained that all other candidates must likewise possess this attribute. The new Prime is sadly deficient here. He is sensitive, and the idea of one man intentionally inflicting pain upon another sickens him. I may add that none of the candidates achieved a perfect count in the last episode. Two others equaled your score—"

Prime evinced interest. "Which are they?"

The Chief Elder pointed them out—a tall hard-muscled man with rock-hewn face standing by the alabaster balustrade gazing moodily out across the sunny distance, and a man of middle age who sat with his legs folded under him, watching a point three feet before him with an expression of imperturbable placidity.

"One is utterly obstinate and hard," said the Chief Elder. "He refused to say a single word. The other assumes an outer objectivity when unpleasantness overtakes him. Others among the candidates fared not so well; mental readjustments and therapy will be necessary in almost all cases."

Their eyes went to the witless creature with vacant eyes who padded up and down the aisle, humming and muttering quietly to himself.

"The tests were by no means valueless," said the Chief Elder. "We learned a great deal. By your system of scoring, the competition rated you most high. By other standards, which we Elders postulated, your place was lower."

With a tight mouth Prime inquired, "Who is this paragon of altruism, kindliness, sympathy and generosity?"

The lunatic wandered close, fell on his hands and knees, crawled whimpering to the wall. He pressed his face to the cool stone, stared blankly up at Prime. His mouth hung loose, his chin was wet, his eyes rolled apparently free of each other.

The Chief Elder smiled in great compassion. Sadly he stroked the mad creature's head. "This is he. Here is the man we select."

The old Galactic Prime sat silent, mouth compressed, eyes burning like far volcanoes.

At his feet the new Prime, Lord of Two Billion Suns, found a dead leaf, put it into his mouth, and began to chew.

THE END

Task To Luna

By ALFRED COPPEL

*Two rocket ships bit into lunar dust. Two men—a Yankee, a Russian—
dueled in nightmare shadow and glare, each eager to destroy the Enemy. What
cosmic joke made them drop their weapons and die laughing?*

THE ROCKETS STARTED almost simultaneously. From
two widely separated points on the great curving surface of Earth
they reached upward and outward—toward the Moon.

It wasn't really so strange a coincidence. Space navigation is
governed by mathematics and logic, not politics. The fact that
man-carrying spaceships happened to be developed concurrently
on two sides of an iron curtain meant little to the Universe. It
happened; that's all. And there is a proper time to launch such
missiles. When that time came, they were launched.

In a manner of speaking it was a race. A race wherein the
prizes were such things as: "gravity gauge" and "surveillance
point" and "impregnable launching sites." The contestants were
earnest, capable men; each certain that the Moon must not fall into
the hands of the opponent. It made a stirring and patriotic picture,
vivid with nationalistic fervor. It was thrilling with its taste of high
adventure and self-sacrifice. For each rocket pilot it was a personal
crusade against the thing he had been raised to regard *as the enemy*…

But somehow under the steady, cold scrutiny of the eternal
stars, they must have looked a little ridiculous…perhaps just a tiny
bit tragic, too.

HARSH WAS THE MOON. There was black and there was
white. Great jagged cliffs and razor-backed mountains slashed the
pocked surface of the crater floor, humping themselves at the huge
unwinking stars. The sun was a stark disc of fire, incredibly white,
hung in the black sky. The shadows were bottomless pools.
Within them there was nothing. In the sunlight, the pumice soil
glared white.

The Russian rocket had crashed on landing. Randick could see the tiny, buckled shape of it high on the mountain. No doubt the pilot was dead, but he had to be sure. The risks were too great for any unsupported assumptions. He had to go up there and see for himself.

Ponderous in his pressure suit, Randick emerged from the open lock of the Anglo-American rocket. He slogged across the pumice of the crater floor toward the spot where the mountain's sheer talus erupted skyward, if there were no trouble from the Russki, he would return to his own ship and begin setting up the first cell of what would soon be the Anglo-American Moon Base. As soon as he signaled a safe landing and no opposition from the Russian, other rockets would come to add their cells, and presently there would be an atomic rocket pointed dead at the heart of every Russian population center. A rocket each for Moscow, Leningrad, Kiev, Vladivostok…

Randick frowned. It would be a lot simpler if the crash had finished the Russian pilot. He knew the Russians had exactly the same plan for the Moon. Only the rockets would be aimed at Washington, London, Paris, San Francisco. The slight weight of the one-man bazooka on Randick's back seemed suddenly very comforting.

Randick knew himself to be on the very edge of known territory. His map showed him that he was in the highest part of the Doerfel Mountains. Behind him lay the two great bowls of Bailly and Schickard, and far to the north he could see, as he climbed higher, the smooth surface of the Mare Humorum. He looked up to the spine-like ridge beyond and slightly above the wreck of the Russian ship. There was a deep pass that slashed like a wound into the backbone of the range. He felt a slight thrill. Beyond that cleft lay…mystery. The other side of the Moon.

The sun's rays beat down brutally. Even through the heavily insulated suit Randick could feel their searing touch. All around him stretched a jumbled nightmare of black and white. He was suddenly very glad that he could not see the Earth in the sky. The homesickness would be unbearable.

Randick found himself frowning. He had no time for such thoughts. He was a soldier. He reminded himself that up there in the tangled wreckage of the Russian spaceship there might be another soldier, ready to kill him. Two human beings on the Moon. Each eager to kill. Randick shook his head angrily. He had no right to let his mind dwell on such things...

He was within a hundred yards of the wreck when a streak of fire and a soundless blast drove him into the shadows. Pumice showered him from the star-shaped depression where the explosive missile had struck. Randick cursed heartily. The Russki was very much alive, and there wasn't a thing wrong with his eyesight. The shot had been uncomfortably close.

Unslinging his bazooka, Randick began to work his way around behind the Russian rocket. A slight movement among the wreckage caught his trained eye and he launched a projectile at it. It flared wickedly, tearing fragments of metal loose and flinging them fantastic distances down the sheer slope of the ridge. There was no return fire.

Randick broke out of the shadow and ran for the cover of a large pumice-stone boulder farther up the draw. A sun-bright flash of fire spattered the loose soil a dozen feet from him. He slid for the darkness on his belly. That one had been a near thing!

Behind the boulder lay a trench-like depression that sloped away up the draw toward the pass. Randick dropped into it and began to crawl laboriously upward. If he could flank the Russki he could finish this with one good shot. Another explosion rocked the boulder he had just left, Randick didn't even look back.

He felt his breath rasping in his throat and his body felt hot and sticky inside the bulky pressure suit. Glancing down and to his right, he could see the proudly erect shape of his own rocket far below on the floor of the crater.

It took him almost thirty minutes to reach the edge of the shadow that spilled from the side of the mountain pass. To his left, not ten feet away, was the sudden white glare of the pumice floor. He was well above and almost behind the wreck of the Russian's ship. His flanks were heaving with the exertion of the climb as he searched the buckled mass of the crash for his opponent.

There seemed to be a dark shape wedged in between two twisted bulkheads. It looked like a man. With pounding heart,

Randick murmured a prayer and lifted his bazooka, aimed, and pressed the firing stud. The shadow vanished in silent white fire.

The return blast almost knocked him down. For a moment Randick was stunned, wondering foggily where the shot had come from. Then his brain cleared and he realized that the Russki too had climbed to the pass, leaving Randick to fire at shadows.

Randick cursed himself for his dangerous stupidity. The other must be among those shadowy rocks directly across the bright floor of the pass. He raised his bazooka carefully, searching the Stygian blackness for some sign of movement. His finger curled around the firing stud...

OUT OF THE CORNER of his eye he saw the flare. The Russian rocket erupted in a gout of bluish flame and the whole mountain seemed to rock. Randick stared stupidly at the glowing crater where the ship had been. For just an instant he thought that perhaps a meteorite had struck it, but the explosion had been unquestionably...atomic.

The Russian must have been stunned, too, for he moved out into the light, empty-handed, his helmet turned woodenly toward the rapidly cooling lake of magma where his spaceship had been.

They both saw the bright arc of fire that raced up from beyond the ridge and curved down gracefully toward the floor of the crater far below. Open-mouthed, Randick watched his ship vanish into flame and he felt the vague tremor of the ground under him as the shock rumbled across the face of the Moon.

The Russian rocket was gone. The Anglo-American rocket was gone. Moon Base was gone before it had ever been.

The weapon fell from Randick's hand, and he stepped unsteadily into the light toward the Russian. Suddenly human companionship was very, very important. Panicky terror was plucking at his throat.

The two men stumbled toward each other across the pass cut deep into the jagged back of the Doerfel mountains. As one they turned and looked out across the vast expanse of the Moon's hidden face.

They were soldiers. They knew an invasion base when they saw one. As far as the eye could see, lines of sleek mammoth spaceships of unknown design stretched away into the distance. The face of the vast unnamed *mare* was covered with them.

Suddenly Randick felt himself beginning to giggle. He tried to stop, but the laughter welled up inside of him, echoing wildly within his confining helmet. He could see that the Russian was laughing too, white teeth gleaming behind the Plexiglas faceplate. They laughed until they gasped. Their sides hurt with laughter, tears rolled down their faces. They were arm in arm and still laughing when the third rocket arced down on them from out of the black and star-flecked sky.

THE END

Everest

By ISAAC ASIMOV

Perhaps you've read how Everest has now been climbed? But have you heard of Planetary Survey? Here's the real truth about it. Everest has been climbed twice...

IN 1952 they were about ready to give up trying to climb Mt. Everest. It was the photographs that kept them going.

As photographs go, they weren't much; fuzzy, streaked and with just dark blobs against the white to be interested in. But those dark blobs were living creatures. The men swore to it.

I said, "What the hell, they've been talking about creatures skidding along the Everest glaciers for forty years. It's about time we did something about it."

Jimmy Robbons (pardon me, James Abram Robbons) was the one who pushed me into that position. He was always nuts on mountain climbing, you see. He was the one who knew all about how the Tibetans wouldn't go near Everest because it was the mountain of the Gods; he could quote me every mysterious man-like footprint ever reported in the ice 25,000 feet up; he knew by heart every tall story about the spindly white creatures, speeding along the crags just over the last heart-breaking camp that the climbers had managed to establish.

It's good to have one enthusiastic creature of the sort at Planetary Survey headquarters.

The last photographs put bite into his words, though. After all, you *might* just barely think they were men.

Jimmy said, "Look, boss, the point isn't that they're there, the point is that they move fast. Look at that figure. It's blurred."

"The camera might have moved."

"The crag here is sharp enough. And the men swear it was running. Imagine the metabolism it must have to run at that oxygen pressure. Look, boss, would you have believed in deep-sea fish if you'd never heard of them? You have fish that are looking for new niches in environment that they can exploit, so they go deeper and deeper into the abyss until one day they find they can't return. They've adapted so thoroughly they can live only under tons of pressure."

"Well—"

"Damn it, can't you reverse the picture? Creatures can be forced up a mountain can't they? They can learn to stick it out in thinner air and colder temperatures. They can live on moss or on occasional birds, just as the deep-sea fish in the last analysis live on the upper fauna that slowly go filtering down. Then, someday, they find they can't go down again. I don't even say they're men. They can be chamois or mountain goats or badgers or anything."

I said stubbornly, "The witnesses said they were vaguely manlike, and the reported footprints are certainly manlike."

"Or bearlike," said Jimmy. "You can't tell."

So that's when I said, "It's about time we did something about it."

Jimmy shrugged and said, "They've been trying to climb Mt. Everest for forty years." And he shook his head.

"For god sake," I said. "All you mountain climbers are nuts that's for sure. You're not interested in getting to the top. You're just interested in getting to the top in a certain way. It's about time we stopped fooling around with picks, ropes, camps and all the paraphernalia of the Gentlemen's Club that sends suckers up the slopes every five years or so."

"What are you getting at?"

"They invented the airplane in 1903, you know?"

"You mean fly over Mt. Everest?" He said it the way an English lord would say "Shoot a fox?" or an angler would say, "Use worms?"

"Yes," I said, "fly over Mt. Everest and let someone down on the top. Why not?"

"He won't live long. The fellow you let down, I mean."

"Why not?" I asked again. "You drop supplies and oxygen tanks, and the fellow wears a spacesuit. Naturally."

It took time to get the Air Force to listen and to agree to send a plane and by that time Jimmy Robbons had swiveled his mind to the point where he volunteered to be the one to land on Everest's peak. "After all," he said in half a whisper, "I'd be the first man ever to stand there."

That's the beginning of the story. The story itself can be told very simply, and in far fewer words.

The plane waited two weeks during the best part of the year (as far as Everest was concerned that is) for a siege of only moderately nasty flying weather, then took off.

They made it. The pilot reported by radio to a listening group exactly what the top of Mt. Everest looked like when seen from above and then he described exactly how Jimmy Robbons looked as his parachute got smaller and smaller.

Then another blizzard broke and the plane barely made it back to base and it was another two weeks before the weather was bearable again.

And all that time Jimmy was on the roof of the world by himself and I hated myself for a murderer.

The plane went back up two weeks later to see if they could spot his body. I don't know what good it would have done if they had, but that's the human race for you. How many dead in the last war? Who can count that high? But money or anything else is no object to the saving of one life, or even the recovering of one body.

They didn't find his body, but they did find a smoke signal; curling up in the thin air and whipping away in the gusts. They let down a grapple and Jimmy came up, still in his spacesuit, looking like hell, but definitely alive.

The P.S. to the story involves my visit to the hospital last week to see him. He was recovering very slowly. The doctors said shock, they said exhaustion, but Jimmy's eyes said a lot more.

I said, "How about it, Jimmy, you haven't talked to the reporters, you haven't talked to the government. All right. How about talking to me?"

"I've got nothing to say," he whispered.

"Sure you have," I said. "You lived on top of Mr. Everest during a two-week blizzard. You didn't do that by yourself, not with all the supplies we dumped along with you. Who helped you, Jimmie boy?"

I guess he knew there was no use trying to bluff. Or maybe he was anxious to get it off his mind.

He said, "They're intelligent, boss. They compressed air for me. They set up a little power pack to keep me warm. They set up the smoke signal when they spotted the airplane coming back."

"I see." I didn't want to rush him. "It's like we thought. They're adapted to Everest life. They can't come down the slopes."

"No, they can't. And we can't go up the slopes. Even if the weather didn't stop us, they would."

"They sound like kindly creatures, so why should they object? They helped *you.*"

"They have nothing against us. They spoke to me, you know. Telepathy."

I frowned. "Well then…"

"But they don't intend to be interfered with. They're watching us, boss. They've got to. We've got atomic power. We're about to have rocket ships. They're worried about us. And Everest is the only place they can watch us from."

I frowned deeper. He was sweating and his hands were shaking.

I said, "Easy, boy. Take it easy. What on Earth are these creatures?"

And he said, "What do you suppose would be so adapted to thin air and subzero cold that Everest would be the only livable place on Earth to them. That's the whole point. They're nothing at all on Earth. They're Martians."

And that's it.

THE END

Grandma's Lie soap

By ROBERT ABERNATHY

*Grandma's soap was a miracle of miracles under the stars. If you don't believe
it—just try lying to the flying saucer folk.*

OF COURSE you'll believe this story. Everybody will. The
funny thing is that it *could* be a lie…

To make that point clearer: A little while ago I happened to be
at a gathering of literary amateurs and critics, one of those
sprawling aimless affairs where people mill around with drinks in
their hands, congealing in little clusters to talk or listen to
somebody talk.

I listened. I heard a serious bespectacled young man discourse
not unintelligently on Proust, and I heard a plump gentleman make
some safe, sound comments on Faulkner.

Nobody disagreed with them.

Nobody argued. Nobody even said, "But—"

I can remember when arguments were the order of the day.

After I'd had a little more of it than I could stand, I spoke up.
"Say what you like about those scribblers," I declared firmly, "none
of them can hold a candle to Wolf."

"Thomas?" someone asked—not with the air of being about to
contradict me, but merely as one sincerely, infuriatingly desiring
instruction.

"No, *Howling,*" I retorted, with flamboyant irony. "Do you
mean to say you never heard of Howling Wolf, the genius of the
North Woods, the greatest author of all time? The one writer who
grasped the human soul in all its depth, breadth, and angular
momentum? Who painted Life in its true colors on a canvas vast
as all Nature, with a non-union brush? Who sounded every note of
emotional experience, and rang all the bells in belles lettres?
Who—"

I ran out of breath, paused, and added, "Of course,
unfortunately all of Wolf's mighty works were written in his native

language, which happened to be Chinook Trade Jargon, and they've never been translated. So if you don't know the Jargon..."

At my age I should have known better. Naturally, every word I uttered was gospel but all I got back were earnest requests for more information about the great Wolf. To explain that I'd just been kidding—that I say such things experimentally and to keep in practice as one of the few remaining liars in a truthful world—would have been worse than useless. It would have been cruelty to talking animals.

I mumbled, "Pardon me," to all the nice, candid, inquisitive, credulous faces. I grabbed my hat and pulled it over my eyes, and ducked out. Not that I imagined I'd get away from the consequences. I could already envisage how the ripples would spread. For a long while to come I'd get inquiries in the mail from literary clubs, collectors, compilers of biographical dictionaries. Probably there'd be a Howling Wolf Commemorative Society organized, and if I told them he was buried at the bottom of the Chicago Drainage Canal, they'd go and strew posies there.

But this is not the story of Howling Wolf. It is the story of Grandma's lie soap.

When I first remember Grandma, back when I was one of the numerous grandchildren—my brothers, sisters, and assorted cousins who overran the old hill-country farm during vacations—she was already a dried-up little old lady who couldn't have weighed ninety pounds, with a brown, wrinkled face and intolerant black eyes.

She ruled the farm with an iron hand and my two taciturn uncles, who did the heavy work, moved silently about, tending to chores, crops, and stock in obedience to her orders. The farm thrived, too. Even in bad years, when other people's corn was stunted and wells ran dry, nothing of the sort befell Grandma.

Sometimes—though I didn't know this until I was older—the neighbors muttered, and insisted, obviously out of envy, there was something queer about Grandma. Queerness they detected, I suppose, in her fondness for cats—which most of the country people tolerated without affection—and in her long walks in the woods by herself, gathering plants that she dried and kept in unlabeled jars.

Too, a tradition had it that back in England in the seventeenth century one of her female ancestors had been accused of bewitching cattle by the celebrated witchfinder, Mr. Samson Broadforks, who fell ill shortly afterward of an ailment believed to be foot-and-mouth disease. Be that as it may, the ancestor in question emigrated to America around that time.

But we children, of course, saw nothing odd about our Grandma. Childishly, we assumed that everybody had a grandmother who kept a piece of lie soap on the high shelf over the washstand.

This was a chunk of strong brown soap, like all the rest of the boiled-fat products that Grandma made in the old iron wash-kettle after hog killing. But it wasn't ordinary soap. It was made separately and privately, from some of the herbs that Grandma had in her jars, from a recipe she kept in her head and nowhere else.

Because, you see, another thing about Grandma was that she couldn't abide being lied to. Not, I'm sure, out of any abstract devotion to Truth, but simply because the idea of anyone fooling her made her furious. If somebody tried it, and that somebody was one of her own grandchildren, she knew what to do...

For instance, I can still vividly recall the time when my city cousin Richard first came visiting on the farm. This Richard was a pale, supercilious brat who lived in New York City. As soon as he made sure that no one else on the farm had been similarly blessed, he sized us up for yokels and set about over-awing us with the marvels of the metropolis.

Grandma, busy round the kitchen range, listened silently for a while. But we who knew her well could see the storm warnings going up—the tightening lips and the dangerous gleam in her eye. Richard didn't see anything, naturally. He finished describing the George Washington Bridge and went on to the skyscrapers.

That did it. Grandma slammed a skillet down and fastened a harpy grip on Richard's collar. "Come along, young man," she said grimly. "You needn't think you can pull *my* leg."

And she wagged him off to the washstand, the rest of us trailing after in delighted horror.

"Oliver—" Grandma addressed me, because I was already a gangling thirteen then—"Reach me down the lie soap."

I did so, gingerly, and before the bawling Richard knew what was happening he was sputtering through a haze of suds, his mouth thoroughly washed out with the strong soap.

"*Now,*" said Grandma briskly, releasing him and stepping back. "Take a dipper of water, and then answer me: Were you or weren't you exaggerating when you said there was buildings there ten miles high?"

Richard opened and closed his mouth. He grew red in the face with effort. He said, "N…N…Yes, ma'am, I was exaggerating."

You could see that he was thunderstruck to find that he couldn't do anything but tell the truth. He had yet to learn what the rest of us knew and took for granted. Once anybody had his mouth washed out with Grandma's lie soap, he could never again in this life speak a falsehood, however much he might want to.

A quarter of an hour later, Grandma had mollified Richard with bread and jam and encouraged him to talk some more. She listened with keen interest as he described the Holland Tunnel, nodding her head occasionally and exclaiming, "My, my! Who would have thought it?"

Now, you see, she knew that every word was true.

If I'd been smarter—but maybe I'm still not smart, except in hindsight—I might have seen the shape of things to come in that incident. But I wasn't, and I didn't.

CHAPTER TWO

AT ONE time or another, all of Grandma's grandchildren got their mouths washed with the lie soap—all but me. Why I was spared, I've often wondered. It wasn't for lack of provocation that's certain. I've thought perhaps Grandma had an intuitive grasp of scientific method, and kept me as a control. Or…well, so far as I know, Grandma was the only one of the family in her generation who possessed the secret of the lie soap, and she didn't pass it on to any of her children, who were all sober, truthful, financially unsuccessful citizens. But I'm pretty sure that Grandma herself never got the lie soap treatment as a child.

I grew up, and summers on the farm receded into memory. I went to college, specialized in chemistry, and emerged with rosy visions of science remaking the world. I fell then, naturally into a research job with Gorley and Gorley, who at that time were one of the bigger companies making chemicals, synthetics, cleansers, pharmaceuticals and the like.

The laboratories that I shared with a number of other young and not-so-young research men were magnificent, their chrome-and-porcelain splendor making the university labs where we'd studied seem small and dingy by comparison.

Here I had the facilities and—assigned work being light at the time—the spare time to follow up a project of which I'd become enamored in school—a line on antibiotic synthesis. I almost lived in that lab for some weeks, at the end of which time I had sufficient promising results to make up a summary of them, together with an urgent request for materials needed to carry the investigation through to a successful conclusion.

I submitted this report to the Coordinator, a fussy, harassed little man, who nervously promised to call it to the attention of the front office, and assigned me to work on the problem of producing a red detergent powder that would not make pink suds.

Time went by, and nothing happened. Naturally I reminded the Coordinator, but he assured me that the matter had merely slipped his mind. To make a sad story short, I finally found out how things worked. Communications between the research department and the front office, i.e. the sales department, went only one way.

When the latter had decided just what sort of epoch-making miracle of modern science the buying public was ripe for, word would come down, and if we happened to have such a miracle on hand, well and good. Otherwise, we could produce it, or a reasonable facsimile thereof, in time for the scheduled start of the advertising campaign.

It was O'Brien who first explained this system in full to me. O'Brien was an Assistant Sales Manager and an advertising man from way back. But he was also a human being.

"Over there with your test tubes, kid," he said bluntly. "You're playing pin-the-tail-on-the-donkey. Sometimes you hit, oftener you miss. But you're never quite sure in advance. Right?"

I had to admit he had hit on a pretty fair description of scientific research in general.

"But," said O'Brien, "by us in Sales it's *hit, hit, hit*, all the time. We can't wait for you boys to get that tail pinned on straight. But sometimes you do, don't you?" He sighed.

"God help us, some of the characters I associate with don't even know that. They can't see any difference between having something to sell and having to sell something. So when you *do* hit, let me know, and I'll see what I can do at my end."

He was as good as his word, too. A couple of times when we'd fumbled around and come up with a product that people really needed, something to keep them from dying, for instance, or to make not dying worth their while, he went to bat for us in the sales department.

I've described at length the situation at Gorley and Gorley, first because it had a direct bearing on what happened later, and second because it was typical of a way of life that is past, and which the younger generation nowadays has difficulty even in imagining. I'm referring, of course, to the middle of the twentieth century with its feverish atmosphere of compulsory Progress or a reasonable facsimile thereof and of the glitter that was sometimes gold.

It was the era of the false front, the false rear and the questionable middle, of scandal, slander, and the Hard Sell. It was also the Age of the Big Lie, as somebody called it. But it was even more the age of the little half-truth.

During those years when I was growing up—a painful process then, though it doesn't seem to be so any more—my education progressed along other lines as well.

There was my baptism of politics. I joined with the enthusiasts working for nomination of a reform slate of candidates against those of the city machine. We were too innocent to know that it was an unpropitious time. For one thing, it wasn't a Presidential year and the vote was bound to be light, and for another, the last reform administration was still too fresh in public memory, and the machine was riding high.

The opposition called us idealistic crackpots, conniving scoundrels, and dimwits who didn't know what it was all about. They had the money and they spent it on a flood of lies from the platform, through the mail, and from sound trucks that rolled bellowing through the streets. Finally, our candidates were snowed under in the primaries and not so much as a reform dogcatcher appeared on the ticket.

That was another bruising experience for an easy bruiser such as I was. After the crescendo of activity, the speeches, the leaflets, the house-to-house canvasses, after the starry-eyed phrases about cleaning up local government as a first step toward cleaning up the country and the world...

I took a freshly disillusioned look at that world. It was a world where the leaders of great nations daily pointed to one another as conspirators plotting to exterminate the human race, and where "security" and fear grew rankly intertwined as the ordinary man learned to swallow the idea that *he* couldn't be trusted with the truth about anything really important. It was a world where, consequently, the scaremongers, the inside scoopers, and the genuine conspirators throve mightily.

And, finally, there was Alice.

Alice was in the bookkeeping department at Gorley and Gorley. She didn't have the kind of looks that make cover photographers and movie scouts drool and lunge. But she had something, a spontaneous allure, a magnetism that must surely have upset the IBM machines she worked with.

I met Alice, was magnetized, polarized, and lost. Lost and happy. When I proposed to her, and she said *Yes,* I felt that my good fortune was *too* good to be true. And it was. Some three weeks later she handed back the ring. She couldn't marry me. It had all been a mistake, and so on.

Two days afterward I encountered her by accident in a corridor at the plant. She wore another ring, with a bigger diamond. I stopped her, and roughly demanded:

"Who?"

Stumblingly, she told me. He was a junior executive, a young--man-who-would-go-far with family connections and stock in the company. Alice was a smart girl, and she'd simply bettered herself. I guess I said some rather bitter things on that subject.

"No, Oliver," she insisted. "It's not like that at all. It's just that I don't love you. I never did." But she wouldn't meet my eyes.

When I'd cooled down a bit, I realized that she was being honest with me after a fashion. She was lying to me in just the same terms she was lying to herself. And at the same time, recalling little details of her behavior, I realized why.

Alice was afraid. Her people had been poor, and she knew what it meant. Anyway, who *wasn't* afraid in those days, except for the feebleminded and some of the insane? So she was looking for security, a place to hide in that world of the nineteen-fifties where there wasn't any place to hide. But what was the use of telling her that?

I did some serious drinking, enough to convince me that I wasn't cut out to make a career of it. It was during the sobering-up process that I got the Idea. I wonder how many of the thoughts that changed the world have been fathered by hangovers?

I had some days' vacation with pay coming, so it was comparatively easy. I took a plane, a train, and a ramshackle bus. I then swung in on a grapevine and there I was, walking up the familiar path to the old farmhouse door, where I hadn't been for a span of years that astonished me when I counted them.

Grandma was out in the backyard hanging out a wash of patched work shirts and faded blue overalls. She said without surprise, "How do, Oliver," and went right on finishing her task, while I watched with suppressed impatience.

Finally she picked up the empty clothesbasket and led the way into the house. It was getting dusk, so she lit a kerosene lamp in the kitchen, where supper was simmering on the cast-iron range.

"Grandma," I fumbled. "I came down here—"

"I can see that," Grandma interrupted. "How do you like my new teeth, Oliver?" She grinned at me alarmingly. "Today's my birthday—ninety-first or ninety-fourth or something like that, I forget—so I went to town and got me my new teeth. Pretty, eh, boy? Figure they ought to do me another ten or twelve years."

"Yes, Grandma," I said, a little dazedly.

She peered at me searchingly. "Well, Oliver? Speak up. You've got troubles written all over you."

I'd more or less rehearsed a persuasive speech, but sitting there in Grandma's lamp-lit kitchen I felt as if the years had fallen away and I was like a little boy who had run away from home and come back sorry.

In considerable disorder I poured out the story of how I'd gone out into the world and what I'd found it like. I covered all of it, my work and how little it amounted to compared to what it could have meant to me, and my experience with the way people were governed—even Alice. Above all, I told her how at every turning I had been lied to, and had heard people lie to one another, and seen them lie to themselves.

Grandma nodded once or twice as she listened, which encouraged me. I remembered a scrap from the arguments I'd meant to muster: "Some philosopher once said that a lie is the Original Sin itself. Without it, all other crimes become impossible."

"So," Grandma broke in, "you want the recipe for my lie soap."

"Uh…yes, that's right," I admitted. "It's the answer. Your ancestors and mine had no right to hold it back this long. Look, Grandma, the company I work for makes mouthwashes, toothpastes, and the like. Millions of people use their products; and if a new 'miracle ingredient' were publicized the right way, other companies with more millions of customers would have to adopt it too."

I was counting on O'Brien. I'd explain it to him squarely, and somehow we'd manage to put it over.

Grandma got up to stir a kettle. She took her time, while I held my breath. Finally she said, "I'm going to give you the recipe, Oliver—"

My heart leaped.

"—but not for ten or twenty years yet. Not until you've learned a mite of caution. I was your age once, myself, and I thought how nice it would be to make the world over tomorrow morning, and sit down and admire it tomorrow afternoon. Now I know better, and so will you."

I pleaded and argued, but it was no use. The old lady was adamant. Finally I fell glumly silent, while Grandma went about setting the table for supper.

On the train coming down I'd bought a newspaper out of sheer habit, and, preoccupied, hadn't even opened it. It lay now on the table, and Grandma picked it up to glance at the headlines. Suddenly I realized she'd been standing motionless, staring at the paper, for a remarkably long time. There was a look I'd never seen before on her wrinkled face.

I heard her whisper to herself, *"The Moon."* But that didn't make any sense until I looked over her shoulder and read:

Air Force Rocket Lands on Moon!

Still I didn't understand Grandma's agitation. I said banally, "Well, we've known for quite a while they were going to try it."

"The Moon," Grandma repeated. She went on wanderingly, "You know that just reminds me of one night in a buggy..." Her voice trailed off, and she brooded darkly, which was strange indeed in her.

Then she let the paper fall, and said briskly, "I've changed my mind, Oliver."

"You mean—"

"Yes. You can have the lie soap. I'll write the recipe out and give it to you for a birthday present."

I said stupidly, "It's not my birthday, though."

"No, it's mine." She cackled with a return of the old merriment. She found a stub of pencil, tore off a corner of newspaper, and began writing in a crabbed hand.

As she wrote she muttered, only half to me: "Evening of the day they dropped the Bomb, your Uncle Henry told me: 'Ma, the time's come.' But I said, 'No.' I said, 'People may be crazy, but they're not crazy enough to blow the whole world up and them on it.'

"But now... If there's a Man in the Moon, and he's got a Bomb in his hand and all he's got to do is fling it, what's to stop him? *Him,* he's safe in the Moon... *There.*" She held out the scrap of paper. "Go on, boy, do what you like with it, and I hope you like what you do. I held back, I never thought I'd live to see times like these. But there's some duties you just can't shirk, boy, I don't have to tell you that."

CHAPTER THREE

BILL, Jerry and I slipped into a booth at the tavern near the plant. Looking across the table at Jerry, I marveled at how well he was keeping up the act, the casual off-hours good-fellowship. As for me, I felt sure my tense nerves were showing.

While Jerry called Bill's attention to the waitress' walk, I dropped a little, fast-dissolving white tablet into Bill's drink.

As he picked it up and sipped, I felt a qualm, which I ruthlessly stifled. This test *had* to be made. We—Jerry and I, since I'd taken him into my confidence as a man I could trust and a wizard at organic chemistry—had studied the lie soap formula backward and forward, we'd analyzed samples of it I'd obtained from Grandma, and isolated—or so we thought—the active ingredients. But we had to know, and we could hardly experiment on animals.

Bill set down an empty glass. I grew tenser. Jerry inquired, "Another?" and when Bill shook his head, asked the sixty-four-thousand-dollar question. "So—you've decided to quit lushing around, and get some work done for a change?"

That was one of the trick questions we'd settled on—a variation of the old "Have you stopped beating your wife?" formula. If Bill had been quite normal, he'd have answered, "Hell no," or, "Yeah, guess I better," or some answer as jocular and meaningless as the question. But if our elixir of lie soap worked, he'd answer with a peculiar, embarrassed gulp of hesitation:

"But I don't lush around, and I get a good deal of work done."

Which was what he *did* say. Because it was the truth, silly and pompous as it sounded there and then.

I could see Jerry rallying himself to ask some more telling questions, and I knew he was feeling an emotion exactly like mine—exultation curiously mixed with shame.

Both of us realized at that moment, I guess, that it was going to mean no more friendly kidding over a couple of beers, no more harmless insults and bragging, no more fish stories... But of course there's always a price.

I went to O'Brien.

He heard me out without changing expression. When I'd laid all the cards on the table, he said slowly, "If this stuff will really do what you say—"

"It will," I assured him. "It has."

"In that case, my young scientific friend, do you realize what you're asking me to do? I've spent twenty years in the advertising game. You might say I've devoted my life to it. Now you want me to help you with a scheme that'll wipe out advertising as we know it—lock, stock, and barrel."

"I—I hadn't thought of it like that."

"In other words," O'Brien went on, "you're offering me the fulfillment of my fondest dreams. Shake on it, kid!"

Then he settled back and grew thoughtful. "But it isn't going to be easy. I guess you still have trouble believing it, but I can't just walk into a sales conference and say, 'See here, I've got wind of a product that's the greatest boon to humanity since fire and the wheel; and expect them to fall all over me. We need a good promotion angle."

"There's got to be some way."

"Keep your shirt on. I'll find one. I haven't been in the business for twenty years for nothing. But one thing anyway. Until this deal is swung, keep your witch's brew away from me."

The convincer came, after all, from an idea I had. But it was O'Brien who saw the possibilities and, by dint of massive doses of double-talk and cajolery, arranged for a test survey of a hundred volunteer subjects. These human guinea pigs were furnished gratis with a thirty days' supply of a new toothpaste—a standard base, plus Grandma's lie soap—and, when the time was up, were quizzed as to their reactions to the experiment.

Almost without exception, they professed themselves well pleased. Of course, that was what the sales department wanted to hear about satisfied customers.

As to *why* our subjects felt better after trying a new dentifrice, they couldn't say because they didn't know. It was merely that their outlook on life seemed to have become sunnier, and their personal relations more agreeable—apart from a few unfortunate domestic upsets, about which, however, the victims themselves seemed remarkably cheerful.

I thought I knew why. My pet theory was working out. Though I was no psychologist, I'd always been sure that a lot of people's mental difficulties and prevailing unhappiness was due solely to their inveterate habit of deceiving themselves. But these people who'd tried Grandma's lie soap couldn't even lie to themselves any more.

This outcome made our brave new world look braver in prospect—as well as likelier. A couple of days later the company's directors made the decision to go into production; and it was rumored that another of the biggest firms was already dickering for a look at the formula.

We had no trouble with the Bureau of Standards. After all, we only had to satisfy them that the stuff was harmless. Presumably they tried it on mice...

To celebrate the directors' decision, I invited Alice and her new fiancé to dinner. I was rather vague about what we were celebrating, so that they left no wiser than when they came. But they were much more candid, since I had a supply of the little white tablets on hand.

I gave the leaven most of the evening to work; and at eleven o'clock called Alice's apartment. I'd timed it correctly. She was in tears, too—judging by her voice.

"You and he must have said some pretty nasty things to each other," I remarked sympathetically. "Too bad about the engagement."

"Oh, it was *awful!* He said—he *admitted* that if it weren't for my b-bosom— And I told him—oh, how could I say *that?* But Oliver, how did you know?"

"I saw it coming. And now you're home all alone, and sort of wishing I was there to console you...aren't you?"

There was one of those pauses I'd learned to recognize. Then she said strangledly, "Y-yes. I was. I am. But *Oliver*—people don't—"

"Sometimes they do," I said. "Hold on. I'll be right up."

When a woman has once told the truth to a man, either everything is over between them, or everything has just begun.

From then on the story is mostly history.

Gorley and Gorley's new improved toothpaste with Verolin began outselling all other brands. Other companies saw that the new ingredient—for reasons nobody quite understood—was becoming more indispensable than chlorophyll had been somewhat earlier, and paid through the nose for the right to use it. G and G added a Verolin mouthwash to their line, and it was also a snowballing success. All the time, of course, Verolin was really Grandma's lie soap.

These products blanketed the country and went into the export market. They went all over civilization, if you define civilization as those regions of the Earth where people use toothbrushes and seek to avoid halitosis—or, anyway, all over what was then called "the free world" by its inhabitants and "the enslaved world" by the publicists of the "free world" on the other side.

The returns began coming in.

CHAPTER FOUR

A WELL-KNOWN radio news commentator paused for a refreshing gargle in the mid-break of his program, was unable to continue broadcasting, and resigned the same day.

Various other commentators and newspaper columnists suffered more or less similar fates, while a good many newspapers and periodicals underwent violent shifts of editorial policy.

Half a dozen magazines having the word "True" in their titles suspended publication.

Quite a few authors, including some more than usually successful ones, abandoned their profession. Surprisingly, those who quit included some who had been praised by the critics for the stark realism of their work, and among those who did not quit were some whose writings were regarded as sheer imaginative flights.

As for the critics, most of them took up useful trades.

A number of university professors conscientiously resigned, stating that they could not teach "facts" that they did not know to be true.

Several hitherto popular and, to their founders, profitable religious cults abruptly disintegrated. In one case there was a riot, when the Prophet of the Luminous Truth appeared in a mass meeting and told his followers some home truths about himself, his doctrines, and themselves.

Most of the churches lost grievously in membership, though at the same time they enjoyed an accession of new converts. Those whose rites included confession complained that, somehow, the act appeared to be losing its deep significance.

Psychoanalysts at first rejoiced over their sudden wholesale success in overcoming their patients' "resistances," and a little later were appalled by their empty waiting rooms.

The divorce rate skyrocketed, then plunged to a permanent record low. Conversely, the marriage rate at first fell off sharply, then climbed gradually back to normal. The birth rate was unaffected.

Innumerable lawyers took down their shingles.

Congressional investigating committees enjoyed a field day, but fell prey to an increasing nervous frustration as witness after witness refused to perjure himself.

In Washington, D. C., a conservatively-dressed gentleman checked into a hotel, came down to the lobby after brushing his teeth, and in response to a commercial traveler's casual question said, "My business? Well, I'm a secret agent for the Soviet Union. And you?"

Police in scores of cities were swamped by confessions of offenses ranging from multiple murder to double parking, and were bewildered by the absence of the expected percentage of false confessions.

For the first time in modern history, the number of homicides exceeded the number of suicides. In general, crimes of stealth virtually ceased to occur, while crimes of violence continued at about their previous level and reported cases of rape declined spectacularly.

Numerous government officials admitted themselves guilty of peculation and malfeasance in office. The business bureaucracy was even harder hit. Among the casualties was a prominent board member of Gorley and Gorley.

To my particular satisfaction, the mayor our local machine had elected made a public speech—apparently unaware that he was doing anything out of the way—in which he thanked by name the boys who had purchased the most votes for him in the last campaign, also those who had put in the strong-arm work.

All the F.B.I. agents doing undercover work in the Communist Party were exposed, and as a result the party went bankrupt for lack of dues paying members.

As O'Brien had predicted, the advertising business collapsed, burying many lesser enterprises under the ruins. But somehow no general financial panic took place.

A man from Texas was heard to confess that he sometimes got tired of hearing about Texas, and even admitted it couldn't be twice as large as the rest of the United States.

Events such as these were the convulsions, the death throes of an old world and the birth pangs of a new.

Their final phase was the breakdown of the international situation, which had continued for over a decade in a sort of deadly balance. The balance was destroyed when U. S. and other Western diplomats adopted a new tact that provoked, in their Eastern-bloc opponents, reactions first of suspicious alarm, then of bafflement, and finally of a dazed conviction that the spirit of Marxian history had at long last delivered the enemy into their hands—which last impression led directly to their undoing.

Forgetting the chiseler's basic precept—you can't cheat an honest man—they set about exploiting the situation by extracting from the West all the technical information they coveted, and which was now theirs for the asking. Along with plutonium refinement methods and guided missile designs, they obtained, naturally, the formula for Grandma's lie soap, alias Verolin.

The counterparts of Gorley and Gorley's sales department, in their government-run industries, were also shrewdly alive to the importance of having satisfied customers. Clearly, they reasoned, studying our records, this is a good thing, this is a valuable bit of *kul'tura*...

From there on developments followed pretty much the pattern that had already established in the West. There were some painful incidents, such as the Kiev massacre of former secret police agents, and the three days when *Pravda* shut down to retool. But on the whole, the reaction was more than anything else like that of a man who comes to the top and takes breath at last, after very nearly drowning.

The Iron Curtain sagged, fell apart, and sank into oblivion. Grandma's lie soap had conquered the world.

CHAPTER FIVE

SINCE I retired, I've been using my leisure in exploration and observation of this world in which I did a good deal to create, this world that differs so much from the one I grew up in and can remember better than most others even of my own generation. They've had the treatment, and they've changed. But I still brush my teeth with a salt-and-soda mixture.

In many ways, the present era answers to the visions that were called Utopian when I was a boy—called that, usually, with a sneer. A lot of the social and political reforms we only dreamed about then have been carried out as a matter of course that was inevitable once people stopped lying themselves and one another black in the face.

Mental diseases, tangled lives, crime have all been swept away— not to mention the threat of war that was the Great Shadow over-lying all the lesser shadows of the old world.

An election campaign now is carried on in an atmosphere of sobriety and statesmanship that would have given an old-time politician the creeps. None of the old bandstand, circus stuff... Speaking of that, one thing I miss is the circus. I used to like to listen to the sideshow barkers—an extinct tribe. I know, they still have circuses, or call them that; but P. T. Barnum would disown them.

But...people look one another in the eyes much more than they ever used to. They don't seem afraid. There's confidence—not the ballooning confidence that led to big economic booms and bigger busts, but a trust resting on solid foundations.

Still, sometimes I wonder.

Not long ago I ran into O'Brien, for the first time in years, in a bar. People don't drink as much as they did, but O'Brien had been drinking a good deal.

"How are you?" I said automatically, the sight of such a long-remembered face making me forget that that particular greeting wasn't used nowadays.

He began a detailed description of his general state of health and present state of intoxication. "Oh," I said. "You've had it."

"Yeah," said O'Brien. "I broke down and took the treatment. I got like everybody else. I couldn't stand the temptation any more. You know what I mean?"

I knew exactly what he meant. For him, with his background, it must have been much worse.

"Maybe," said O'Brien thickly, "I could have been dictator of the world if I'd wanted. But this way's better." He signaled the waiter, then looked at me curiously. "You—not yet?"

"Not yet," I said. "Maybe never. I like to watch things."

"Watch the sheep run," mumbled O'Brien. "All sheep…"

He was drunk, but he'd had Grandma's lie soap, and he spoke the truth.

Perhaps there's too much confidence.

Once in a while I yield a little to that temptation O'Brien mentioned, but always in harmless ways, merely for amusement or out of curiosity to see just how much people will swallow. Like in that fabrication of Howling Wolf, the genius of the North Woods that I told you about in the beginning. More and more I find that they'll believe almost anything, especially the younger generation. Older people still have a residuum of skepticism.

Now it's plain—using hindsight—that we should easily have foreseen the secondary effect. But it developed very slowly. No physiological effect, this, but a psychological one—or simply logical. Once people stop lying, they'll also stop suspecting deceit. They'll believe as they expect to be believed. Little by little, particularly as the young ones who don't remember grow up, they'll become totally gullible, it used to be called.

A while back, down South, there was an unwashed prophet who made converts right and left to a weird sect of his own devising—until somebody seduced him into heathenish ways and he tried brushing his teeth. But incidents like that don't really disturb me. As the example shows, they all come out in the wash.

Yet there is something that bothers me. Back before Grandma's lie soap, we used to get sporadic reports of "mysterious airships," "flying saucers," or similarly named equivalents for unexplained objects in the sky. We laughed them off, mostly, because people were always starting crazy rumors... After the great change, those reports might have been expected to stop coming.

But they didn't.

And more recently there have been some queer phenomena noted by the space station and the bubbles on the Moon.

So suppose we're not alone in the Universe or even in the Solar System? And suppose that whoever is out there—circling us, observing us with immense caution for so long—are beings like we used to be—fierce, wary, enormously suspicious as their behavior suggests, capable of any falsehood, any treachery?

Wolves, circling the sheep...

Perhaps it's all my imagination.

I can't be sure. There's only one way I can be sure even of what I think myself.

Pretty soon now I'll go into the bathroom and wash my mouth with Grandma's lie soap. Then I'll look into the mirror and ask myself, face to face, with no possibility of deception: *Did I do right?*

What will my answer be?

THE END

The Voyage That Lasted 600 Years

By DON WILCOX

Both Robert A. Heinlein's "Universe" (1941) and A. E. Van Vogt's "Far Centaurus" (1944) are rightfully considered to be s-f landmarks in the development of the interstellar theme—the Heinlein because it shows what might happen if the purpose of the voyage were lost, the Van Vogt because it beautifully delineates what ironies can follow if one form of travel were to supersede another. But Don Wilcox's "The Voyage That Lasted 600 Years" (Amazing, 1940) shows that sometimes a very popular writer can introduce the same two variants in a single story before more illustrious contemporaries make classics out of them—and still receive little or no recognition—until now.

CHAPTER ONE

THEY gave us a gala sendoff, the kind that keeps your heart bobbing up at your tonsils.

"It's a long, long way to the Milky Way!" the voices sang out. The band thundered the chorus over and over. The golden trumpaphones blasted our eardrums wide open. Thousands of people clapped their hands in time.

There were thirty-three of us—that is, there was supposed to be. As it turned out, there were thirty-five.

We were a dazzling parade of red, white and blue uniforms. We marched up the gangplank by couples, every couple a man and wife, every couple young and strong, for the selection had been rigid.

Captain Sperry and his wife and I—I being the odd man—brought up the rear. Reporters and cameramen swarmed at our heels. The microphones stopped us. The band and the crowd hushed.

"This is Captain Sperry telling you good-by" the amplified voice boomed. "On behalf of the thirty-three, I thank you for your grand farewell. We'll remember this hour as our last contact with our beloved Earth."

The crowd held its breath. The mighty import of our mission struck through every heart.

"We go forth into space to live—and to die," the captain said gravely. "But *our children's children,* born in space and reared in the light of our vision, will carry on our great purpose. And in centuries to come, your *children's children* may set forth for the Robinello planets, knowing that you will find an American colony already planted there."

The captain gestured good-by and the multitude responded with a thunderous cheer. Nothing so daring as a six-century nonstop flight had ever been undertaken before.

An announcer nabbed me by the sleeve and barked into the microphone, "And now one final word from Professor Gregory Grimstone, the one man who is supposed to live down through the six centuries of this historic flight and see the journey through to the end."

"Ladies and gentlemen," I choked, and the echo of my swallow blobbed back at me from distant walls, "as Keeper of the Traditions, I give you my word that the S. S. *Flashaway* shall carry your civilization through to the end, unsoiled and unblemished!"

A cheer stimulated me and I drew a deep breath for a burst of oratory. But Captain Sperry pulled at my other sleeve.

"That's all. We're set to slide out in two minutes."

The reporters scurried down the gangplank and made a center rush through the crowd. The band struck up. Motors roared sullenly.

One lone reporter who had missed out on the interviews blitzkrieged up and caught me by the coattail.

"Hold it, Butch. Just a coupla words so I can whip up a column of froth for the *Star*— Well, I'll be damned. If it ain't 'Crackdown' Grimstone..."

I scowled. The reporter before me was none other than Bill Broscoe, one of my former pupils at college and a star athlete. At heart I knew that Bill was a right guy, but I'd be the last to tell him so.

"Broscoe," I snarled. "Tardy as usual. You finally flunked my history course, didn't you?"

"Now, Crackdown," he whined, "don't go hopping on me. I won that Thanksgiving game for you, remember?"

He gazed at my red, white and blue uniform.

"So you're off for Robinello," he grinned.

"Son, this is my last minute on Earth, and *you* have to haunt me, of all people—"

"So you're the one that's taking the refrigerated sleeper, to wake up every hundred years—"

"And stir the fires of civilization among the crew—yes. Six hundred years from now when your bones have rotted, I'll still be carrying on."

"Still teaching 'em history? God forbid." Broscoe grinned.

"I hope I have better luck than I did with you."

"Let 'em off easy on dates, Crackdown. Give them 1066 for William the Conqueror and 2066 for the *Flashaway* take-off. That's enough. Taking your wife, I suppose?"

At this impertinent question I gave Broscoe the cold eye.

"Pardon me," he said, suppressing a sly grin—proof enough that he had heard the devastating story about how I missed my wedding and got the air. "Faulty alarm clock, wasn't it? Too bad, Crackdown. And you always ragged *me* about being tardy."

With this jibe Broscoe exploded into laughter. Some people have the damnedest notions about what constitutes humor. I backed into the entrance of the space ship uncomfortably. Broscoe followed.

The automatic door cut past me. I jerked Broscoe through barely in time to keep him from being bisected.

Zzzzippp!

"Tardy as usual, my friend," I hooted. "You've missed your gangplank. That makes you the first castaway in space."

We took off like a shooting star, and the last I saw of Bill Broscoe, he stood at a rear window cursing as he watched the earth and the moon fall away into the velvety black heavens. And the more I laughed at him, the madder he got. No sense of humor.

Was that the last time I ever saw him? Well, no, to be strictly honest I had one more unhappy glimpse of him.

It happened just before I packed myself away for my first one hundred years' sleep.

I had checked over the "Who's Who Aboard the *Flashaway*"—the official register—to make sure that I was thoroughly acquainted with everyone on board; for these sixteen couples were to be the great-grandparents of the next generation I would meet. Then I had promptly taken my leave of Captain Sperry and his wife, and gone directly to my refrigeration plant, where I was to suspend my life by instantaneous freezing.

I clicked the switches, and one of the two huge horizontal wheels—one in reserve, in the event of a breakdown—opened up for me like a door opening in the side of a gigantic doughnut, or better, a tubular merry-go-round. There was my nook waiting for me to crawl in.

Before I did so I took a moment and cast a backward glance toward the ballroom. The one-way glass partition, through which I could see but not be seen, gave me a clear view of the scene of merriment. The couples were dancing. The journey was off to a good start.

"A grand gang," I said to myself. No one doubted that the ship was equal to the six-hundred-year journey. The success would depend upon the people. Living and dying in this closely circumscribed world would put them to a severe test. All credit, I reflected, was due the planning committee for choosing such a congenial group.

"They're equal to it," I said optimistically. If their children would only prove as sturdy and adaptable as their parents, my job as Keeper of the Traditions would be simple.

But how, I asked myself, as I stepped into my life-suspension merry-go-round, would Bill Broscoe fit into this picture? Not a half bad guy. Still—

My final glance through the one-way glass partition slew me. Out of the throng I saw Bill Broscoe dancing past with a beautiful girl in his arms. The girl was Louise—*my* Louise—the girl I had been engaged to marry!

In a flash it came to me—but not about Bill. I forgot him on the spot. About Louise.

Bless her heart, she'd come to find me. She must have heard that I had signed up for the *Flashaway*, and she had come aboard, a stowaway, to forgive me for missing the wedding—to marry me! Now—

A warning click sounded, a lid closed, my refrigerator merry-go-round whirled—blackness.

CHAPTER TWO
Babies, Just Babies

In a moment—or so it seemed—I was again gazing into the light of the refrigerating room. The lid stood open.

A stimulating warmth circulated through my limbs. Perhaps the machine, I half consciously concluded, had made no more than a preliminary revolution.

I bounded out with a single thought. I must find Louise. We could still be married. For the present I would postpone my entrance into the ice. And since the machine had been equipped with two merry-go-round freezers as an emergency safeguard—ah! Happy thought—perhaps Louise would be willing to undergo life suspension with me?

I stopped at the one-way glass partition, astonished to see no signs of dancing in the ballroom. I could scarcely see the ballroom, for it had been darkened.

Upon unlocking the door (the refrigerator room was my own private retreat) I was bewildered. An unaccountable change had come over everything. What it was, I couldn't determine at the moment. But the very air of the ballroom was different.

A few dim green light bulbs burned along the walls—enough to show me that the dancers had vanished. Had time enough elapsed for night to come on? My thoughts spun dizzily. Night, I reflected, would consist simply of turning off the lights and going to bed. It had been agreed in our plan that our twenty-four hour Earth day would be maintained for the sake of regularity.

But there was something more intangible that struck me. The furniture had been changed about, and the very walls seemed *older*. Something more than minutes had passed since I left this room.

Strangest of all, the windows were darkened.

In a groggy state of mind I approached one of the windows in hopes of catching a glimpse of the solar system. I was still puzzling over how much time might have elapsed. Here, at least, was a sign of very recent activity.

"Wet Paint" read the sign pinned to the window. The paint was still sticky. What the devil—

The ship, of course, was fully equipped for blind flying. But aside from the problems of navigation, the crew had anticipated enjoying a wonderland of stellar beauty through the portholes. Now, for some strange reason, every window had been painted opaque.

I listened. Slow measured steps were pacing in an adjacent hall-way. Nearing the entrance, I stopped, halted by a shrill sound from somewhere overhead. It came from one of the residential quarters that gave on the ballroom balcony.

It was the unmistakable wail of a baby.

Then another baby's cry struck up; and a third, from somewhere across the balcony, joined the chorus. Time, indeed, must have passed since I left this roomful of dancers.

Now some irate voices of disturbed sleepers added rumbling basses to the symphony of wailings. Grumbles of "Shut that little devil up!" and poundings of fists on walls thundered through the empty ballroom. In a burst of inspiration I ran to the records room, where the ship's "Who's Who" was kept.

The door to the records room was locked, but the footsteps of some sleepless person I had heard now pounded down the dimly lighted hallway. I looked upon the aged man. I had never seen him before. He stopped at the sight of me; then snapping on a brighter light, came on confidently.

"Mr. Grimstone?" he said, extending his hand. "We've been expecting you. My name is William Broscoe—"

"William Broscoe, the second. You knew my father, I believe."

I groaned and choked.

"And my mother," the old man continued, "always spoke very highly of you. I'm proud to be the first to greet you."

He politely overlooked the flush of purple that leaped into my face. For a moment nothing that I could say was intelligible.

He turned a key and we entered the records room. There I faced the inescapable fact. My full century had passed. The original crew of the *Flashaway* were long gone. A completely new generation was on the register.

Or, more accurately, three new generations: the children, the grandchildren, and the great grandchildren of the generation I had known.

One hundred years had passed—and I had lain so completely suspended, owing to the freezing that only a moment of my own life had been absorbed.

Eventually I was to get used to this; but on this first occasion I found it utterly shocking—even embarrassing. Only a few minutes ago, as my experience went, I was madly in love with Louise and had hopes of yet marrying her.

But now—well, the leatherbound "Who's Who" told all. Louise had been dead twenty years. Nearly thirty children now alive aboard the S. S. *Flashaway* could claim her as their great-grandmother. These carefully recorded pedigrees proved it.

And the patriarch of that fruitful tribe had been none other than Bill Broscoe, the fresh young athlete who had always been tardy for my history class. I gulped as if I were swallowing a baseball.

Broscoe—tardy! And I had missed my second chance to marry Louise—by a full century.

My fingers turned the pages of the register numbly. William Broscoe II misinterpreted my silence.

"I see you are quick to detect our trouble," he said, and the same deep conscientious concern showed in his expression that I had remembered in the face of his mother, upon our grim meeting after my alarm clock had failed and I had missed my own wedding.

Trouble? Trouble aboard the S. S. *Flashaway*, after all the careful advance planning we had done, and after all our array of budgeting and scheduling and vowing to stamp our systematic ways upon the oncoming generations? This, we had agreed, would be the world's most unique colonizing expedition; for every last trouble that might crop up on the six-hundred-year voyage had already been met and conquered by advance planning.

"They've tried to put off doing anything about it until your arrival," Broscoe said, observing respectfully that the charter invested in me the authority of passing upon all important policies.

"But this very week three new babies arrived, which brings the trouble to a crisis. So the captain ordered a blackout of the heavens as an emergency measure."

"Heavens?" I grunted. "What have the heavens got to do with babies?"

"There's a difference of opinion on that. Maybe it depends upon how susceptible you are."

"Susceptible—to what?"

"The romantic malady."

I looked at the old man, much puzzled. He took me by the arm and led me toward the pilots' control room. Here were unpainted windows that revealed celestial glories beyond anything I had ever dreamed. Brilliant planets of varied hues gleamed through the blackness, while close at hand—almost close enough to touch—were numerous large moons, floating slowly past as we shot along our course.

"Some little show," the pilot grinned, "and it keeps getting better."

He proceeded to tell me just where we were and how few adjustments in the original time schedules he had had to make, and why this non-stop flight to Robinello would stand unequalled for centuries to come.

And I heard virtually nothing of what he said. I simply stood there, gazing at the unbelievable beauty of the skies. I was hypnotized, enthralled, shaken to the very roots. One emotion, one thought dominated me. I longed for my dear beloved Louise.

"The romantic malady, as I was saying," William Broscoe resumed, "may or may not be a factor in producing our large population. Personally, I think it's pure buncombe."

"Pure buncombe," I echoed, still thinking of Louise. If she and I had had moons like these—

"But nobody can tell Captain Dickinson anything..."

There was considerable clamor and wrangling that morning as the inhabitants awakened to find their heavens blacked out. Captain Dickinson was none too popular anyway. Fortunately for him, many of the people took their grouches out on the babies who had caused the disturbance in the night.

Families with babies were supposed to occupy the rear staterooms—but there weren't enough rear staterooms. Or rather, there were too many babies.

Soon the word went the rounds that the Keeper of the Traditions had returned to life. I was duly banqueted and toasted and treated to lengthy accounts of the events of the past hundred years. And during the next few days many of the older men and women would take me aside for private conferences and spill their worries into my ears.

CHAPTER THREE
Boredom

What's the world coming to?" these granddaddies and grandmothers would ask. And before I could scratch my head for an answer, they would assure me that this expedition was headed straight for the rocks.

"It's all up with us. We've lost our grip on our original purposes. The Six-Hundred-Year Plan is nothing but a dead scrap of paper."

I'll admit things looked plenty black. And the more parlor conversations I was invited in on, the blacker things looked. I couldn't sleep nights.

"If our population keeps on increasing, we'll run out of food before we're halfway there," William Broscoe II repeatedly declared. "We've got to have a compulsory program of birth control. That's the only thing that will save us."

A delicate subject for parlor conversations, you think? This older generation didn't think so. I was astonished, and I'll admit I was a bit proud as well, to discover how deeply imbued these old graybeards were with _Flashaway_ determination and patriotism. They had missed life in America by only one generation, and they were unquestionably the staunchest of flag wavers on board.

The younger generations were less outspoken, and for the first week I began to deplore their comparative lack of vision. They, the possessors of families, seemed to avoid these discussions about the oversupply of children.

"So you've come to check upon our American traditions, Professor Grimstone," they would say casually. "We've heard all about this great purpose of our forefathers, and I guess it's up to us to put it across. But gee whiz, Grimstone, we wish we could have seen the earth... What's it like, anyhow?"

"Tell us some more about the earth..."

"All we know is what we get second hand..."

I told them about the earth. Yes, they had books galore, and movies and phonograph records, pictures and maps; but these things only excited their curiosity. They asked me questions by the thousands. Only after I had poured out several encyclopedia-loads of Earth memories did I begin to break through their masks.

Back of this constant questioning, I discovered, they were watching me. Perhaps they were wondering whether they were not being subjected to more rigid discipline here on shipboard than their cousins back on Earth. I tried to impress upon them that they were a chosen group, but this had little effect. It stuck in their minds that they had had no choice in the matter.

Moreover, they were watching to see what I was going to do about the population problem, for they were no less aware of it than their elders.

Two weeks after my "return" we got down to business.

Captain Dickinson preferred to engineer the matter himself. He called an assembly in the movie auditorium. Almost everyone was present.

The program began with the picture of the Six-Hundred-Year Plan. Everyone knew the reels by heart. They had seen and heard them dozens of times, and were ready to snicker at the proper moments—such as when the stern old committee chairman, charging the unborn generations with their solemn obligations, was interrupted by a friendly fly on his nose.

When the films were run through, Captain Dickinson took the rostrum, and with considerable bluster he called upon the Clerk of the Council to review the situation. The clerk read a report that went about as follows:

To maintain a stable population, it was agreed in the original Plan that families should average two children each. Hence, the original 16 families would bring forth approximately 32 children; and assuming that they were fairly evenly divided as to sex, they would eventually form 16 new families. These 16 families would, in turn, have an average of two children each—another generation of approximately 32.

By maintaining these averages, we were to have a total population, at any given time, of 32 children, 32 parents and 32 grandparents. The great-grandparents may be left out of account, for owing to the natural span of life they ordinarily die off before they accumulate in any great numbers.

The three living generations, then, of 32 each would give the *Flashaway* a constant active population of 96, or roughly, 100 persons.

The Six-Hundred-Year Plan has allowed for some flexibility in these figures. It has established the safe maximum at 150 and the safe minimum at 75.

If our population shrinks below 75, it is dangerously small. If it shrinks to 50, a crisis is at hand.

But if it grows above 150, it is dangerously large; and if it reaches the 200 mark, as we all know, a crisis may be said to exist.

The clerk stopped for an impressive pause, marred only by a baby from some distant room.

"Now, coming down to the present-day facts, we are well aware that the population has been dangerously large for the past seven years—"

"Since we entered this section of the heavens," Captain Dickinson interspersed with a scowl.

"From the first year in space, the population plan has encountered some irregularities," the clerk continued. "To begin with, there were not sixteen couples, but seventeen. The seventeenth couple—" here the clerk shot a glance at William Broscoe, "did not belong to the original compact, and after their marriage they were not bound by the sacred traditions—"

"I object!" I shouted, challenging the eyes of the clerk and the captain squarely. Dickinson had written that report with a touch of malice. The clerk skipped over a sentence or two.

"But however the Broscoe family may have prospered and multiplied, our records show that nearly all the families of the present generation have exceeded the per-family quota."

At this point there was a slight disturbance in the rear of the auditorium. An anxious-looking young man entered and signaled to the doctor. The two went out together.

"*All* the families," the clerk amended. "Our population this week passed the two hundred mark. This concludes the report."

The captain opened the meeting for discussion, and the forum lasted far into the night. The demand for me to assist the Council with some legislation was general. There was also hearty sentiment against the captain's blacked-out heavens from young and old alike.

This, I considered, was a good sign. The children craved the fun of watching the stars and planets; their elders desired to keep up their serious astronomical studies.

"Nothing is so important to the welfare of this expedition," I said to the Council on the following day, as we settled down to the job of thrashing out some legislation, "as to maintain our interests in the outside world. Population or no population, we must not become ingrown."

I talked of new responsibilities, new challenges in the form of contests and campaigns, new leisure-time activities. The discussion went on for days.

"Back in my times—" I said for the hundredth time; but the captain laughed me down. My times and these times were as unlike as black and white, he declared.

"But the principle is the same," I shouted. "We had population troubles, too."

They smiled as I referred to twenty-first century relief families who were overrun with children. I cited the fact that some industrialists who paid heavy taxes had considered giving every relief family an automobile as a measure to save themselves money in the long run; for they had discovered that relief families with cars had fewer children than those without.

"That's no help," Dickinson muttered. "You can't have cars on a space ship."

"You can play bridge," I retorted. "Bridge is an enemy of the birthrate too. Bridge, cars, movies, checkers—they all add up to the same thing. They lift you out of your animal natures."

The Councilmen threw up their hands. They had bridged and checkered themselves to death.

"Then try other things," I persisted. "You could produce your own movies and plays—organize a little theater—create some new drama—"

"What have we got to dramatize?" the captain replied sourly. "All the dramatic things happen on the earth."

This shocked me. Somehow it took all the starch out of this colossal adventure to hear the captain give up so easily.

"All our drama is second hand," he grumbled. "Our ship's course is cut and dried. Our world is bounded by walls. The only dramatic things that happen here are births and deaths."

A doctor broke in on our conference and seized the captain by the hand.

"Congratulations, Captain Dickinson, on the prize crop of the season. Your wife has just presented you with a fine set of triplets—three boys!"

That broke up the meeting.

Captain Dickinson was so busy for the rest of the week that he forgot all about his official obligations. The problem of population limitation faded from his mind.

I wrote out my recommendations and gave them all the weight of my dictatorial authority. I stressed the need for more birth control forums, and recommended that the heavens be made visible for further studies in astronomy and mathematics.

I was tempted to warn Captain Dickinson that the *Flashaway* might incur some serious dramas of its own—poverty, disease and the like—unless he got back on the track of the Six-Hundred-Year Plan in a hurry. But Dickinson was preoccupied with some family washings when I took my leave of him, and he seemed to have as much drama on his hands as he cared for.

I paid a final visit to each of the twenty-eight great-grand-children of Louise, and returned to my ice.

CHAPTER FOUR
Revolt!

My chief complaint against my merry-go-round freezer was that it didn't give me any rest. One whirl into blackness, and the next thing I knew I popped out of the open lid again with not so much as a minute's time to reorganize my thoughts.

Well, here it was 2266—two hundred years since the take-off.

A glance through the one-way glass told me it was daytime in the ballroom.

As I turned the key in the lock I felt like a prize fighter on a vaudeville tour who, having just trounced the tough local strong man, steps back in the ring to take on his cousin.

A touch of a headache caught me as I reflected that there should be four more returns after this one—if all went according to plan. *Plan.* That word was destined to be trampled underfoot.

Oh, well (I took a deep optimistic breath) the *Flashaway* troubles would all be cleared up by now. Three generations would have passed. The population should be back to normal.

I swung the door open, stepped through, locked it after me.

For an instant I thought I had stepped in on a big movie "take"—a scene of a stricken multitude. The big ballroom was literally strewn with people—if creatures in such a deplorable state could be called people.

There was no movie camera. This was the real thing.

"Grimstone's come," a hoarse voice cried out.

"Grimstone. Grimstone." Others caught up the cry. Then "Food. Give us food. We're starving. For God's sake—"

The weird chorus gathered volume. I stood dazed, and for an instant I couldn't realize that I was looking upon the population of the *Flashaway*.

Men, women and children of all ages and all states of desperation joined in the clamor. Some of them stumbled to their feet and came toward me, waving their arms weakly. But most of them hadn't the strength to rise.

In that stunning moment an icy sweat came over me.

"Food! Food! We've been waiting for you, Grimstone. We've been holding on—"

The responsibility that was strapped to my shoulders suddenly weighed down like a locomotive. You see, I had originally taken my job more or less as a lark. That Six-Hundred-Year Plan had looked so airtight. I, the Keeper of the Traditions, would have a snap.

I had anticipated many a pleasant hour acquainting the oncoming generations with noble sentiments about George Washington; I had pictured myself filling the souls of my listeners by reciting the Gettysburg address and lecturing upon the mysteries of science.

But now those pretty bubbles burst on the spot, nor did they ever re-form in the centuries to follow.

And as they burst, my vision cleared. My job had nothing to do with theories or textbooks or speeches. My job was simply to get to Robinello—to get there with enough living, able-bodied, sane human beings to start a colony.

Dull blue starlight sifted through the windows to highlight the big roomful of starved figures. The mass of pale blue faces stared at me. There were hundreds of them. Instinctively I shrank as the throng clustered around me, calling and pleading.

"One at a time," I cried. "First I've got to find out what this is all about. Who's your spokesman?"

They designated a handsomely built, if undernourished, young man. I inquired his name and learned that he was Bob Sperry, a descendant of the original Captain Sperry.

"There are eight hundred of us now," Sperry said.

"Don't tell me the food has run out?"

"No, not that—but six hundred of us are not entitled to regular meals."

"Why not?"

Before the young spokesman could answer, the others burst out with an unintelligible clamor. Angry cries of "That damned Dickinson!" and "Guns!" and "They'll shoot us!" were all I could distinguish.

I quieted them and made Bob Sperry go on with his story. He calmly asserted that there was a very good reason that they shouldn't be fed, all sentiment aside; namely, because they had been born outside the quota.

Here I began to catch a gleam of light.

"By Captain Dickinson's interpretation of the Plan," Sperry explained, "there shouldn't be more than two hundred of us altogether."

This Captain Dickinson, I learned, was a grandson of the one I had known.

Sperry continued, "Since there are eight hundred, he and his brother—his brother being Food Superintendent—launched an emergency measure a few months ago to save food. They divided the population into the two hundred, who had a right to be born, and the six hundred who had not."

So the six hundred starving persons before me were theoretically the excess population. The vigorous ancestry of the sixteen—no, seventeen—original couples, together with the excellent medical care that had reduced infant mortality and disease to the minimum, had wrecked the original plan completely.

"What do you do for food? You must have *some* food…"

"We live on charity."

The throng again broke in with hostile words. Young Sperry's version was too gentle to do justice to their outraged stomachs. In fairness to the two hundred, however, Sperry explained that they shared whatever food they could spare with these, their less fortunate brothers, sisters and offspring.

Uncertain what should or could be done, I gave the impatient crowd my promise to investigate at once. Bob Sperry and nine other men accompanied me.

The minute we were out of hearing of the ballroom, I gasped:

"Good heavens, men, how is it that you and your six hundred haven't mobbed the storerooms long before this?"

"Dickinson and his brother have got the drop on us."

"Drop? What kind of drop?"

"Guns."

I couldn't understand this. I had believed these new generations of the *Flashaway* to be relatively innocent of any knowledge of firearms.

"What kind of guns?"

"The same kind they use in our Earth-made movies—that make a loud noise and kill people by the hundreds."

"But there aren't any guns aboard... That is..."

I knew perfectly well that the only firearms the ship carried had been stored in my own refrigerator room, which no one could enter but myself. Before the voyage, one of the planning committee had jestingly suggested that if any serious trouble ever arose, I should be master of the situation by virtue of one hundred revolvers.

"They made their own guns," Sperry explained, "just like the ones in our movies and books."

Inquiring whether any persons had been shot, I learned that three of their number, attempting a raid on the storerooms, had been killed.

"We heard three loud bangs, and found our men dead with bloody skulls."

Reaching the upper end of the central corridor, we arrived at the captain's headquarters.

The name of Captain Dickinson carried a bad flavor for me. A century before I had developed a distaste for a certain other Captain Dickinson, his grandfather. I resolved to swallow my prejudice. Then the door opened, and my resolve stuck in my throat. The former Captain Dickinson had merely annoyed me; but this one I hated on sight.

"Well?" the captain roared at the eleven of us.

Well-uniformed and neatly groomed, he filled the doorway with an impressive bulk. In his right hand he gripped a revolver. The gleam of that weapon had a magical effect upon the men. They shrank back respectfully. Then the captain's cold eye lighted on me.

"Who are you?"

"Gregory Grimstone, Keeper of the Traditions."

The captain sent a quick glance toward his gun and repeated his "Well?"

For a moment I was fascinated by that intricately shaped piece of metal in his grip.

"Well," I echoed. "If 'well' is the only reception you have to offer, I'll proceed with my official business. Call your Food Superintendent."

"Why?"

"Order him out. Have him feed the entire population without further delay."

"We can't afford the food," the captain growled.

"We'll talk that over later, but we won't talk on empty stomachs. Order out your Food Superintendent."

"Crawl back in your hole," Dickinson snarled.

At that instant another bulky man stepped into view. He was almost the identical counterpart of the captain, but his uniform was that of the Food Superintendent. Showing his teeth with a sinister snarl, he took his place beside his brother. He too jerked his right hand up to flash a gleaming revolver.

I caught one glimpse—and laughed in his face. I couldn't help it.

"You fellows are good," I roared. "You're damned good actors. If you've held off the starving six hundred with nothing but those two dumb imitations of revolvers, you deserve an Academy award."

The two Dickinson brothers went white.

Back of me came low mutterings from ten starving men.

"Imitations—dumb imitations—what the hell?"

Sperry and his nine comrades plunged with one accord. For the next ten minutes the captain's headquarters was simply a whirlpool of flying fists and hurtling bodies.

I have mentioned that these ten men were weak from lack of food. That fact was all that saved the Dickinson brothers; for ten minutes of lively exercise was all the ten men could endure, in spite of the circumstances.

But ten minutes left an impression. The Dickinsons were the worst beaten-up men I have ever seen, and I have seen some bad ones in my time. When the news echoed through the ship, no one questioned the ethics of ten starved men attacking two overfed ones.

Needless to say, before two hours passed, every hungry man, woman and child ate to his gizzard's content. And before another hour passed, some new officers were installed. The S. S. *Flashaway's* trouble was far from solved; but for the present the whole eight hundred were one big family picnic. Hope was restored, and the rejoicing lasted through many thousand miles of space.

There was considerable mystery about the guns. Surprisingly, the people had developed an awe of the movie guns as if they were instruments of magic.

Upon investigating, I was convinced that the captain and his brother had simply capitalized on this superstition. They had a sound enough motive for wanting to save food. But once their gun bluff had been established, they had become uncompromising oppressors. And when the occasion arose that their guns were challenged, they had simply crushed the skulls of their three attackers and faked the noises of explosions.

But now the firearms were dead. And so was the Dickinson regime.

But the menacing problem of too many mouths to feed still clung to the S. S. *Flashaway* like a hungry ghost determined to ride the ship to death.

Six full months passed before the needed reform was forged.

During that time everyone was allowed full rations. The famine had already taken its toll in weakened bodies, and seventeen persons—most of them young children—died. The doctors, released from the Dickinson regime, worked like Trojans to bring the rest back to health.

The reform measure that went into effect six months after my arrival consisted of outright sterilization.

The compulsory rule was sterilization for everyone except those born "within the quota"—and that quota, let me add, was narrowed down one half from Captain Dickinson's two hundred to the most eligible one hundred. The disqualified one hundred now joined the ranks of the six hundred.

And that was not all. By their own agreement, every within-the-quota family, responsible for bearing the *Flashaway's* future children, would undergo sterilization operations after the second child was born.

The seven hundred out-of-quota citizens, let it be said, were only too glad to submit to the simple sterilization measures in exchange for a right to live their normal lives. Yes, they were to have three squares a day. With an assured population decline in prospect for the coming century, this generous measure of food would not give out. Our surveys of the existing food supplies showed that these seven hundred could safely live their four-score years and die with full stomachs.

Looking back on the six months work, I was fairly well satisfied that the doctors and the Council and I had done the fair, if drastic, thing. If I had planted seeds for further trouble with the Dickinson tribe, I was little concerned about it at the time.

My conscience was, in fact, clear—except for one small matter. I was guilty of one slight act of partiality.

I incurred this guilt shortly before I returned to the ice. The doctors and I, looking down from the balcony into the ballroom, chanced to notice a young couple who were obviously very much in love.

The young man was Bob Sperry, the handsome, clear-eyed descendant of the *Flashaway's* first and finest captain, the lad who had been the spokesman when I first came upon the starving mob.

The girl's name—and how it had clung in my mind!—was Louise Broscoe. Refreshingly beautiful, she reminded me for all the world of my own Louise (mine and Bill Broscoe's).

"It's a shame," one of the doctors commented, "that fine young blood has to fall outside the quota. But rules are rules."

With a shrug of the shoulders he had already dismissed the matter from his mind—until I handed him something I had scribbled on a piece of paper.

"We'll make this one exception," I said perfunctorily. "If any question ever arises, this statement relieves you doctors of all responsibility. This is my own special request."

CHAPTER FIVE
Wedding Bells

One hundred years later my rash act came back to haunt me— and how! Bob Sperry had married Louise Broscoe, and the births of their two children had raised the unholy cry of *"Favoritism."*

By the year 2366, Bob Sperry and Louise Broscoe were gone and almost forgotten. But the enmity against me, the Keeper of the Traditions who played favorites, had grown up into a monster of bitter hatred waiting to devour me.

It didn't take me long to discover this. My first contact after I emerged from the ice set the pace.

"Go tell your parents," I said to the gang of brats that were playing ball in the spacious ballroom, "that Grimstone has arrived."

Their evil little faces stared at me a moment, then they snorted.

"Faw! Faw! Faw!" and away they ran.

I stood in the big bleak room wondering what to make of their insults. On the balcony some of the parents craned over the railings at me.

"Greetings," I cried. "I'm Grimstone, Keeper of the Traditions. I've just come—"

"Faw!" the men and women shouted at me. "Faw! Faw!"

No one could have made anything friendly out of those snarls. "Faw," to them, was simply a vocal manner of spitting poison.

Uncertain what this surly reception might lead to, I returned to my refrigerator room to procure one of the guns. Then I returned to the volley of catcalls and insults, determined to carry out my duties, come what might.

When I reached the forequarter of the ship, however, I found some less hostile citizens who gave me a civil welcome. Here I established myself for the extent of my 2366-67 sojourn, an honored guest of the Sperry family.

This, I told myself, was my reward for my favor to Bob Sperry and Louise Broscoe a century ago. For here was their grandson, a fine upstanding gray-haired man of fifty, a splendid pilot and the father of a beautiful twenty-one year old daughter.

"Your name wouldn't be Louise by any chance?" I asked the girl as she showed me into the Sperry living room.

"Lora-Louise," the girl smiled. It was remarkable how she brought back memories of one of her ancestors of three centuries previous.

Her dark eyes flashed over me curiously.

"So you are the man that we Sperrys have to thank for being here."

"You've heard about the quotas?" I asked.

"Of course. You're almost a god to our family."

"I must be a devil to some of the others," I said, recalling my reception of catcalls.

"Rogues," the girl's father snorted, and he thereupon launched into a breezy account of the past century.

The sterilization program, he assured me, had worked—if anything, too well. The population was the lowest in Flashaway history. It stood at the dangerously low mark of *fifty*.

Besides the sterilization program, a disease epidemic had taken its toll. In addition three ugly murders, prompted by jealousies, had spotted the record. And there had been one suicide.

As to the character of the population, Pilot Sperry declared gravely that there had been a turn for the worse.

"They fight each other like damned anarchists," he snorted.

The Dickinsons had made trouble for several generations. Now it was the Dickinsons against the Smiths; and these two factions included four-fifths of all the people. They were about evenly divided—twenty on each side—and when they weren't actually fighting each other, they were "fawing" at each other.

These bellicose factions had one sentiment in common: they both despised the Sperry faction. And—here my guilt cropped up again—their hatred stemmed from my special favor of a century ago, without which there would be no Sperrys now. In view of the fact that the Sperry faction lived in the forequarter of the ship and held all the important offices, it was no wonder that the remaining forty citizens were jealous.

All of which gave me enough to worry about. On top of that, Lora-Louise's mother gave me one other angle of the set-up.

"The trouble between the Dickinsons and the Smiths has grown worse since Lora-Louise has become a young lady," Mrs. Sperry confided to me.

We were sitting in a breakfast nook. Amber starlight shone softly through the porthole, lighting the mother's steady imperturbable gray eyes.

"Most girls have married at eighteen or nineteen," her mother went on. "So far, Lora-Louise has refused to marry."

The worry in Mrs. Sperry's face was almost imperceptible, but I understood. I had checked over the "Who's Who" and I knew the seriousness of this population crisis. I also knew that there were four young unmarried men with no other prospects of wives except Lora-Louise.

"Have you any choice for her?" I asked.

"Since she must marry—and I know she *must*— I have urged her to make her own choice."

I could see that the ordeal of choosing had been postponed until my coming, in hopes that I might modify the rules. But I had no intention of doing so. The *Flashaway* needed Lora-Louise. It needed the sort of children she would bear.

That week I saw the two husky Dickinson boys. Both were in their twenties. They stayed close together and bore an air of treachery and scheming. Rumor had it that they carried weapons made from table knives.

Everyone knew that my coming would bring the conflict to a head. Many thought I would try to force the girl to marry the older Smith—"Batch", as he was called in view of his bachelorhood. He was past thirty-five, the oldest of the four unmarried men.

But some argued otherwise. For Batch, though a splendid specimen physically, was slow of wit and speech. It was common knowledge that he was weak-minded.

For that reason, I might choose his younger cousin, "Smithy," a roly-poly overgrown boy of nineteen who spent his time bullying the younger children.

But if the Smiths and the Dickinsons could have their way about it, the Keeper of the Traditions should have no voice in the matter. Let me insist that Lora-Louise marry, said they; but whom she should marry was none of my business.

They preferred a fight as a means of settlement. A free-for-all between the two factions would be fine. A showdown of fists among the four contenders would be even better.

Best of all would be a battle of knives that would eliminate all but one of the suitors. Not that either the Dickinsons or the Smiths needed to admit that was what they preferred; but their barbaric tastes were plain to see.

Barbarians. That's what they had become. They had sprung too far from their native civilization. Only the Sperry faction, isolated in their monasteries of control boards, physicians' laboratories and record rooms, kept alive the spark of civilization.

The Sperrys and their associates were human beings out of the twenty-first century. The Smiths and the Dickinsons had slipped. They might have come out of the Dark Ages.

What burned me up more than anything else was that obviously both the Smiths and the Dickinsons looked forward with sinister glee toward dragging Lora-Louise down from her height to their own barbaric levels.

One night I was awakened by the sharp ringing of the pilot's telephone. I heard the snap of a switch. An *emergency* signal flashed on throughout the ship.

Footsteps were pounding toward the ballroom. I slipped into a robe, seized my gun, made for the door.

"The Dickinsons are murdering up on them," Pilot Sperry shouted to me from the door of the control room.

"I'll see about it," I snapped.

I bounded down the corridor. Sperry didn't follow. Whatever violence might occur from year to year within the hull of the *Flashaway*, the pilot's code demanded that he lock himself up at the controls and tend to his own business.

It was a free-for-all. Under the bright lights they were going to it, tooth and toenail.

Children screamed and clawed, women hurled dishes, old tottering granddaddies edged into the fracas to crack at each other with canes.

The appalling reason for it all showed in the center of the room—the roly-poly form of young "Smithy" Smith. Hacked and stabbed, his nightclothes ripped, he was a veritable mess of carnage.

I shouted for order. No one heard me, for in that instant a chase thundered on the balcony. Everything else stopped. All eyes turned on the three racing figures.

Batch Smith, fleeing in his white nightclothes, had less than five yards' lead on the two Dickinsons. Batch was just smart enough to run when he was chased, not smart enough to know he couldn't possibly outrun the younger Dickinsons.

As they shot past blazing lights the Dickinsons' knives flashed. I could see that their hands were red with Smithy's blood.

"*Stop!*" I cried. "Stop or I'll *shoot!*"

If they heard, the words must have been meaningless. The younger Dinkinson gained ground. His brother darted back in the opposite direction, crouched, waited for his prey to come around the circular balcony.

"Dickinson! Stop or I'll shoot you dead!" I bellowed.

Batch Smith came on, his eyes white with terror. Crouched and waiting, the older Dickinson lifted his knife for the killing stroke.

I shot.

The crouched Dickinson fell in a heap. Over him tripped the racing form of Batch Smith, to sprawl headlong. The other Dickinson leaped over his brother and pounced down upon the fallen prey, knife upraised.

Another shot went home.

Young Dickinson writhed and came toppling down over the balcony rail. He lay where he fell, his bloody knife sticking up through the side of his neck.

It was ugly business trying to restore order. However, the magic power of firearms, which had become only a dusty legend, now put teeth into every word I uttered.

The doctors were surprisingly efficient. After many hours of work behind closed doors, they released their verdicts to the waiting groups. The elder Dickinson, shot through the shoulder, would live. The younger Dickinson was dead. So was Smithy. But his cousin, Batch Smith, although too scared to walk back to his stateroom, was unhurt.

The rest of the day the doctors devoted to patching up the minor damages done in the free fight. Four-fifths of the *Flashaway* population were burdened with bandages, it seemed. For some time to come both the warring parties were considerably sobered over their losses. But most of all they were disgruntled because the fight had settled nothing.

The prize was still unclaimed. The two remaining contenders, backed by their respective factions, were at a bitter deadlock.

Nor had Lora-Louise's hatred for either the surviving Dickinson or Smith lessened in the slightest.

Never had a duty been more oppressive to me. I postponed my talk with Lora-Louise for several days, but I was determined that there should be no more fighting. She must choose.

We sat in an alcove next to the pilot's control room, looking out into the vast sky. Our ship, bounding at a terrific speed though it was, seemed to be hanging motionless in the tranquil star-dotted heavens.

"I must speak frankly," I said to the girl. "I hope you will do the same."

She looked at me steadily. Her dark eyes were perfectly frank, her full lips smiled with childlike simplicity.

"How old are you?" she asked.

"Twenty-eight," I answered. I'd been the youngest professor on the college faculty. "Or you might say three hundred and twenty-eight. Why?"

"How soon must you go back to your sleep?"

"Just as soon as you are happily married. That's why I must insist that you—"

Something very penetrating about her gaze made my words go weak. To think of forcing this lovely girl—so much like the Louise of my own century—to marry either the brutal Dickinson or the moronic Smith—

"Do you really want me to be *happily* married?" she asked.

I don't remember that any more words passed between us—

A few days later she and I were married—and *most* happily.

The ceremony was brief. The entire Sperry faction and one representative from each of the two hostile factions were present. The aged captain of the ship, who had been too ineffectual in recent years to apply any discipline to the fighting factions, was still able with vigorous voice to pronounce us man and wife.

A year and a half later I took my leave.

I bid fond good-by to the "future captain of the *Flashaway*," who lay on a pillow kicking and squirming. He gurgled back at me. If the boasts and promises of the Sperry grandparents and their associates were to be taken at full value, this young prodigy of mine would in time become an accomplished pilot and a skilled doctor as well as a stern but wise captain.

Judging from his talents at the age of six months, I was convinced he showed promise of becoming Food Superintendent as well.

I left reluctantly but happily.

CHAPTER SIX
The Final Crisis

The year 2466 was one of the darkest in my life. I shall pass over the hopeless situation, I found, briefly.

The captain met me personally and conveyed me to his quarters without allowing the people to see me.

"Safer for everyone concerned," he muttered. I caught glimpses as we passed through the shadows. I seemed to be looking upon ruins.

Not until the captain had disclosed the events of the century did I understand how things could have come to such a deplorable state. And before he finished his story, I saw that I was helpless to right the wrongs.

"They've destroyed most everything," the hard-bitten old captain rasped. "And they have not overlooked *you*. They've destroyed you completely. *You are an ogre.*"

I wasn't clear on his meaning. Dimly in the back of my mind the hilarious farewell of four centuries ago still echoed.

"The *Flashaway* will go through," I insisted.

"They destroyed all the books, phonograph records, movie films. They broke up clocks and bells and furniture—"

And I was supposed to carry this interspatial outpost of American civilization through *unblemished*. That was what I had promised so gayly four centuries ago.

"They even tried to break out the windows," the captain went on. "'Oxygen be damned!' they'd shout. They were mad. You could not tell them anything. If they could have got into this end of the ship, they'd have murdered us and smashed the control boards to hell."

I listened with bowed head. "Your son tried like the devil to turn the tide. But God, what chance did he have? The dam had busted loose. They wanted to kill each other. They wanted to destroy each other's property and starve each other out. No captain in the world could have stopped either faction. They had to get it out of their systems…"

He shrugged helplessly. "Your son went down fighting…" For a time I could hear no more. It seemed but minutes ago that I had taken leave of the little tot.

The war—if a mania of destruction and murder between two feuding factions could be called a war—had done one good thing, according to the captain. It had wiped the name of Dickinson from the records.

Later I turned through the musty pages to make sure. There were Smiths and Sperrys and a few other names still in the running, but no Dickinsons. Nor were there any Grimstones. My son had left no living descendants.

To return to the captain's story, the war (he said) had degraded the bulk of the population almost to the level of savages. Perhaps the comparison is an insult to the savage. The instruments of knowledge and learning having been destroyed, beliefs gave way to superstitions, memories of past events degenerated into fanciful legends.

The rebound from the war brought a terrific superstitious terror concerning death. The survivors crawled into their shells, almost literally; the brutalities and treacheries of the past hung like storm clouds over their imaginations.

As year after year dropped away, the people told and retold the stories of destruction to their children. Gradually the legend twisted into a strange form in which all the guilt for the carnage was placed upon *me*.

I was the one who had started all the killing. *I, the ogre*, who slept in a cave somewhere in the rear of the ship, came out once upon a time and started all the trouble.

I, the Traditions Man, dealt death with a magic weapon. I cast the spell of killing upon the Smiths and the Dickinsons that kept them fighting until there was nothing left to fight for.

"But that was years ago," I protested to the captain. "Am I still an ogre?" I shuddered at the very thought.

"More than ever. Stories like that don't die out in a century. They grow bigger. You've become the symbol of evil. I've tried to talk the silly notion down, but it has been impossible. My own family is afraid of you."

I listened with sickening amazement. I was the Traditions Man; or rather, the "Traddy Man" the bane of every child's life.

Parents, I was told, would warn them, "If you don't be good, the Traddy Man will come out of his cave and get you."

And the Traddy Man, as every grown-up knew, could storm out of his cave without warning. He would come with a strange gleam in his eye. That was his evil will. When the bravest, strongest men would cross his path, he would hurl instant death at them. Then he would seize the most beautiful woman and marry her.

"Enough," I said. "Call your people together. I'll dispel their false ideas—"

The captain shook his head wisely. He glanced at my gun.

"Don't force me to disobey your orders," he said. "I can believe you're not an ogre—but they won't. I know this generation. You don't. Frankly I refuse to disturb the peace of this ship by telling the people you have come. Nor am I willing to terrorize my family by letting them see you."

For a long while I stared silently into space.

The captain dismissed a pilot from the control room and had me come in.

"You can see for yourself that we are straight on our course. You have already seen that all the supplies are holding up. You have seen that the population problem is well cared for. What more do you want?"

What more did I want? With the whole population of the *Flashaway* steeped in ignorance—immorality—superstition—savagery?*

Again the captain shook his head. "You want us to be like your friends of the twenty-first century. *We can't be.*"

He reached in his pocket and pulled out some bits of crumpled papers.

"Look. I save every scrap of reading matter. I learned to read from the primers and charts that your son's grandparents made. Before the destruction, I tried to read about the Earth-life. I still piece together these torn bits and study them. But I can't piece together the Earth-life that they tell about. All I really know is what I've seen and felt and breathed right here in my native *Flashaway* world.

"That's how it's bound to be with all of us. We can't get back to your notions about things. Your notions haven't any real truth for us. You don't belong to our world," the captain said with honest frankness.

"So I'm an outcast on my own ship?"

"That's putting it mildly. You are a menace and a troublemaker—*an ogre*. It's in their minds as tight as the bones in their skulls."

The most I could do was secure some promises from him before I went back to the ice. He promised to keep the ship on its course, to do his utmost to fasten the obligation upon those who took over the helm.

"Straight relentless navigation." We drank a toast to it. He didn't pretend to appreciate the purpose or the mission of the *Flashaway*, but he took my word for it that it would come to some good.

"To Robinello in 2666." Another toast. Then he conducted me back, in utmost secrecy, to my refrigerator room.

I awoke to the year of 2566, keenly aware that I was not Gregory Grimstone, the respected Keeper of the Traditions. If I was anyone at all, I was the Traddy Man—the ogre.

---

* Professor Grimstone is obviously astounded that his charges, with all the necessities of life on board their space ship, should have degenerated so completely. It must be remembered, however, no other outside influence ever entered the *Flashaway* in all its long voyage through space. In the space of centuries, the colonists progressed not one whit.

On a very much reduced scale, the *Flashaway* colonists are a more or less accurate mirror of a nation in transition. Sad but true it is that nations, like human beings, are born, wax into bright maturity, grow into comfortable middle age and oft times linger on until old age has impaired their usefulness.

In the relatively short time that man has been a thinking, building animal, many great empires—many great nations—have sprung from humble beginnings to grow powerful and then wane into oblivion, sometimes slowly, sometimes with tragic suddenness.

Grimstone, however, has failed to take the lessons of history into account through the mistaken conception that because the colonists' physical wants were taken care of that was all they required to keep them healthy and contented-Ed.

But perhaps by this time—and I took hope with the thought—I had been completely forgotten.

I tried to get through the length of the ship without being seen. I had watched through the one-way glass for several hours for a favorable opportunity, but the ship seemed to be in a continual state of daylight, and shabby looking people roamed about as aimlessly as sheep in a meadow.

The few persons who saw me as I darted toward the captain's quarters shrieked as if they had been knifed. In their world there was no such thing as a strange person. I was the impossible, the unbelievable. My name, obviously, had been forgotten.

I found three men in the control room. After minutes of tension, during which they adjusted themselves to the shock of my coming, I succeeded in establishing speaking terms. Two of the men were Sperrys.

But at the very moment I should have been concerned with solidifying my friendship, I broke the calm with an excited outburst. My eye caught the position of the instruments and I leaped from my seat.

"How long have you been going *that* way?"

"Eight years."

"Eight—" I glanced at the huge automatic chart overhead. It showed the long straight line of our centuries of flight with a tiny shepherd's crook at the end. Eight years ago we had turned back sharply.

"That's sixteen years lost, gentlemen."

I tried to regain my poise. The three men before me were perfectly calm, to my astonishment. The two Sperry brothers glanced at each other. The third man, who had introduced himself as Smith, glared at me darkly.

"It's all right," I said. "We won't lose another minute. I know how to operate—"

"No, you don't." Smith's voice was harsh and cold. I had started to reach for the controls. I hesitated. Three pairs of eyes were fixed on me.

"We know where we're going," one of the Sperrys said stubbornly. "We've got our own destination."

"This ship is bound for Robinello," I snapped. "We've got to colonize. The Robinello planets are ours—America's. It's our job to clinch the claim and establish the initial settlement—"

"Who said so?"

"America."

"When?" Smith's cold eyes tightened.

"Five hundred years ago."

"That doesn't mean a thing. Those people are all dead."

"I'm one of those people," I growled. "And I'm not dead by a damned sight."

"Then you're out on a limb."

"Limb or no limb, the plan goes through." I clutched my gun. "We haven't come five hundred years in a straight line for nothing."

"The plan is dead," one of the Sperrys snarled. "We've killed it."

His brother chimed in, "This is our ship and we're running it. We've studied the heavens and we're out on our own. We're through with this straight-line stuff. We're going to see the universe."

"You can't! You're bound for Robinello."

Smith stepped toward me, and his big teeth showed savagely.

"We had no part in that agreement. We're taking orders from no one. I've heard about you. You're the Traddy Man. Go back in your hole—and stay there."

I brought my gun up slowly. "You've heard of me? Have you heard of my gun? Do you know that this weapon shoots men dead?"

Three pairs of eyes caught on the gleaming weapon. But three men stood their ground staunchly.

"I've heard about guns," Smith hissed. "Enough to know that you don't dare shoot in the control room—"

"I don't dare *miss.*"

I didn't want to kill the men. But I saw no other way out. Was there any other way? Three lives weren't going to stand between the *Flashaway* and her destination.

Seconds passed, with the four of us breathing hard. Eternity was about to descend on someone. Any of the three might have been splendid pioneers if they had been confronted with the job of building a colony. But in this moment, their lack of vision was as deadly as any deliberate sabotage. I focused my attack on the most troublesome man.

"Smith, I'm giving you an order. Turn back before I count to ten or I'll kill you. One...two...three..."

Not the slightest move from anyone.

"Seven...eight...nine

Smith leaped at me—and fell dead at my feet.

The two Sperrys looked at the faint wisp of smoke from the weapon. I barked another sharp command, and one of the Sperrys marched to the controls and turned the ship back toward Robinello.

CHAPTER SEVEN
Time Marches On

For a year I was with the Sperry brothers constantly, doing my utmost to bring them around to my way of thinking. At first I watched them like hawks. But they were not treacherous. Neither did they show any inclination to avenge Smith's death. Probably this was due to a suppressed hatred they had held toward him.

The Sperrys were the sort of men, being true children of space, who bided their time. That's what they were doing now. That was why I couldn't leave them and go back to my ice.

As sure as the *Flashaway* could cut through the heavens, those two men were counting the hours until I returned to my nest. The minute I was gone, they would turn back toward their own goal.

And so I continued to stay with them for a full year. If they contemplated killing me, they gave no indication. I presume I would have killed them with little hesitation, had I had no pilots whatsoever that I could entrust with the job of carrying on.

There were no other pilots, nor were there any youngsters old enough to break into service.

Night after night I fought the matter over in my mind. There was a full century to go. Perhaps one hundred and fifteen or twenty years. And no one except the two Sperrys and I had any serious conception of a destination.

These two pilots and I—*and one other*, whom I had never for a minute forgotten. If the *Flashaway* was to go through, it was up to me and *that one other*—

I marched back to the refrigerator room, people fleeing my path in terror. Inside the retreat I touched the switches that operated the auxiliary merry-go-round freezer. After a space of time the operation was complete.

Someone very beautiful stood smiling before me, looking not a minute older than when I had packed her away for safe keeping two centuries before.

"Gregory," she breathed ecstatically. "Are my three centuries up already?"

"Only two of them, Lora-Louise." I took her in my arms. She looked up at me sharply and must have read the trouble in my eyes.

"They've all played out on us," I said quietly. "It's up to us now."

I discussed my plan with her and she approved.

One at a time we forced the Sperry brothers into the icy retreat, with repeated promises that they would emerge within a century. By that time Lora-Louise and I would be gone—but it was our expectation that our children and grandchildren would carry on.

And so the two of us, plus firearms, plus Lora-Louise's sense of humor, took over the running of the *Flashaway* for its final century.

As the years passed the native population grew to be less afraid of us. Little by little a foggy glimmer of our vision filtered into their number minds.

The year is now 2600. Thirty-three years have passed since Lora-Louise and I took over. I am sixty-two, she is fifty-six. Or if you prefer, I am 562, she is 256. Our four children have grown up and married.

We have realized down through these long years that we would not live to see the journey completed. The Robinello planets have been visible for some time; but at our speed they are still sixty or eighty years away.

But something strange happened nine or ten months ago. It has changed the outlook for all of us—even me, the crusty old Keeper of the Traditions.

A message reached us through our radio receiver.

It was a human voice speaking in our own language. It had a fresh vibrant hum to it and a clear-cut enunciation. It shocked me to realize how sluggish our own brand of the King's English had become in the past five-and-a-half centuries.

"Calling the S. S. *Flashaway!*" it said. "Calling the S. S. *Flashaway!* We are trying to locate you, S. S. *Flashaway*. Our instruments indicate that you are approaching. If you can hear us, will you give us your exact location?"

I snapped on the transmitter. "This is the *Flashaway*. Can you hear us?"

"Dimly. Where are you?"

"On our course. Who's calling?"

"This is the American colony on Robinello," came the answer. "American colony, Robinello, established in 2550—fifty years ago. We're waiting for you, *Flashaway*."

"How the devil did you get there?" I may have sounded a bit crusty but I was too excited to know what I was saying.

"Modern space ships," came the answer. "We've cut the time from the earth to Robinello down to six years. Give us your location. We'll send a fast ship out to pick you up."

I gave them our location. That, as I said, was several months ago. Today we are receiving a radio call every five minutes as their ship approaches.

One of my sons, supervising the preparations, has just reported that all persons aboard are ready to transfer—including the Sperry brothers who have emerged successfully from the ice. The eighty-five *Flashaway* natives are scared half to death and at the same time as eager as children going to a circus.

Lora-Louise has finished packing our boxes, bless her heart. That teasing smile she just gave me was because she noticed the "Who's Who Aboard the *Flashaway*" tucked snugly under my arm.

THE END

On The Fourth Planet

BY J. F. BONE

*To Kworn the object was a roadblock, threatening his life. But it was also a
high road to a magnificent future!*

THE UL Kworn paused in his search for food, extended his
eye and considered the thing that blocked his path.

He hadn't notice the obstacle until he had almost touched it.
His attention had been focused upon gleaning every feeder large
enough to be edible from the lichens that covered his feeding strip.
But the unexpected warmth radiating from the object had startled
him. Sundown was at hand. There should be nothing living or
non-living that radiated a fraction of the heat that was coming from
the gleaming metal wall that lay before him. He expanded his
mantle to trap the warmth as he pushed his eye upward to look
over the top. It wasn't high, just high enough to be a nuisance. It
curved away from him toward the boundaries of his strip,
extending completely across the width of his land.

A dim racial memory told him that this was an artifact, a product of the days when the Folk had leisure to dream and time to
build. It had probably been built by his remote ancestors millennia
ago and had just recently been uncovered from its hiding place
beneath the sand. These metal objects kept appearing and
disappearing as the sands shifted to the force of the wind. He had
seen them before, but never a piece so large or so well preserved.
It shone as though it had been made yesterday, gleaming with a
soft silvery luster against the blue-black darkness of the sky.

As his eye cleared the top of the wall, he quivered with shock
and astonishment. For it was not a wall as he had thought.
Instead, it was the edge of a huge metal disc fifty raads in diameter.
And that wasn't all of it. Three thick columns of metal extended
upward from the disc, leaning inward as they rose into the sky.
High overhead, almost beyond the range of accurate vision, they
converged to support an immense cylinder set vertically to the
ground. The cylinder was almost as great in diameter as the disc

upon which his eye first rested. It loomed overhead, and he had a queasy feeling that it was about to fall and crush him. Strange jointed excrescences studded its surface, and in its side, some two-thirds of the way up, two smaller cylinders projected from the bigger one. They were set a little distance apart, divided by a vertical row of four black designs, and pointed straight down his feeding strip.

The UL Kworn eyed the giant structure with disgust and puzzlement. The storm that had uncovered it must have been a great one to have blown so much sand away. It was just his fortune to have the thing squatting in his path! His mantle darkened with anger. Why was it that everything happened to him? Why couldn't it have lain in someone else's way, upon the land of one of his neighbors? It blocked him from nearly three thousand square raads of life-sustaining soil. To cross it would require energy he could not spare. Why couldn't it have been on the Ul Caada's or the Ul Varsi's strip—or any other of the numberless Folk? Why did he have to be faced with this roadblock?

He couldn't go around it since it extended beyond his territory and, therefore, he'd have to waste precious energy propelling his mass up the wall and across the smooth shining surface of the disc—all of which would have to be done without food, since his eye could see no lichen growing upon the shiny metal surface.

THE chill of evening had settled on the land. Most of the Folk were already wrapped in their mantles, conserving their energy until the dawn would warm them into life. But Kworn felt no need to estivate. It was warm enough beside the wall.

The air shimmered as it cooled. Microcrystals of ice formed upon the legs of the structure, outlining them in shimmering contrast to the drab shadowy landscape, with its gray-green over of lichens stippled with the purple balls of the lichen feeders that clung to them. Beyond Kworn and his neighbors, spaced twenty raads apart, the mantled bodies of the Folk stretched in a long single line across the rolling landscape, vanishing into the darkness. Behind this line, a day's travel to the rear, another line of the Folk was following. Behind them was yet another. There were none ahead, for the Ul Kworn and the other Ul were the elders of the

Folk and moved along in the first rank where their maturity and ability to reproduce had placed them according to the Law.

Caada and Varsi stirred restlessly, stimulated to movement by the heat radiating from the obstacle, but compelled by the Law to hold their place in the ranks until the sun's return would stimulate the others. Their dark crimson mantles rippled over the soil as they sent restless pseudopods to the boundaries of their strips.

They were anxious in their attempt to communicate with the Ul Kworn.

But Kworn wasn't ready to communicate. He held aloof as he sent a thin pseudopod out toward the gleaming wall in front of him. He was squandering energy; but he reasoned that he had better learn all he could about this thing before he attempted to cross it tomorrow, regardless of what it cost.

It was obvious that he would have to cross it, for the Law was specific about encroachment upon a neighbor's territory. *No member of the Folk shall trespass the feeding land of another during the Time of Travel except with published permission. Trespass shall be punished by the ejection of the offender from his place in rank.*

And that was equivalent to a death sentence.

He could ask Caada or Varsi for permission, but he was virtually certain that he wouldn't get it. He wasn't on particularly good terms with his neighbors. Caada was querulous, old and selfish. He had not reproduced this season and his vitality was low. He was forever hungry and not averse to slipping a sly pseudopod across the boundaries of his land to poach upon that of his neighbor. Kworn had warned him some time ago that he would not tolerate encroachment and would call for a group judgment if there was any poaching. And since the Folk were physically incapable of lying to one another, Caada would be banished. After that Caada kept his peace, but his dislike for Kworn was always evident.

BUT Varsi who held the land on Kworn's right was worse. He had advanced to Ul status only a year ago. At that time there had been rumors among the Folk about illicit feeding and stealing of germ plasm from the smaller and weaker members of the race. But that could not be proved, and many young Folk died in the grim process of growing to maturity. Kworn shrugged. If Varsi was an example of the younger generation, society was heading hell-bent toward Emptiness. He had no love for the pushing, aggressive youngster who crowded out to the very borders of his domain, pressing against his neighbors, alert and aggressive toward the slightest accidental spillover into his territory. What was worse, Varsi had reproduced successfully this year and thus had rejuvenated. Kworn's own attempt had been only partially successful. His energy reserves hadn't been great enough to produce a viable offspring, and the rejuvenation process in his body had only gone to partial completion. It would be enough to get him to the winter feeding grounds. But as insurance he had taken a place beside Caada, who was certain to go into Emptiness if the feeding en route was bad.

Still, he hadn't figured that he would have Varsi beside him.

He consoled himself with the thought that others might have as bad neighbors as he. But he would never make the ultimate mistake of exchanging germ plasm with either of his neighbors, not even if his fertility and his position depended upon it. Cells like theirs would do nothing to improve the sense of discipline and order he had so carefully developed in his own. His offspring were courteous and honorable, a credit to the Folk and to the name of Kworn. A father should be proud of his offspring, so that when they developed to the point where they could have descendants, he would not be ashamed of what they would produce. An U1, Kworn thought grimly, should have some sense of responsibility toward the all-important future of the race.

His anger died as he exerted synergic control. Anger was a waster of energy, a luxury he couldn't afford. He had little enough as it was. It had been a bad year. Spring was late, and winter had come early. The summer had been dry and the lichens in the feeding grounds had grown poorly. The tiny, bulbous lichen feeders, the main source of food for the Folk, had failed to ripen to their usual succulent fullness. They had been poor, shrunken things, hardly worth ingesting. And those along the route to the winter feeding grounds were no better.

Glumly he touched the wall before him with a tactile filament. It was uncomfortably warm, smooth and slippery to the touch. He felt it delicately, noting the almost microscopic horizontal ridges on the wall's surface. He palpated with relief. The thing was climbable. But even as he relaxed, he recoiled, the filament writhing in agony. The wall had burned his flesh! Faint threads of vapor rose from where he had touched the metal, freezing instantly in the chill air. He pinched off the filament in an automatic protective constriction of his cells. The pain ceased instantly, but the burning memory was so poignant that his mantle twitched and shuddered convulsively for some time before the reflexes died.

THOUGHTFULLY he ingested his severed member. With a sense of numbing shock he realized that he would be unable to pass across the disc. The implications chilled him. If he could not pass, his land beyond the roadblock would be vacant and open to preemption by his neighbors. Nor could he wait until they had passed and rejoin them later. The Law was specific on that point. *If one of the Folk lags behind in his rank, his land becomes vacant and open to his neighbors. Nor can one who has lagged behind reclaim his land by moving forward. He who abandons his position, abandons it permanently.*

Wryly, he reflected that it was this very Law that had impelled him to take a position beside the Ul Caada. And, of course, his neighbors knew the Law as well as he. It was a part of them, a part of their cells even before they split off from their parent. It would be the acme of folly to expect that neighbors like Varsi or Caada would allow him to pass over their land and hold his place in rank.

Bitterness flooded him with a stimulation so piercing that Caada extended a communication filament to project a question. "What is this thing which lies upon your land and mine?" Caada asked. His projection was weak and feeble. It was obvious that he would not last for many more days unless feeding improved.

"I do not know. It is something of metal, and it bars my land. I cannot cross it. It burns me when I touch it."

A quick twinge of excitement rushed along Caada's filament. The old Ul broke the connection instantly, but not before Kworn read the flash of hope that Kworn had kindled. There was no help in this quarter, and the wild greed of Varsi was so well known that there was no sense even trying that side.

A surge of hopelessness swept through him. Unless he could find some way to pass this barrier he was doomed.

He didn't want to pass into Emptiness. He had seen too many others go that way to want to follow them. For a moment he thought desperately of begging Caada and Varsi for permission to cross into their land for the short time that would be necessary to pass the barrier, but reason asserted itself. Such an act was certain to draw a flat refusal and, after all, he was the Ul Kworn and he had his pride. He would not beg when begging was useless.

And there was a bare possibility that he might survive if he closed his mantle tightly about him and waited until all the ranks had passed. He could then bring up the rear…and, possibly, just possibly, there would be sufficient food left to enable him to reach the winter feeding grounds.

And it might still be possible to cross the disc. There was enough warmth in it to keep him active. By working all night he might be able to build a path of sand across its surface and thus keep his tissues from being seared by the metal. He would be technically violating the law by moving ahead of the others, but if he did not feed ahead, no harm would be done.

HE MOVED closer to the barrier and began to pile sand against its base, sloping it to make a broad ramp to the top of the disc. The work was slow and the sand was slippery. The polished grains slipped away and the ramp crumbled time after time. But he worked on, piling up sand until it reached the top of the disc. He looked across the flat surface that stretched before him.

Fifty raads!

It might as well be fifty zets. He couldn't do it. Already his energy level was so low that he could hardly move, and to build a raad-wide path across this expanse of metal was a task beyond his strength. He drooped across the ramp, utterly exhausted. It was no use. What he ought to do was open his mantle to Emptiness.

He hadn't felt the communication filaments of Caada and Varsi touch him. He had been too busy, but now with Caada's burst of glee, and Varsi's cynical, "A noble decision, Ul Kworn. You should be commended," he realized that they knew everything.

His body rippled hopelessly. He was tired, too tired for anger. His energy was low. He contemplated Emptiness impassively. Sooner or later it came to all Folk. He had lived longer than most, and perhaps it was his time to go. He was finished. He accepted the fact with a cold fatalism that he never dreamed he possessed. Lying there on the sand, his mantle spread wide, he waited for the end to come.

It wouldn't come quickly, he thought. He was still far from the cellular disorganization that preceded extinction. He was merely exhausted, and in need of food to restore his energy.

With food he might still have an outside chance of building the path in time. But there was no food. He had gleaned his area completely before he had ever reached the roadblock.

Lying limp and relaxed on the ramp beside the barrier, he slowly became conscious that the metal wasn't dead. It was alive! Rhythmic vibrations passed through it and were transmitted to his body by the sand.

A wild hope stirred within him. If the metal were alive it might hear him if he tried to communicate. He concentrated his remaining reserves of energy, steeled himself against the pain and pressed a communication filament against the metal.

"Help me," he projected desperately. "You're blocking my strip! I can't pass!"

Off to one side he sensed Varsi's laughter and on the other felt Caada's gloating greed.

"I cannot wake this metal," he thought hopelessly as he tried again, harder than before, ignoring the pain of his burning flesh.

Something clicked sharply within the metal, and the tempo of the sounds changed.

"It's waking," Kworn thought wildly.

THERE was a creaking noise from above. A rod moved out from the cylinder and twisted into the ground in Varsi's territory, to the accompaniment of clicking, grinding noises. A square grid lifted from the top of the cylinder and began rotating. And Kworn shivered and jerked to the tremendous power of the words that flowed through him. They were words, but they had no meaning, waves of sound that hammered at his receptors in an unknown tongue he could not understand. The language of the Folk had changed since the days of the ancients, he thought despairingly.

And then, with a mantle-shattering roar, the cylinders jutting overhead spouted flame and smoke. Two silvery balls trailing thin, dark filaments shot out of the great cylinder and buried themselves in the sand behind him. The filaments lay motionless in the sand as Kworn, wrapped defensively in his mantle, rolled off the ramp to the ground below.

The silence that followed was so deep that it seemed like Emptiness had taken the entire land.

Slowly Kworn loosened his mantle. "In the name of my first ancestor," he murmured shakily, "what was that?" His senses were shocked and disorganized by the violence of the sound. It was worse even than the roar and scream of the samshin that occasionally blew from the south, carrying dust, lichens, feeders and even Folk who had been too slow or too foolish to hide from the fury of the wind.

Gingerly, Kworn inspected the damage to his mantle. It was minor. A tiny rip that could easily be repaired, a few grains of sand that could be extruded. He drew himself together to perform the repairs with the least possible loss of energy, and as he did, he was conscious of an emanation coming from the filaments that had been hurled from the cylinder.

Food!

And such food...

It was the distilled quintessence of a thousand purple feeders. It came to his senses in a shimmering wave of ecstasy so great that his mantle glowed a bright crimson. He stretched a pseudopod toward its source, and as he touched the filament his whole body quivered with anticipation. The barrier was blotted from his thoughts by an orgy of shuddering delight almost too great for flesh to endure. Waves of pleasure ran through his body as he swiftly extended to cover the filament. It could be a trap, he thought, but it made no difference. The demands of his depleted body and the sheer vacuole-constricting delight of this incredible foodstuff made a combination too potent for his will to resist, even if it had desired to do so. Waves of pleasure rippled through him as more of his absorptive surface contacted the filament. He snuggled against it, enfolding it completely, letting the peristaltic rushes sweep through him. He had never fed like this as long as he could recall. His energy levels swelled and pulsed as he sucked the last delight from the cord, and contemplated the further pleasure waiting for him in that other one lying scarcely twenty raads away.

Sensuously, he extended a pseudopod from his upper surface and probed for the other filament. He was filled to the top of his primary vacuole but the desire for more was stronger than ever— despite the fact that he knew the food in the other filament would bring him to critical level, would force him to reproduce. The thought amused him. As far back as he could remember, no member of the Folk had ever budded an offspring during the Time of Travel. It would be unheard of, something that would go down through the years in the annals of the Folk, and perhaps even cause a change in the Law.

The pseudopod probed, reached and stopped short of its goal. There was nothing around it but empty air.

FEAR drove the slow orgasmic thoughts from his mind. Absorbed in gluttony, he hadn't noticed that the filament had tightened and was slowly drawing back into the cylinder from whence it came. And now it was too late... He was already over the rim of the metal disc.

Feverishly, he tried to disengage his absorptive surfaces from the filament and crawl down its length to safety, but he couldn't move. He was stuck to the dark cord by some strange adhesive that cemented his cells firmly to the cord. He could not break free.

The line moved steadily upward, dragging him inexorably toward a dark opening in the cylinder overhead. Panic filled him. Desperately he tried to loosen his trapped surfaces. His pseudopod lashed futilely in the air, searching with panic for something to grip, something to clutch that would stop this slow movement to the hell of pain that waited for him in the metal high overhead.

His searching flesh struck another's, and into his mind flooded the Ul Caada's terrified thought. The old one had reacted quicker than he, perhaps because he was poaching, but like himself he was attached and could not break free.

"Serves you right," Kworn projected grimly. "The thing was on my land. You had no right to feed upon it."

"Get me loose," Caada screamed. His body flopped at the end of a thick mass of digestive tissue, dangling from the line, writhing and struggling in mindless terror. It was strange, Kworn thought, that fear should be so much stronger in the old than in the young.

"Cut loose, you fool," Kworn projected. "There isn't enough of you adhered to hurt if it were lost. A little body substance isn't worth your life. Hurry! You'll be too late if you don't. That metal is poisonous to our flesh."

"But it will be pain to cut my absorbing surface," Caada protested.

"It will be death if you don't."

"Then why don't you?"

"I can't," Kworn said hopelessly. "All my surface is stuck to the filament. I can't cut free." He was calm now, resigned to the inevitable. His greed had brought him to this. Perhaps it was a fitting punishment. But Caada need not die if he would show courage.

He rotated his eye to watch his struggling neighbor. Apparently Caada was going to take his advice. The tissue below the part of him stuck to the filament began to thin. His pseudopod broke contact. But his movements were slow and hesitant. Already his body mass was rising above the edge of the disc.

"Quick, you fool!" Kworn projected. "Another moment and you're dead!"

But Caada couldn't hear. Slowly his tissues separated as he reluctantly abandoned his absorptive surface. But he was already over the disc. The last cells pinched off and he fell, mantle flapping, full on the surface of the disc. For a moment he lay there quivering, and then his body was blotted from sight by a cloud of frozen steam, and his essence vanished screaming into Emptiness.

KWORN shuddered. It was a terrible way to die. But his own fate would be no better. He wrapped his mantle tightly around him as his leading parts vanished into the dark hole in the cylinder. In a moment he would be following Caada on the journey from which no member of the Folk had ever returned. His body disappeared into the hole.

–and was plunged into paradise!

His foreparts slipped into a warm, thick liquid that loosened the adhesive that bound him to the cord. As he slipped free, he slowly realized that he was not to die. He was bathed in liquid food. He was swimming in it! He was surrounded on all sides by incredible flavors so strange and delicious that his mind could not classify them. The filament had been good, but this—this was indescribable! He relaxed, his mantle spreading through the food, savoring, absorbing, digesting, metabolizing, excreting. His energy levels peaked. The nuclei of his germ plasm swelled, their chromosomes split, and a great bud formed and separated from his body. He had reproduced.

Through a deadening fog of somatic sensation, he realized dully that this was wrong, the time wasn't right, the space was limited, and that the natural reaction to abundant food supply was wrong. But for the moment he didn't care.

For thousands of seasons he had traveled the paths between equator and pole in a ceaseless hunt for food, growing and rejuvenating in good seasons, shrinking and aging in bad. He had been bound to the soil, a slave to the harsh demands of life and Nature. And now the routine was broken.

He luxuriated in his freedom. It must have been like this in the old days, when the waters were plentiful and things grew in them that could be eaten, and the Folk had time to dream young dreams and think young thoughts, and build their thoughts and dreams into the gleaming realities of cities and machines. Those were the days when the mind went above the soil into the air and beyond it to the moons, the sun and the evening stars.

But that was long ago.

He lay quietly, conscious of the change within him as his cells multiplied to replace those he had lost, and his body grew in weight and size. He was rejuvenated. The cells of his growing body, stimulated by the abundance of food, released memories he had forgotten he had ever possessed. His past ran in direct cellular continuity to the dawn of his race, and in him was every memory he had experienced since the beginning. Some were weak, others were stronger, but all were there awaiting an effort of recall. All that was required was enough stimulation to bring them out of hiding.

And for the first time in millennia the stimulus was available. The stimulus was growth, the rapid growth that only an abundant food supply could give, the sort of growth that the shrunken environment outside could not supply. With sudden clarity he saw how the Folk had shrunk in mind and body as they slowly adapted to the ever-increasing rigor of life. The rushing torrent of memory and sensation that swept through him gave him a new awareness of what he had been once and what he had become. His eye was lifted from the dirt and lichens.

WHAT he saw filled him with pity and contempt. Pity for what the Folk had become; contempt for their failure to recognize it. Yet he had been no better than the others. It was only through the accident of this artifact that he had learned. The Folk couldn't know what the slow dwindling of their food supply had done to them. Over the millennia they had adapted, changing to fit the changing conditions, surviving only because they were more intelligent and more tenacious than the other forms of life that had become extinct. A thousand thousand seasons had passed since the great war that had devastated the world. A million years of slow adaptation to the barren waste that had been formed when the ultimate products of Folk technology were loosed on their creators, had created a race tied to a subsistence level of existence, incapable of thinking beyond the basic necessities of life.

The Ul Kworn sighed. It would be better if he would not remember so much. But he could suppress neither the knowledge nor the memories. They crowded in upon him, stimulated by the food in which he floated.

Beside him, his offspring was growing. A bud always grew rapidly in a favorable environment, and this one was ideal. Soon it would be as large as himself. Yet it would never develop beyond an infant. It could not mature without a transfer of germ plasm from other infants of the Folk. And there were no infants.

It would grow and keep on growing because there would be no check of maturity upon its cells. It would remain a partly sentient lump of flesh that would never be complete. And in time it would be dangerous. When it had depleted the food supply it would turn on him in mindless hunger. It wouldn't realize that the Ul Kworn was its father, or if it did, it wouldn't care. An infant is ultimately selfish, and its desires are the most important thing in its restricted universe.

Kworn considered his situation dispassionately.

It was obvious that he must escape from this trap before his offspring destroyed him. Yet he could think of no way to avoid the poison metal. He recognized it now, the element with the twelve protons in its nucleus, a light metal seldom used by the Folk even in the days of their greatness because of its ability to rapidly oxidize and its propensity to burst into brilliant flame when heated. With sudden shock he realized that the artifact was nothing less than a gigantic torch.

Why had it been built like this? What was its function? Where had it come from? Why hadn't it spoke since it had released that flood of unintelligible gibberish before it had drawn him inside? Ever since he had entered this food tank it had been quiet except for a clicking, chattering whir that came from somewhere above him. He had the odd impression that it was storing information about him and the way he reacted in the tank.

And then, abruptly, it broke into voice. Cryptic words poured from it, piercing him with tiny knives of sound. The intensity and rapidity of the projections shocked him, left him quivering and shaking when they stopped as abruptly as they had begun.

In the quiet that followed, Kworn tried to recall the sequence of the noise. The words were like nothing he had ever heard. They were not the language of the Folk either past or present. And they had a flow and sequence that was not organic. They were mechanical, the product of a metal intelligence that recorded and spoke but did not think. The Folk had machines like that once.

How had it begun? There had been a faint preliminary, an almost soundless voice speaking a single word. Perhaps if he projected it, it would trigger a response. Pitching his voice in the same key and intensity he projected the word as best he could remember it.

And the voice began again.

KWORN quivered with excitement. Something outside the artifact was forcing it to speak. He was certain of it. As certain as he was that the artifact was recording himself and his offspring. But who—or what—was receiving the record? And why?

This could be a fascinating speculation, Kworn thought. But there would be time enough for that later. His immediate need was to get out. Already the food supply was running low, and his offspring was becoming enormous. He'd have to leave soon if he was ever going to. And he'd have to do something about his own growth. Already it was reaching dangerous levels. He was on the ragged edge of another reproduction, and he couldn't afford it.

Regretfully, he began moving the cornified cells of his mantle and his under layer toward his inner surfaces, arranging them in a protective layer around his germ plasm and absorptive cells. There would be enough surface absorption to take care of his maintenance needs, and his body could retain its peak of cellular energy. Yet the desire to feed and bud was almost overpowering. His body screamed at him for denying it the right that food would give it, but Kworn resisted the demands of his flesh until the frantic cellular urges passed.

Beside him his offspring pulsed with physical sensation. Kworn envied it even as he pitied it. The poor mindless thing could be used as a means to the end of his escape, but it was useless for anything else. It was far too large, and far too stupid, to survive in the outside world. Kworn extruded a net of hair-like pseudopods and swept the tank in which they lay. It was featureless, save for a hole where the filament had not completely withdrawn when it had pulled him into this place. A few places in the wall had a different texture than the others, probably the sense organs of the recorder. He rippled with satisfaction. There was a grille of poison metal in the top of the tank through which flowed a steady current of warm air. It would be pleasant to investigate this further, Kworn thought, but there was no time. His offspring had seen to that.

He placed his eye on a thin pseudopod and thrust it through the hole in the wall of the tank. It was still night outside, but a faint line of brightness along the horizon indicated the coming of dawn. The artifact glittered icily beneath him, and he had a feeling of giddiness as he looked down the vertiginous drop to the disc below. The dark blotch of Caada's burned body was almost invisible against the faintly gleaming loom of the still-warm disc. Kworn shuddered. Caada hadn't deserved a death like that. Kworn looked down, estimating the chances with his new intelligence, and then slapped a thick communication fibril against his offspring's quivering flesh and hurled a projection at its recoiling mass.

Considering the fact that its cells were direct derivations of his own, Kworn thought grimly, it was surprising how hard it was to establish control. The youngster had developed a surprising amount of individuality in its few xals of free existence. He felt a surge of thankfulness to the old Ul Kworn as the youngster yielded to his firm projection. His precursor had always sought compliant germ plasm to produce what he had called "discipline and order." It was, in fact, weakness. It was detrimental to survival. But right now that weakness was essential.

UNDER the probing lash of his projection the infant extruded a thick mass of tissue that met and interlocked with a similar mass of his own. As soon as the contact firmed, Kworn began flowing toward his eye, which was still in the half-open hole in the side of the tank.

The outside cold struck his sense centers with spicules of ice as he flowed to the outside, clinging to his offspring's gradually extending pseudopod. Slowly he dropped below the cylinder. The infant was frantic. It disliked the cold and struggled to break free, but Kworn clung limpet-like to his offspring's flesh as it twisted and writhed in an effort to return to the warmth and comfort into which it was born.

"Let go," his offspring screamed. "I don't like this place."

"In a moment," Kworn said as he turned the vague writhings into a swinging pendulum motion. "Help me move back and forth."

"I can't. I'm cold. I hurt. Let me go!"

"Help me," Kworn ordered grimly, "or hang out here and freeze."

His offspring shuddered and twitched. The momentum of the swing increased. Kworn tightened his grip.

"You promised to let go," his offspring wailed. "You prom—"

The infant's projection was cut off as Kworn loosed himself at the upward arc of the swing, spread his mantle and plummeted toward the ground. Fear swept through him as his body curved through the thin air, missing the edge of the disc and landing on the ground with a sense-jarring thud. Behind and above him up against the cylinder, the thick tendril of his offspring's flesh withdrew quickly from sight. For a moment the Ul Kworn's gaze remained riveted on the row of odd markings on the metal surface, and then he turned his attention to life.

There was no reason to waste the pain of regret upon that half sentient mass of tissue that was his offspring. The stupid flesh of his flesh would remain happy in the darkness with the dwindling food until its flesh grew great enough to touch the poison metal in the ceiling of the tank.

And then—

With a harsh projection of horror, the Ul Kworn moved, circling the artifact on Caada's vacated strip. And as he moved he concentrated energy into his high-level communication organs, and projected a warning of danger.

"Move," he screamed. "Move forward for your lives!"

The line rippled. Reddish mantles unfolded as the Folk reacted. The nearest, shocked from estivation, were in motion even before they came to full awareness. Alarms like this weren't given without reason.

Varsi's reaction, Kworn noted, was faster than any of his fellows. The young Ul had some favorable self-preservation characteristics. He'd have to consider sharing some germ plasm with him at the next reproduction season, after all.

In a giant arc, the Folk pressed forward under the white glow of emerging dawn. Behind them the artifact began to project again in its strange tongue. But in mid-cry it stopped abruptly. And from it came a wail of mindless agony that tore at Kworn's mind with regret more bitter because nothing could be done about it.

His offspring had touched the poison metal.

Kworn turned his eye backwards. The artifact was shaking on its broad base from the violence of his offspring's tortured writhings. As he watched a brilliant burst of light flared from its top. Heat swept across the land, searing the lichens and a scattered few of the Folk too slow to escape. The giant structure burned with a light more brilliant than the sun and left behind a great cloud of white vapor that hung on the air like the menacing cloud of a samshin. Beneath the cloud the land was bare save for a few twisted pieces of smoking metal.

The roadblock was gone.

KWORN moved slowly forward, gleaning Caada's strip and half of his own, which he shared with Varsi.

He would need that young Ul in the future. It was well to place him under an obligation. The new thoughts and old memories weren't dying. They remained, and were focused upon the idea of living better than at this subsistence level. It should be possible to grow lichens, and breed a more prolific type of lichen feeder. Water channeled from the canals would stimulate lichen growth a thousand-fold. And with a more abundant food supply, perhaps some of the Folk could be stimulated to think and apply ancient buried skills to circumvent Nature.

It was theoretically possible. The new breed would have to be like Varsi, tough, driving and selfishly independent. In time they might inherit the world. Civilization could arise again. It was not impossible.

His thoughts turned briefly back to the artifact. It still bothered him. He still knew far too little about it. It was a fascinating speculation to dream of what it might have been. At any rate, one thing was sure. It was not a structure of his race. If nothing else, those cabalistic markings on the side of the cylinder were utterly alien.

Thoughtfully he traced them in the sand. What did they mean?

THE END

Tydore's Gift

By ALFRED COPPEL

So unpredictable, these dead-world Tower Dwellers! Take old Tydore who placed such an inestimably valuable gift in the greed-hands of one he hated.

THE sun was a shrunken red disk against the star fields, a distant pale luminosity surrendering to the encroachment of the falling night. Hoarfrost crunched under Marley's feet as he walked by the still black waters of the canal, and then thin wind whispered over the sand and across the breasts of the ancient hills. Starlight gleamed in the dark water as the day faded. Earth hung low in the sky, like an emerald pendant over the bosom of a sleeping woman.

Marley pulled his silks and furs closer about his shoulders. The air was sharp and cold. His breath froze wraithlike in the icy evening as he hurried down the path toward Tydore's tower.

The green planet shone like a beacon in his eyes. Home. The thought brought impatience and a longing to walk again under a pale sky and a warm sun. He looked about him with faint distaste. This peace—this solitude of low red hills and blue-black nights—was alien to Marley. It was unreal. Mars was a dream. An ancient wasted slumbering dream.

Marley's lips compressed as he thought of Tydore and their last meeting. It seemed that Tydore laughed at him. Tydore withheld too much, and there was so little time left. There was an acrid core of decadence in the old Martian, Marley thought. A consciousness of too many millennia of civilization and decay. Devious was the word, perhaps, though it seemed a pallid one for the reality of the Martian's intricate mind. It was always impossible to know what he was thinking—how much he knew. About Marley being a spy. About the war on Earth. In spite of himself, Marley smiled. It sounded so melodramatic that way, but it was the way it really was. The Martians held the perfect weapon. Marley needed that weapon, and his nation had put forth a gigantic effort to get him to Mars so that he might steal it.

Tydore's tower loomed up before him in the fading light, a fey filigree of minaret's and graceful flying buttresses too delicate for a grosser world than Mars. The tower's reflection shimmered in the still dark waters of the canal like an alter ego extending deep into the liquid depths.

Marley descended the steps of delicately wrought stone that led to the tower's underground entrance with care, for the drifted ferric sand made them treacherous. How like the Martians, he thought irritatedly, to make it necessary to travel down in order to enter a tower. Everything the long way, the hard and devious way.

The outer doorway was shaped like a fleur-de-lis and it opened from the top down, sliding into a recess of ancient, oily machinery. It would be far too simple to make a door that looked and worked like a door. Everything Marley had seen during his months on Mars served only to increase his sense of alienage. He had seen only Tydore, of course, of the living Martians. There were only a handful left and they lived in their isolated towers along the still canals surrounded by their tissue-thin manuscripts and ancient, reed-like music spools that filled the air of their retreats with skeins of weird and enharmonic melody.

The weapon was Tydore's. He had rebuilt it from plans drawn by some ensorcelled armorer dead over five thousand years. Rebuilt it in the paradoxical way that Martians seemed to do everything, for if there was one thing that no Martian needed it was a weapon. No strife had marred the planet's peace for millennia. But build it he had, and Marley's hands itched for the sleek deadliness of it—the smooth grained stock, the oddly wrought, ornate muzzle. There was a vicious, tangy violence frozen into every line of the weapon. And it was the only handgun Marley had ever seen that chained the forces of the atom. With such weapons an army could be invincible.

TYDORE STOOD to greet him. With the elaborate courtesy of his kind, he performed the ritual gestures of welcome, his slender, finely veined hands tracing the ancient symbols in the air.

"The gods of sand and wind have brought you safely to my house, man of Earth. I give thanks and pray you find peace and wisdom within my walls."

The old Martian's chanting voice was like the fluting grace of a Scarlatti choral. It was one with the miniscule paintings that covered the walls, the finely wrought carvings on the antique flagstones under his feet. Marley was not at home in the fluid Martian tongue, but the very sound of the words conjured for him the serried ranks of spectral generations that had reached their culmination in this one robed ancient.

And yet, he thought with irritation, Tydore's words mean not at all what they said. Through the finely polished phrases of welcome ran a thread of hidden, mockery—even hate—for Marley and everything he represented. Never once had Tydore, by word or deed, indicated that he felt anything but friendship for his visitor from the silvery ship out on the desert, and yet there was no mistaking the nuance of contempt. Tydore despised Marley as an out world savage. One with the despoilers of the holy places of Mars.

Not that the Martians had gods. They had lived too long for that, and their deities existed only in their beautifully turned phrases and their hyper-cultured ritual. But the first men from Earth had looted the libraries and shattered the soaring towers. It was a thing no Martian would ever forget—or forgive. It marked Earthmen for what they were. In Martian eyes—precocious barbarians. Targets for Martian subtlety.

"I give thanks for your welcome," Marley said slowly, his tongue clumsy on the singing syllables.

Tydore inclined his head slightly and indicated that Marley should follow him up the winding ramp that pierced the core of the tower. Each time Marley came, the ritual was the same, as unchanging as the still waters of the dark canals or the frozen loneliness of the red hills beyond. They would pass the first level, where the old engines supplied Tydore with what little heat and sustenance he needed. They would go on to the second level, where the music spools lay in ordered confusion amid the sonic transcribers that Tydore used to weave the sounds of the Martian night into atonal poems of melody. And then they would reach the level of the weapon.

It would still be in its crystal case, guarded by a lock of bronze. A lock to which there was one key, and that one key on a silver chain around Tydore's neck. They would pass the weapon by and seek the top level, a platform shielded against the frigid night by a crystal canopy. And there they would begin their nightly fencing with words and ideas under the guise of friendship.

Marley's heart was pounding suddenly as he drew near to the weapon. His patience was failing him at long last, he knew. He was sick of Mars, sick of Tydore. Sick of posing as a humble seeker after knowledge. If he could not trick the Martian into parting with the weapon soon, he knew that he must chance violence. He had not dared it before, because he could never be sure that Tydore and his kind were as defenseless as they seemed. It was paradoxical that they should possess a weapon such as the weapon and yet be unwilling or unable to use it.

Still it seemed to Marley that such must be the case. He could only explain it to himself by saying that they had lived too long, amid too much deviousness and inverted purpose to be quite virile. They were—the word came readily to mind from the days of his training on Earth—decadent. And the meek did not inherit the earth or anything else, he told himself with satisfaction. Only the militant, the ruthless.

THE TIME HAD COME, Marley thought, for the calculated risk. Direct action. He could scarcely contain himself as they passed the weapon and climbed to the top level.

"You seem preoccupied tonight, Marley," Tydore said, pouring two tiny goblets of wine. "Can it be that you grow tired of Mars?"

Marley sipped the wine thoughtfully. To him it seemed completely insipid and without flavor. Subtlety again? He doubted it. "I mean to ask a favor of you, Tydore," he said. "And I but ponder how I should begin."

"My house is yours," the Martian replied softly. "And all that it contains."

Marley's eyes narrowed. Did he imagine the accent on the last phrase, or was it actually there? He decided to be very cautious. "I came here, as you know," he said, "to learn everything I might about your kind. As you know, we of Earth are a young race, still much in need of guidance and knowledge."

"You have learned much," Tydore said.

Marley's tone grew harder. "But not enough."

Tydore's eyebrows arched delicately. "So? You have read my books, listened to my music. You have tasted the wines and eaten the fruits of Mars. You have seen the stars and the sand, the waters and the lichens. Have you not known my world?"

"I want more," Marley said flatly.

Tydore smiled. In that smile Marley saw a flash of more distilled venom and ancient hatred than he could have imagined existed. The utter virulence of it left him shaken and his illogical fear brought anger.

He got to his feet, the tiny goblet in his hand. It was old and delicate, a tiny gem of carved jade and ivory. To one such as Tydore—priceless. Brutally, Marley crushed it to shards in his hands and dropped it to the flagstones. The fragments tinkled as they fell.

"So it must always be," said Tydore in a soft voice.

"I have not come here to listen to music," Marley said. "Nor to read your books or to know your world. You have one thing that I want. You will give it to me, or I will take it from you." He ground his heel onto the remains of the goblet with a grating sound.

"The weapon," the Martian said. "You want the weapon. You may have it. You need not have broken my goblet..."

Marley was almost sorry that he had won so easily. He suddenly wanted to crush the old Martian as he had crushed the goblet. In both there was a quality that eluded him, and it was maddening.

Tydore handed him the key. "Come, we will get it together."

Marley followed him cautiously, alert for any trickery. Presently they stood before the case and Marley unlocked it, reaching greedily for the polished stock. He cradled the gun in his arms lovingly, savoring triumph. With this in his hands, he could defy a world.

"There is no other like it, nor any but I to make one," Tydore said with a strange smile.

"Why did you make it?" asked Marley,

"I made it for you."

Marley laughed aloud. It was an alien sound in the thin, cold air of the tower. "You're a liar, Tydore. You built this weapon long before I ever left Earth and you know it."

"By you, I meant simply men like you," Tydore said. "When the first Earthmen came and befouled Mars with their presence, I knew that I must make the weapon." He smiled, showing even white teeth. "A small triumph, but things are not to be measured by whether they are great or small. Rather by their flavor, their grace, and their neatness, Marley."

"You speak of triumph, old man," snorted Marley derisively, "while your precious weapon is in my hands."

Tydore shrugged. "As I knew it would be one day when I spread the tales of what the weapon would do. It drew you as a lodestone draws a sliver of iron."

Marley felt a pang of panic. "You mean this thing is a fake?"

Tydore shook his head . "No counterfeit. It will do what I said it would do. Kill. What more can one ask of a weapon?"

It was Marley's turn to smile. "Nothing. And there is only this one. And if you were to die…"

Tydore smiled a veiled smile. "It is as the gods of sand and wind decree."

Marley pointed the weapon at Tydore. He had only to kill the old Martian and return to his ship. The mission was over. Completed. He was done with Mars and with Tydore and his subtle scorn.

He cradled the weapon lovingly, laying his cheek to the carven stock. Old Tydore had built well. There was perfect balance in the feel of it. His finger curled around the trigger and he sighted carefully down the long barrel at the robed figure of the Martian. Tydore was smiling in the face of death, and Marley wanted to laugh out loud. This is the way the world ends, he was thinking. Not with a bang, but a whimper. He squeezed the trigger…

The universe exploded in Marley's face. There was a streak of searing pain that carried away half his face, and as he fell he could hear a strange sound. For the first time, Tydore was laughing aloud. It was a hideous sound. A voice for the torment and hatred of a race that had lived too long, planned too much. Marley felt the tower pinwheel around him, the flagstones leapt up to meet him, greeting the searing agony of his face with the soundless laughter of a million intricate patterns of lonely death. And blackness welled up out of the stones to engulf him, but not before he knew—

Tydore had made the weapon with the muzzle resembling the stock. It was as simple as that.

THE END

Little Green Man

BY NOEL LOOMIS

The little green man claimed he represented the population of the Cold Belt, here on Uranus—all five of them. And he wanted the Earthlings to depart at once...

THE LITTLE green man with the pink eyebrows and the peacock-feather tail appeared upon the porcelain bench in the chemical laboratory. "I am giving you," he told Engar, "one last warning. If you Earth-people don't get this station off of Uranus within three days, I am going to take steps."

He talked with a peculiar bird-like whistle, and his appearance was so odd that Engar never had been able entirely to get rid of the feeling that the being was talking to hear his head rattle—except for the little man's golden eyes.

Ordinarily, those eyes were soft and gentle, and in keeping with his general appearance; but at this moment, the little man was obviously angry. His golden eyes were burning with a strange fire that gave Engar a very uncomfortable feeling. Surely there was nothing the being could do to injure Earth-people—but he seemed so sure of himself.

Engar, sitting on his chromium stool with the tape-recorder log before him, watching the shifting colors up and down the hundred-foot ion-exchange columns as the rare-earth solutions seeped down through the synthetic resins, was distinctly uncomfortable. He squirmed a little on the stool, making a mental note that No. 3 column was about ready for a draw-off; he mustn't let the little man distract him, for this draw-off would be chemically pure praseodymium—the end toward which the columns had been working for weeks.

"I am afraid," the other man said—and his bird-like voice went up an octave—"that you are not giving serious attention to my words."

"Yes, I am," replied Engar, watching the peach-colored ring beginning to form near the bottom of the column. He looked up at the little green man and started to protest his friendship, but the light from those golden eyes was too intense for him; he had to look away. "After all," he said, "I'm only a laboratory-technician here."

"Technically," the Uranian said, "you are telling the truth; but morally you are evading the fact that you are a very high-type man for an Earthman."

Engar was a proud young man, but also rather modest. He didn't answer, but kept his eyes on the column and its shifting colors.

"It would be obvious to anybody but a Frogman that Earth would send only the pick of her scientists to an outpost like this."

"That might be true," Engar agreed, "but it still is a fact that I am actually nothing but a worker here."

"You have a superior, haven't you?"

"Yes," said Engar, seeing now, instead of the ion-exchange column, the heart-shaped face of Corinne Madison with her black hair and clean white skin, and her constant attempts to be business-like, instead of feminine. One look at Corinne was enough to tell anybody that such a transformation was hardly suited to her—and Engar had taken that look. "But she would not have authority to dismantle the plant here."

"Then somebody back on Earth has," the being said, and his insistence began to be annoying. Suddenly Engar wished he would go away; it was utterly ridiculous that such a creature should be making threats. After all, Earth had attained a technological development far beyond anything found in the Solar System. Of course, there were individuals—and seven species here and there on the various planets—who had some rather unusual personal powers; but those, on the whole, were as nothing compared to the combined resources of Earth technology. For a moment Engar was tempted to speak sharply to the little man and get rid of him; but then he remembered they were constrained to be courteous to all peoples no matter what the circumstances. He said, "Very well, I will relay your message to Earth."

THE LITTLE man's voice went down to its normal tone. "I'll be back tomorrow."

Engar was getting ready to touch the button to set the draw-off in motion. "Your day," he pointed out, "is less than eleven hours, and it will take around three hours for a message to make a one-way trip to Earth by microwave. Two billion miles, you see, is a long distance, and—"

"Six hours for communication," the little man snapped, and added, "tomorrow will give you plenty of time anyway."

"They will have to think it over there on Earth," Engar pointed out.

The little man's golden eyes began radiating again with a brilliance that hurt Engar. "You call yourselves a race of intelligent creatures. Does it take days, then, for your great minds to reach a decision?"

It was apparent that the Uranian, living in a portion of the big planet where there were few other inhabitants—if any—would have difficulty understanding how things were done on Earth, where conferences had to be called and men from all parts of the Earth had to meet for an important matter such as this. Furthermore, it was scarcely conceivable that Earth, after spending twenty years and several billion dollars preparing for this work, would reverse herself and withdraw the entire installation at the behest of one little green man. As a matter of fact, Engar had no idea that the station's director would even transmit such a message to Earth.

There was one other factor to be considered: the ion-exchange columns represented Engar Jarvin's lifework. Ion-exchange was his specialty; he had studied it exhaustively and that was why he had been picked for the station on Uranus. The huge, hundred-foot columns with their ten-thousand gallon charges that lasted for weeks, were his special babies; he couldn't go away and leave them. And there was the minor and personal factor: how would he ever be able to pick up his career back on Earth if he left this station for no reason that would bear explanation? Hardheaded scientists on Earth would never accept his story of the little green man—and nobody else had seen the Uranian. No, back on Earth they would be very polite, but at their luncheons they would say in casual tones, "Engar Jarvin cracked up out there on Uranus. Too bad. He was headed for a great career."

Well—Engar took a deep breath. What he wanted to do right now was get rid of the little man without making him angry. He liked the being—had liked him ever since the first day the little man had appeared in the laboratory out of nowhere to ask questions. Engar had answered him courteously because, after all, the little man had been on Uranus first. At least, Engar assumed that.

THE SELENIUM CELL flashed a warning, and Engar started the draw-off. Then he looked up at the little man. "Who shall I say is requesting our—er—withdrawal from Uranus?" he asked.

"Nolos."

"It would help," Engar suggested, "if I could say that you represent some substantial body of Uranians."

Nolos began to fume. "Naturally, I cannot represent the Spiders who live in the warm-spot; you may say I represent the Cold Belt of Uranus."

"About how many citizens?"

"All five of them."

"Did you say five?"

"Five."

Engar sighed. There was so little ground for understanding between them that it was hopeless. Five opposed to five billion… "I will give your message to my director," Engar said finally.

Nolos seemed somewhat mollified. "I shall be back in exactly three days," he announced, and added, "The most stupid person in the ten planets should be able to make up his mind in that length of time."

The draw-off had started. Engar watched the peach-colored liquid pouring out of the spigot at the base of the column for a moment. Then, puzzled, he looked up at Nolos. How did Nolos know there were ten planets? It was the year 2402, and Stygia had been discovered less than fifty years before. Engar felt certain the being had had no contact with humans until Engar himself had come with the first shipment of material to establish the station on Uranus.

The Earthman remembered what a headache he had had, trying to check in all the stuff; moving around through Uranus' methane atmosphere with a plastic-bubble over his head; dreading almost constantly the red flash of his indicators that would mean his heating power had gone off—for Uranus' temperature at the surface was minus nearly four hundred degrees Fahrenheit. It was so cold that all the ammonia in Uranus atmosphere had frozen solid, long ago; if the power supply in a suit-heater went off, a man had better start running at top speed for the dome.

One workman had seen the red flash, but had finished lifting a shovel full of dirt—frozen ammonia—and then started to walk to the dome. He hadn't made it; it was less than fifty feet, but by the time they got him picked up he was like a stone statue, only not as heavy.

That was one good thing about Uranus: although it was five times the diameter of Earth, its density was considerably less; and owing to its size, gravitational pull at the surface was about equal to that on Earth.

ENGAR REMEMBERED how they had put the body in the outer hold of one of the supply-cruisers for shipment back to Earth. He had thought it a long way to send a body just for burial, but there was sentiment to be considered; the man had a family. Besides, the ships wouldn't have loads going back, anyway.

He had watched the blazing trail of the rockets in their transorbital arc—a path of foaming red and yellow flame through the sea-green atmosphere—and he wondered then how many more men would go back to Earth the same way. He sat on a campstool in the dome, after everybody else had gone to bed, with his log in his lap—that was when the little green man had appeared out of nowhere. He stood just inside the plastic door of the dome, his golden eyes glowing, and Engar wondered fleetingly how he had come through the cold.

The peacock-feathered tail spread wide and the being said, "What are you doing here?"

It had taken Engar aback for a moment, because the surveyors' reports had shown no living entities on Uranus proper, except for the big Spiders who lived in Uranus' only warm spot—which was fifty thousand miles away, near the pole that pointed always toward the Sun.

Engar studied the little man, as much as he could do so politely, observing the sea-greenness of his skin, the pink of his eyebrows, the bird-like whistle of his talk, and realizing at last that the little man had spoken Earth-language. Then he realized, too, that the little man had asked him a question.

"Earth has been forced to go to other planets for many of the rare elements," said Engar. "It happens that Uranus is peculiarly rich in some of them."

"Which ones?"

"All of the rare earths—especially praseodymium."

"What good is praseodymium to you?"

"With its molecules properly aligned by the application of very high-voltage and high-frequency current, and when properly alloyed with certain other elements, it forms a substance that acts as a gravitational shield."

"Why," asked the little man, "do you need to protect yourselves from gravity?"

"So we can, for instance, go to other planets."

The other looked disgusted. "You want praseodymium—so you can go to other planets to find more praseodymium. Is that it?"

"It rather sounds like an over simplification," said Engar.

"I am beginning to wonder," the being retorted, "if anything can be made too simple for the mind of an Earthman."

But Engar pointed out, "I am hardly responsible for the forces that move Earthmen. They do as they do, and they always have done that way."

"That," said the little man, "is the first sensible statement you have made."

Engar kept discreetly silent.

The little man fanned his tail out a couple of times. Then he said, "I don't know if I'm going to like it. We'll wait and see."

He appeared a number of times after that—always when Engar was alone. He talked rather generally, but always with that air of condescension that was hard to put a finger on—perhaps because it seemed, well, *justified.* And occasionally he asked some very sharp questions especially when the tall ion-exchange columns went up; and either he knew what Engar was talking about, or he didn't have the faintest ideal for he didn't not pursue the subject of ion-exchange. He seemed more interested in Earthmen as individuals.

He appeared a number of times, and there were several things he didn't like: the big shovels biting through Uranus' frozen-ammonia soil to get at the rare-earth minerals beneath; the rocket ships with their reaction-motors searing great molten paths along Uranus' surface; the waste-gases from the processing-plant at the station. But, Engar recalled, the little man had not become wrought up until about the time Corinne Madison came to the station as director. Perhaps the being had felt Engar's own perturbation over that—for Corinne was two years younger than Engar; and certainly with no better background. Engar had resented it for a while, and it was during that period that the little green man had begun to talk in an unfriendly manner.

NOW ENGAR looked at him, wondering just what the Uranian thought he could do against Earth's technology. Nolos was ruffling his tail feathers; the "eyes" in the feathers grew larger and more iridescent, until they shone like fire; then the being collapsed them, and Engar knew he was getting ready to go back to wherever he had come from.

He did. Engar glanced at the column and saw that the draw-off was nearly complete; his finger went to the button. When he looked up again, the little man was gone. Engar stopped the draw-off, feeling rather pleased with the operation of the ion-exchange column. He thought that this batch—some twenty liters—when distilled would be a very good grade of praseodymium, usable without further refining. He checked the columns and saw that presently No. 6 would be ready for a draw-off too.

But the pneumatic door to the director's office whispered, and Corinne Madison came out, walking rather hard on her heels. "Mr. Jarvin," she said crisply, "I have asked you before to notify me when you are contemplating any sort of activity that will generate intensive radiation."

Engar looked up at her. Her black hair was glossy against the white starched linen of her jacket, and she knew how to make good use of it too, for—

"Mr. Jarvin?" Her brown eyes narrowed.

"Yes, Miss Madison?" He glanced at No.6 column and set the warning cell, then stood up. He couldn't help it if he was a head taller than she was.

Now she had to bend her head back to look at him.

"As you well know," he said, "there is no radiation connected with the ion-exchange columns."

"I know a number of things," she said indignantly, "and none of them are good."

"Please enumerate, Miss Madison."

"One," she said, "you superintended the construction of this entire plant. Two, you designed and built the ion-exchange columns. Three, you are well aware of your importance on Uranus. Four, you resented my coming here as your superior. Five, I have no doubt you could make those columns radiate if you chose to. Six, you are too damned handsome, and you know it."

He looked down at her and took a full breath. For a moment he felt like putting his arms around her, but restrained himself; after all, she was his boss, and one did not go around hugging one's boss, did one—or did one? He was unable at the moment to recall a comparable situation.

SHE WENT on, "This is the third time hard radiation has thrown my calculator out of adjustment and this time I have traced it to *you*, Mr. Jarvin." Triumphantly she held up a five-by-seven negative. "You can see for yourself."

He glanced at it. "Those streaks do look like radiation, Miss, but—"

"After the last time, when it became apparent that someone was deliberately creating trouble for me, I began to investigate, Mr. Jarvin. I found, among other things, that you yourself—at one time—expected to be made director of this station."

"But—"

"Don't try to alibi," she said. "I know now that you would stoop to any sort of scurvy trick to get me out of here. I do not doubt that you would even try to get the post closed entirely, if you thought you could—just to get rid of me."

He began to feel uncomfortable.

"It may interest you to know my own reasons for coming to Uranus, Mr. Jarvin."

"It certainly would," he said warmly. "A lone girl—and, I might say, a beautiful girl—asking to be sent to Uranus with seventeen men—"

She colored, and he hastened on. "Certainly your conduct is above reproach, Miss Madison, but it does seem a long way for a young girl to come from Hollywood and Vine."

"I certainly did not come here from Hollywood," she informed him. "I was a nuclear physicist at the University of California, and I had some ideas to work out in regard to a catalyst that would change fission-energy into some form of energy besides heat—so that it could be used directly as a power source. Do you follow me?"

"I rather think so," he murmured, watching the movements of her expressive lips.

"It was essential that I establish a laboratory at some place where there would be no interference from radiation originating in, or caused by, the Sun. This plant was being installed, and I applied for a post here, expecting to do my experimental work in my spare time. And I assure you, Mr. Jarvin that I was quite astonished when they appointed me director of the plant. They told me it was the only post open that would give me time to pursue my other work."

He nodded, watching her.

"I was also astonished when I reached here to find that I was to be over the man who had built the plant, but I assumed the board back on Earth knew what it was doing, and I went to work. Then various little annoyances cropped up, culminating in the radiation that makes it impossible to use my calculator. So the last time this disturbance happened," she informed him, "I laid a trap. I put film at various places around the walls—and here is the proof. This negative was in the center of my wall on your side, Mr. Jarvin."

Engar glanced at No. 6 and saw there was plenty of time left. "I'm very sorry, Miss Madison, but I know nothing about it," he said at last.

"It took you long enough to think up that evasion," she retorted.

HE ANSWERED slowly. "Miss Madison, my lifework is bound up in these columns; it is my duty to make them do the job they were designed for. Otherwise I know nothing about all this." He took the negative and examined it more closely. "There is more hard radiation," he conceded again. "Not enough to bother anyone who has had a full immunization, of course, but certainly enough to throw your calculator off."

"Of that fact," she said icily, "I am well aware. What I want to know is what are you going to do about it?"

He said without much hope, "I'll go over the ion-exchange lab, but I don't think it will turn up anything."

"Probably not," she said acidulously.

"Why don't you come in and check for yourself?"

"How do you think it would look," she asked, "for the director of the Earth-station on Uranus to run around with a Geiger counter looking for stray radiation?"

He assumed it was a rhetorical question. "I'm just trying to be helpful."

Too late he saw that she was furious. The fire rose in those brown eyes and she did not back away an inch. "The next time this happens Mr. Jarvin, I shall expect your resignation."

He opened his mouth but closed it again, kept his indignation in check. "This is a strange planet, Miss. I would suggest we do not know all about it."

Her grim smile was his answer. He kept his lips tightly closed. She spun on one high heel and marched stiffly from the room. He watched the many colors and hues from the columns reflected from the stiff white starch of her uniform as she passed them, and he wondered what was throwing her calculator out of adjustment.

He picked up the negative from his bench as he sat down. There was plenty of hard radiation—the straight marks of gamma rays; the curved lines of charged particles; the sprayed burst of a large atom hit head-on by a cosmotron. He frowned and laid the negative down. No. 14 was giving an alarm. He thought it likely that the next day or so would be very busy for him, for all of the columns had been charged at about the same time...

It was the next day—Uranian day, that is—before he remembered the little green man with the pink eyebrows—Nolos, he had called himself. By that time Engar was tired and sleepy and hardly able to think clearly; but he remembered Nolos' warning, and he also remembered Corinne Madison's ultimatum over the radiation. One thing was quite certain: after Corinne's statement that she thought he would go to any length to get rid of her, or words to that effect, it was not even to be hoped that she would entertain the idea of sending a message suggesting discontinuance of the station...

TWO DAYS later the columns were working down through the salts of illinium. Engar was beginning to relax, when the little green man appeared again.

"Hello," said Engar. "Glad to see you."

"Are you indeed?" asked Nolos. His golden, glowing eyes took in the ion-exchange laboratory at a glance. "You are still operating the columns," he said in his bird-like voice. "Am I to assume that the answer from Earth was negative?"

Engar swallowed, then allowed himself the luxury of prevarication. After all, it was what the answer would have been anyway. "I am afraid so," he said.

The peacock-feather tail opened up and pulsed slowly, but the little man's golden eyes did not burn as they had the time before. "I am sorry," Nolos said finally. "It is going to take a terrific expenditure of energy by the five of us to get you off of Uranus."

Engar looked at the being's wide fanning tail and then at the glowing eyes; he felt uneasy. "I don't understand why you are so set against our being here. I know there are some things you don't like, but we aren't actually hurting you, are we?"

"Not too much—right now," conceded Nolos. "But what about tomorrow?"

"Tomorrow?"

"Today you want praseodymium. Perhaps tomorrow you will want ammonia. What will happen to Uranus, then? Isn't Earth's history one continuous record of a people wanting something owned by somebody else?"

Engar frowned. "It is true that Earth-people as a whole are aggressive. But that is a biological drive, and not something we can put down at will. Moreover, there are many of us who think that eventually that drive will be turned to good use for the entire Solar System."

But Nolos did not seem to be interested in argument. He disappeared.

It was two days later that the headman on the big shovels, Chuck Delbert, came into the ion-exchange lab pulling off his heated gloves. "I thought you might be interested, Mr. Jarvin, in something that's going on out there—seeing that you're the oldest man in the place and sort of daddy to the station."

"I am interested in everything around here," said Engar. "After all we know very little about Uranus, and whenever there is a chance to increase that knowledge—"

"Well," said Chuck, "it's like this; there's stuff growing out of that frozen ammonia."

"Growing?"

Chuck nodded positively, "Growing."

"What kind of stuff?"

"Grass," said Chuck. "Red grass."

Engar stared at him. "Red?"

"Like this here." A blade of grass lay in Chuck's big palm. It was wide and coarse, and it was red. Engar took it thoughtfully. "I don't understand," he said. "The chlorophyll reaction—"

"Me neither," said Chuck. "My business is running the shovels. Just thought you'd like to know."

"I'm very much interested," said Engar studying the blade of grass. "Thanks for bringing it in. If there are any further developments, I'd be pleased to hear about them."

Chuck was on his way to the lockers with his bubble under his arm. "I'll let you know, Mr. Jarvin."

ENGAR NODDED. He was already absorbed in the blade. He took it to a microscope and found out it was exactly like any other grass blade, except that it was red. Of course there were many plants on Earth that turned red in the fall. He glanced at the thermometer: it showed three hundred and sixty-one below. *Not exactly Indian summer,* he thought wryly. Anyway, this stuff was just *starting* to grow, and it was growing out of frozen ammonia. He laid the leaf on the porcelain bench. It seemed to turn darker; it began to curl. Suddenly it ignited and went up in a puff of flame.

Engar nodded. Entirely to be expected.

He drew the tape log toward him, but a crisp voice came from behind. "Mr. Jarvin, you are not a botanist, are you?"

He turned to Corinne Madison. "No, I am not," he said.

"I am," she said. "Botany was my minor. Furthermore, I do not like things going on behind my back."

"I only—"

She held out a very small white hand. "The blade of grass, please."

He bit his lower lip rather softly. "I am afraid it is too late."

Her hand dropped to her side. Her eyes flashed. "Why is it too late, Mr. Jarvin?" He pointed to the bench and the tiny pile of ashes.

She drew herself up. "This is rank insubordination, Mr. Jarvin."

"You would hardly expect a leaf that survived outside, there, to retain its composition under what must—to it—be a pretty hot fire. Remember, there is a difference of anywhere up to five hundred degrees."

"No," she said. "I would not expect it, nor would I expect red grass to grow out of frozen ammonia."

Engar looked down. "It's a strange planet, Miss, and we know very little—"

"I think you've told me that before. I do not want to have trouble with you, Mr. Jarvin. The next time something like this occurs, I expect to be notified before—not after—the cremation."

He didn't answer. It was not a situation that lent itself to an answer. If she had not had such white skin and such black hair— he sighed. But he thought probably he did have a limit, and he wondered if Miss Madison was not pushing him toward it.

Two days later Chuck Delbert was in again, a frown between his eyes. "That red grass," he said, lifting the bubble over his head, "is getting thicker. The whole plain outside is covered with it."

"In which direction, Chuck?"

"All directions. I took the ice-sled and made a run around the dome. There's a regular field of it."

"Can you tell how far it reaches from the dome?"

"A long ways—beyond the searchlights, anyway."

"It may be a sort of seasonal thing," said Engar.

"It wasn't here last year."

"Well, no…but seasons may be quite different on Uranus. It takes this planet eighty-four of our years to go around the Sun, so the seasons might be much longer."

"Yeah, maybe. It's funny," said Chuck. "The grass seems to be sort of closing in on the dome."

"That might be your imagination."

"Not me," said Chuck. "My teachers always said I never had no imagination a-tall."

THAT EVENING, when the columns were quiet for a while, Engar got up in the observation post in the top of the dome and turned on the big searchlight. He probed the Uranian darkness in all directions. Everywhere it was the same—a frozen white plain, level and vast. Except for one thing: the red grass that looked black in the light was within two hundred yards on all sides.

It startled Engar; he didn't quite know what to make of it. The red grass was almost like an advancing army. Miss Madison's voice, in his ear, startled him more. "I hope there is a good reason for this juvenile playing with the searchlight, Mr. Jarvin."

He looked down at her. At first he was annoyed. But the tiny space at the top of the dome necessitated their being quite close together, and he overlooked his annoyance. "It is not necessary constantly to assert your authority with me, Miss Madison," he said gently, and pointed at the fringe of red grass. "I don't like it," he said.

She stared, swung the small telescope into position and focused it. Finally she announced, "It does seem to be red grass, Mr. Jarvin, but is that anything to get excited about? After all, you've said yourself it's a strange planet."

He smiled. "Those were my exact words, I believe. However—" he turned sober—"there is the business of the little green man."

"The little what?"

He rubbed his chin with the back of his wrist, frowning in the direction of the searchlight's beam. "I don't ask you to believe this, Miss Madison; it's fantastic."

"I am becoming used to fantasy," she told him.

"This little man with the pink eyebrows and peacock-feather tail—"

"An utterly horrid combination, Mr. Jarvin." She suppressed a half-smile. "Could it be that your imagination is playing tricks on you?"

He looked at her and took a deep breath. "Perhaps you are right. I'll keep it to myself."

"You have aroused my curiosity. Do continue, please."

"He started appearing soon after we landed here with the first shipload of supplies, and he usually shows up about once a week."

"Coming from where—the great frozen outside?" she asked gaily.

"I don't know, he said he was a Uranian."

"I notice you speak Uranian with a slight accent, Mr. Jarvin."

His eyes narrowed. "If you are trying to provoke me," he said, "you are closer to success than you might believe."

She smiled archly. "What would you do, Mr. Jarvin, if I provoked you?"

"That's hard to answer. I can't seem to recall a comparable situation."

"Do you mean you've never been provoked?"

He answered cautiously, "Not enough to do anything—desperate, at least not since I was a kid."

She led the way down the ladder. She was wearing a white nylon blouse, and her shoulders looked very nice in it. "Now tell me more about the little green man, Mr. Jarvin."

"He was here about a week ago and demanded that we abandon the station," Engar said. "I told him it wouldn't be done without authority from Earth. He demanded that I send a message asking that authority." Engar looked down at Corinne. "Then you

192

stormed in, and I decided it was best not to mention it just then."
He stopped, looking away.

"And—" she prompted.

"He appeared again and said he would have to take steps, or
something to that effect."

She studied him as if trying to decide whether to believe him.
Then she looked at the plastic walls of the dome. "I doubt," she
said, "that the red grass has any power to harm our station."

BUT A FEW days later the red grass was growing out of the
frozen ammonia at the very edge of the plastic dome. "The thing I
do not understand," said Miss Madison, "is where it gets energy for
growth."

Engar took a step toward her. She was very lovable when she
wasn't trying to assert authority. But at that moment he heard the
whistle of the air chamber, and a few moments later Chuck Delbert
appeared. His forehead was wrinkled with trying to understand
something that was beyond him. "There's *plants* growing out there
now, Mr. Jarvin—red plants."

"Red plants?" asked Corinne.

"Yes, ma'am. They seem to be growing toward the dome. A
quarter of a mile away they are just breaking through the ground;
but at the limits of the searchlight they look as high as a man. They
have big, droopy leaves, and there seems to be a kind of golden
glow comes from the middle somewhere."

Engar remembered the being's eyes. "A glow," he said
thoughtfully.

Within another week, they could pick up the strange plants in
the searchlight from the observation tower. It was about time for a
new series of drawing from the ion-exchange columns, but Engar
took time out to study the plants with Corinne. "They're coming
closer," he told her.

She began to look worried. "What can we do?"

"Nothing right now," he said.

The plants came closer. They began, one might say, to burst
into bloom. As they matured, they emanated that golden glow
from the top, and the Earth-people soon found that they were not
able to watch it closely. The brilliance was unendurable.

Then came the day when Chuck Delbert's men started out, took a turn in the four-hundred-below temperature, and came clattering back with their big mechanical shovels.

Corinne met Chuck at the air lock. "Why are you back?"

Chuck set a small black box on the table. "Look at that counter, Miss Madison; our contract specifically states that we are not to work in radiation like that."

She glanced at the paper chart, and frowned at the extreme height of the recording line. "Why, this is more than an immunized person can stand; this is up to ten roentgens a day."

"That's what I'm sayin', Miss."

"Very well," she said. "You may take the day off."

Engar looked at the chart over her shoulder. "Where's it coming from?" he wondered.

She looked outside. "From the plants, I suppose. That golden glow may be the signal of some sort of nuclear action."

Engar was watching No. 8 column with one eye.

"You'd better take care of your draw-off, Mr. Jarvin. I'll see if I can work out the answer to this."

He nodded, moving toward the button. The peach-colored band didn't look right to him. Vaguely he heard through the open door to the director's office, the soft shuttling and clicking of the calculator, then an exclamation of exasperation from Miss Madison. But he did not have time to investigate. The calculator was giving her trouble again, but he had to watch the color bands on No.8.

The peach-colored band turned unexpectedly to a sort of gray-brown. Engar frowned and shook his head.

He got out his own counter. The gamma discharge was rising toward the danger-zone; the neutron line was beginning to go up. He went to Miss Madison's office. She was not there. The black box was still on her desk. She had been trying to operate the calculator, but a forest of tiny red lights indicated that it was completely out of adjustment.

He looked around. The door to her personal locker was open, and her spacesuit was gone. He ran out. The big pumps were thumping, and the gauge on the compression-chamber showed a build-up that would keep out the deadly methane when the outer door was opened. Engar pounded on the wall. "Don't do that!" he shouted.

Of course she couldn't hear him. He ran to his locker and got into his suit and put on the bubble. He saw that the heating-unit was working. By that time the air lock was empty; he closed it and stepped inside and started the pumps.

A moment later he was outside. He saw her in the glow from his breast-lamp, leaning into the strong wind, walking toward the red plants. The frozen ammonia was slippery, but he hurried. The nearest sun-plant was two hundred yards away, and she was halfway there, a small, slender figure bending against the Uranian wind. He reached her, and put a hand on her arm. "Come back," he said.

She pulled away and looked at him through the bubble. Her voice in the suit-com sounded odd and a little frantic. "I've got to have a specimen of that plant."

He shook his head. "If you get close enough to touch one," he said, "the radioactive poisons will kill you."

He was standing between her and the plants. She looked over his shoulder, then back at the dome, and seemed resigned. He relaxed, and at the same time she darted around him.

At that moment the dome's searchlights came on and lighted up the entire area. There was the field of red plants growing out of the frozen white ammonia, and from each full-grown plant emanated that intense golden glow.

He ran after her, but she was quick on her feet. She was reaching toward a red leaf when he caught her. She tried to pull away, but this time he held her firmly. They slipped and slid on the ice, but he didn't turn loose. Finally she quit fighting, but she was so furious her face was white. He got them both into the air lock. He was puffing a little. He turned on the pumps.

When they walked out into the ion lab she faced him. "I don't suppose you would care to know why I went out there."

"Of course I would," he said, fascinated by her color.

"Those plants," she said, "those red plants must have a catalyst corresponding to chlorophyll."

"Chlorophyll turns sunlight into plant-energy—sugars and so on," he remembered.

"You get an A," she said sarcastically. "But out here on Uranus there is very little sunlight. The energy has to come from somewhere else—frozen ammonia—and the red color indicates a catalyst that enables the plant to turn ammonia into fission-energy."

"The little green man was right," Engar said sadly. "As soon as you find out how to do that, then Earth will start digging up Uranus' ammonia and hauling it away."

CHUCK DELBERT was coming down from the observation-tower; he looked at them curiously, and went across the lab into the mechanics' quarters.

Corinne began to storm again. "Is it necessary that you take such a narrow view? If that red catalyst will turn ammonia into nuclear energy, then it probably will provide a clue to the reverse-reaction—or to such things as turning nuclear energy directly into electrical energy or something else that we can use. With nuclear energy available, we could use sunlight. There must be some way to use radiant energy directly—and those plants hold the answer."

"I'm sorry," he said. "You would not live more than a few days, if at all, after you touched one of those plants. Even if the nuclear reaction is carried on by no more than a pinpoint of matter, the radiation would be deadly—to say nothing of the heat."

Her tone changed unexpectedly. "You know," she said, "that these plants are coming closer and closer. It is only a question of a very short time until the radiation in the dome itself will be at a level that we cannot stand for more than a few hours. And what will be left for me then? You and I both will lose our positions and will be discredited. I want something to make up for it; a catalyst, such as those plants contain, would be the answer."

"I'm sorry," he said. "It's important to me, too—but neither one of us will be worth much dead."

"What about the sun-plants? We can't even stop them."

"Yes, I think we can." He went to the laboratory bench and looked in the cabinet beneath. "Yes, I think we can stop them. We *must* stop them if we want to live."

He spent the next half-hour up in the observation-tower. He called Chuck Delbert to help him. "Swing that searchlight around the dome in all directions," Engar said, "just as if you were spraying the plants out there."

"It doesn't make any light," said Chuck.

Engar nodded. "It makes a light all right—black light—infrared. And I think you'll be able to follow its path. Now you start to work; mow down everything within reach—and that should be about half a mile. I've got to go outside."

He was out of the dome when the sun-plants began to burst into flame. The long red leaves glowed with a blue fire that seemed to break out in a thousand places at once. The first plant went up in flames. There was a burst of intense light; the wind from the explosion almost knocked him over, and the heat was intense. There was an ascending orange-blue ball of fire, and then the familiar mushroom-shaped cloud—all on a very small scale compared to the nuclear explosions on Earth.

"It's lucky for us," Engar told Corinne when he came inside, "that there is no more than a pinpoint of matter in each plant."

For now they sat side by side and watched through the window as the field of sun-plants went up in fire and smoke. It was like a gigantic display of fireworks, and Chuck Delbert was very thorough. In a few hours the radiation-levels had gone down. Corinne was once more able to use her calculator, and Engar set in motion a draw-off on No.5.

It was then the little green man appeared again. His golden eyes were dim now, as if he was exhausted, and his peacock-feather tail was drooping. "You played unfairly," he said in his bird-like voice. "There are too many of you for us. We are only five, and we used up all of our energy creating the field of sun-plants—which you destroyed in a few hours."

"I'm sorry," Engar said, "but we do have to live."

"Dubious," said the being. "Dubious."

"Oh," said a feminine voice, and Corinne stood behind Engar. Engar could see her white nylon sleeve from the corner of his eye.

The other looked up, but he didn't disappear as Engar had feared he might. He glanced at Corinne and back at Engar. "The female of the species, I take it."

Engar found Corinne's hand. "You are quite right," he said warmly.

The little green man sighed. "Once," he said, "we had females, too; but now there are only we five old men."

"I'm terribly sorry," said Corinne.

The little green man looked at her. His golden eyes began to glow. "You needn't be," he said. "I've already had a long life and a very good one. I was born, in fact, before you Earth-people were even writing history."

"We'll try to see that your planet is not usurped," Corinne said gently.

"Don't. You can't fight evolutionary forces; you can't even fight the force that draws you two together."

Engar looked up at her. "Maybe he's right."

"Maybe."

Engar looked back. The little green man was gone. Engar got up. No. 5's draw-off was finished, and he re-set the warning signal.

"There's just one thing," Corinne said. "If I could have saved some of those leaves before Mr. Delbert finished his extermination—"

Engar looked down at her. "Wouldn't the red grass do just as well?"

She brightened. "Why, yes—" Then her face fell. "But the red grass burned up with the plants."

"Not all of it," he told her. "You remember the grass approached the dome first?"

"Yes."

"I slipped outside," he told her, "and gathered a few handfuls of the grass while Chuck was getting the infra-red lamp in operation. It's stowed away in the air lock now."

She looked up at him, her dark eyes shining. "You *darling,*" she breathed.

Her nylon blouse rustled as she moved into his arms. He kissed her. There was no comparable situation that he could recall, but he kissed her anyway.

THE END

If you've enjoyed this book, you will not want to miss these terrific titles…

ARMCHAIR SCI-FI & HORROR DOUBLE NOVELS, $12.95 each

D-51   **A GOD NAMED SMITH** by Henry Slesar
WORLDS OF THE IMPERIUM by Keith Laumer

D-52   **CRAIG'S BOOK** by Don Wilcox
EDGE OF THE KNIFE by H. Beam Piper

D-53   **THE SHINING CITY** by Rena M. Vale
THE RED PLANET by Russ Winterbotham

D-54   **THE MAN WHO LIVED TWICE** by Rog Phillips
VALLEY OF THE CROEN by Lee Tarbell

D-55   **OPERATION DISASTER** by Milton Lesser
LAND OF THE DAMNED by Berkeley Livingston

D-56   **CAPTIVE OF THE CENTAURIANESS** by Poul Anderson
A PRINCESS OF MARS by Edgar Rice Burroughs

D-57   **THE NON-STATISTICAL MAN** by Raymond F. Jones
MISSION FROM MARS by Rick Conroy

D-58   **INTRUDERS FROM THE STARS** by Ross Rocklynne
FLIGHT OF THE STARLING by Chester S. Geier

D-59   **COSMIC SABOTEUR** by Frank M. Robinson
LOOK TO THE STARS by Willard Hawkins

D-60   **THE MOON IS HELL!** by John W. Campbell, Jr.
THE GREEN WORLD by Hal Clement

ARMCHAIR SCIENCE FICTION CLASSICS, $12.95 each

C-16   **THE SHAVER MYSTERY, Book Three**
by Richard S. Shaver

C-17   **THE PLANET STRAPPERS**
by Raymond Z. Gallun

C-18   **THE FOURTH "R"**
by George O. Smith

ARMCHAIR SCI-FI & HORROR GEMS SERIES, $12.95 each

G-5   **SCIENCE FICTION GEMS, Vol. Three**
C. M. Kornbluth and others

G-6   **HORROR GEMS, Vol. Three**
August Derleth and others

If you've enjoyed this book, you will not want to miss these terrific titles…

ARMCHAIR SCI-FI & HORROR DOUBLE NOVELS, $12.95 each

D-121   **THE GENIUS BEASTS** by Frederik Pohl
THIS WORLD IS TABOO by Murray Leinster

D-122   **THE COSMIC LOOTERS** by Edmond Hamilton
WANDL THE INVADER by Ray Cummings

D-123   **ROBOT MEN OF BUBBLE CITY** by Rog Phillips
DRAGON ARMY by William Morrison

D-124   **LAND BEYOND THE LENS** by S. J. Byrne
DIPLOMAT-AT-ARMS by Keith Laumer

D-125   **VOYAGE OF THE ASTEROID, THE** by Laurence Manning
REVOLT OF THE OUTWORLDS by Milton Lesser

D-126   **OUTLAW IN THE SKY** by Chester S. Geier
LEGACY FROM MARS by Raymond Z. Gallun

D-127   **THE GREAT FLYING SAUCER INVASION** by Geoff St. Reynard
THE BIG TIME by Fritz Leiber

D-128   **MIRAGE FOR PLANET X** by Stanley Mullen
POLICE YOUR PLANET by Lester del Rey

D-129   **THE BRAIN SINNERS** by Alan E. Nourse
DEATH FROM THE SKIES by A. Hyatt Verrill

D-139   **CRY CHAOS** by Dwight V. Swain
THE DOOR THROUGH SPACE By Marion Zimmer Bradley

ARMCHAIR SCIENCE FICTION CLASSICS, $12.95 each

C-55   **UNDER THE TRIPLE SUNS**
by Stanton A. Coblentz

C-56   **STONE FROM THE GREEN STAR**
by Jack Williamson

C-57   **ALIEN MINDS**
by E. Everett Evans

ARMCHAIR MASTERS OF SCIENCE FICTION SERIES, $16.95 each

G-13   **SCIENCE FICTION GEMS, Vol. Seven**
Jack Vance and others

G-14   **HORROR GEMS, Vol. Seven**
Robert Bloch and others

www.ingramcontent.com/pod-product-compliance
Lightning Source LLC
Chambersburg PA
CBHW030327180626
46810CB00003B/1252